PRAISE FOR CASSIDY_

If I could send one book to every sci-fi reader in the world, I think I would choose this one. ... I loved the characters, the plot, the world, and the overall tone of this book. All of it was pulled off so well. I definitely need to check out more from Jo Cassidy. She is one of my new favourite authors.

- NATHANIEL, @HECTICREADINGLIFE,
INSTAGRAM

Harper is a book I definitely think young female readers would REALLY enjoy! The MC is snarky, can kick butt, and has a strong love for her family.

- LAURA A. GRACE, AUTHOR OF DEAR AUTHOR:
LETTERS FROM A BOOKISH FANGIRL

I can honestly say I was sad when this book ended because I love the characters and want to keep adventuring with them.

- TECH GIRL, AMAZON

I do hope that this is not the last we see of Harper and her rag tag group of friends. I love how she is proud of her humble background, her father has a knack for fixing things, her mother is ill and will likely never get better, but Harper loves them and appreciates the time she has with them.

This book taught me to "Stay on Mission."

I needed something to read for when I had some spare time and had this suggested to me. Once I started reading, it sucked me in and I finished it in one weekend.

Loved reading this book. I loved the banter-romance between Harper and Akiro. Most of the scenes had me laughing out loud. The action and mystery kept me reading way past my bedtime. I also loved that it was a clean, uplifting book.

There is a lot to like about Harper, the book and the character. It's a fun read, and Harper—the character—is on my list of favorites. I love the details Jo gives her characters. I'm in for Harper 2.

I loved Harper's loyalty to her family and ability to take down the "bad guys." If you enjoy sass, action, and romance, Harper is for you!

I've loved all of Jo Cassidy's novels, but this one stands out as my absolute favorite. I know I'll be reading it many times. Once is definitely not enough.

Harper sucks you into her life and carries you along on her adventures. Was worth missing a night's sleep.

HARPER UNHINGED

JO CASSIDY

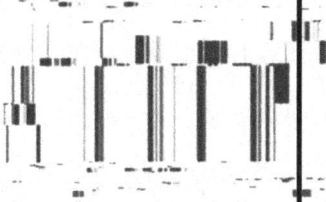

MONSTER IVY
PUBLISHING

To all you adventurous souls.

CHAPTER ONE_

FUNERALS SUCK.

They're full of random people coming up to you, offering self-centered sympathies that in no way help the grieving person. It just makes the sympathizer feel better, like they've done a heroic deed for reaching out to the heartbroken soul, the one who just lost the person they love most in this stupid world, the one person that knew them better than anyone else and still loved them despite their snarky manners and a tendency to take things that don't belong to them.

I don't need to be reminded how amazing my mom was because I already know. I don't need to hear how they met her or their favorite memory of her because *I don't care*. Those are their memories, not mine.

I want to soak in *my* memories, all the good times we had, all the times she made me smile on the days where I just wanted to beat the crap out of everyone.

Like today. The next person who tells me 'time heals all wounds' or 'I know what you're going through' is going to get a solid punch right in their condescending face. Yeah, you once lost your mom, dad, brother, sister, uncle, dog, former roommate, ex that you suddenly care about, but that doesn't help *me*. It's just another way to turn it back to themselves. Am I supposed to offer my condolences? Hey, I know my mom just died, but I'm so sorry you lost your pet hamster back in the third grade.

The whole scene before me is bleak. Dad is kneeling next to Mom's coffin, arms draped over the top, sobbing harder than I've ever seen. Rain is pouring down, the grass beneath my feet turning into a swamp. Uncle Forest—Mom's brother—is standing over Dad, one hand resting on Dad's shoulder, the other holding an umbrella to offer them at least some protection. Fog is rolling in, something straight out of a horror movie. I shift back and forth where I stand, water seeping into the flats I'm wearing.

I almost curse myself for wearing them. They're Mom's. Her favorites. She bought them a few months ago from the earnings she'd made selling her fingerless gloves. As much as my friend Pearl drives me crazy, she's done a great job of spreading the word about my mom's business. Although, now I have to see all those idiots at school walking around, wearing the things.

I adjust the gloves on my hands, ignoring the sweat lining my palms from the summer heat. Mine are the only ones with owls crocheted in them. She had to make me a new pair after I lost my last ones in a fight with a beefy idiot named Wyatt Mitchell. Thankfully, he's behind bars now and out of my life.

I made Mom promise to keep that design only for me.

"I'd never make this design for anyone other than my girl," she'd said. I can still hear her soft voice.

My fists clench, and I jam my hands into my raincoat pockets so I won't punch something.

My boyfriend, Akiro, stands next to me, holding an umbrella over us. His spiked hair is taller than when I first met him, sticking straight up thanks to all the gel. He's trying to set some sort of record for tallest hair. I told him ninjas don't have hair that obvious, but he shrugged it off.

Everyone else has already left, heading back to the house. Thank goodness for Akiro's mom—Mrs. Fukunaga —who took the luncheon into her trusty hands. It was basically the last thing Dad and I wanted to think about. Picking out her dress, then putting it on her corpse, was bad enough.

I shiver, despite the heat. I hate that that's one of the last images I have of her. I want to remember her smile, color in her cheeks, her musical laugh.

Nowadays, most people are cremated. They've been running out of places to bury people. But Everly Stuart inserted herself into the picture in typical Evs fashion. She's the lady who pretty much owns San Diego and I did a job for her last year. All she had to do was make some calls and she snatched us a spot to bury Mom. I tried to talk Dad out of it, but he couldn't say no to Everly. She's done way too much for our family, like build us a house fully equipped to handle Mom and her cancer, and she offered Dad a job. The idea of burning Mom's body to a crisp was too much for him anyway. Guess he wants to tell himself she's just lying peacefully six feet under the earth so he can sleep better at night.

Won't change the fact that she's dead.

Son of a terrorist, I hate this whole thing. I hate that she's gone.

I do love the fact that Akiro hasn't said a peep next to me. He's just stayed at my side, offering moral support and running interference when someone says something incredibly stupid to me. If it weren't for him, at least four people would be leaving the funeral with a broken nose.

Someone steps up beside me and I turn to see Scarlett, one of the owners of the company I work for—Dogwood Protection Services. She's recently dyed her hair a blood red, matching with her tough, yet sexy, exterior.

"Baby girl," she drawls, all grit and scratch, "standing out here in the rain won't bring her back." She bumps my arm. "Let's get you home."

I shake my head. "So a bunch of people can keep annoying me? No, thanks. I'd rather stab myself repeatedly in the eye with those cheap chopsticks from the Golden Dragon."

"That's kind of graphic," Akiro mumbles under his breath. "And very specific."

4

Scarlett chuckles, low and throaty. "Akiro and I can sneak you into your room. We'll tell people you have a headache."

I scoff. "Or you could just tell them the truth, and I'd be happier if they just left my house and never spoke to me again."

Aside from my other boss, Rigg, the only people I care about are with me. I don't need anyone else.

Dad's sobs are slowing, but they don't look like they'll be stopping anytime soon. I'm not leaving him, and I won't force him to stop grieving his dead wife. I'll stay with him all night if I must.

A message from Rigg hovers above Scarlett's watch, the text in a deep red.

Just carry her to the car.

He's sitting in his truck somewhere behind me, so I twist my arm that way and flip him off.

Scarlett pats me on the shoulder. "Take all the time you need. We'll see you at the house." With a wink, she leaves me alone with Akiro.

Akiro sniffs, wiping at his nose. "What do you need me to do? I can have someone bring all of us dry clothes, a tent, water, food, portable air conditioner. We can totally camp here. Oh, maybe some knee pads for your dad."

The briefest of smiles tugs at my lips.

For the longest time, the only two people I loved were

my mom and dad. Scarlett worked her way onto the list a while ago, reading me better than anyone else. Rigg's on there, too, but I'll never admit that out loud.

Akiro could easily become the fifth.

My skin pricks, all my hairs standing on end. I feel someone staring in our direction. When I turn, I spot a guy behind a tree, snapping pictures of Mom's coffin.

My mind flips into hyper-active mode and I calculate the distance between me and the man, plus draw up my plan of attack. Ripping off my shoes, I shove them into Akiro's chest and then take off, ignoring his shouts of confusion behind me.

Warm water squishes under my bare feet as I sprint across the grass, heading for the guy. His focus is on my dad and the casket, so he doesn't see me coming. Rain pounds down on me, soaking me through.

When I'm only a few feet away, I leap, throwing my body into the guy and sending him sprawling to the ground. I get off two solid blows to his face before I slip off, all the rain making it difficult to stay in place.

Plus, like a total idiot, I wore a dress, so I'm trying to remain somewhat modest here. Dresses are seriously one of the most impractical inventions, ever.

The guy is scrambling for his 3D camera, more worried about it than me. Whoever he is, he's a total amateur and has no idea who he's dealing with.

With all the pent-up anger inside me, I turn him over

and punch him right in the nuts. The man groans, folding inward and cupping his hands over his groin.

I wait for him to finish whining like a baby before asking, "Who are you?"

When he doesn't answer, I reach under my dress, yank out the knife strapped to my thigh, flip it open, and hold the sharp blade against the man's neck, just barely pricking the skin, a small amount of blood escaping. "What are you doing here?"

The man just glares at me, doing a weak version of a snarl. It's then that I notice the gold and diamonds laughing up at me. I rip the tie clip off him and wrap my fist around it. I know exactly who it belongs to, and he should be thanking all the stars above that he isn't here for me to jam it down his thick throat.

Burly. Aka, Wyatt Mitchell.

Son of a locked-up terrorist.

CHAPTER TWO

AFTER GETTING OFF ANOTHER BLOW—KNOCKING the guy unconscious—I take off, heading for the exit of the cemetery, folding my knife so the blade isn't exposed, and then shooting Akiro a quick message. I need to go to Wyatt and question him. Why does he have someone spying on Mom's funeral? Especially an incompetent fool. It's insulting.

I leap over an old-school headstone, barely clearing the top. That family should really invest in a projected gravestone instead. Less clutter in the graveyard and easier to run around.

I thought I'd seen the last of Wyatt at Everly's gala. I mean, yeah, I blew his entire operation wide open, stabbed him in the arm, shot him in the leg, and got him arrested, but I've already moved on. So should he.

Two steps onto the road, Rigg's massive truck is suddenly there, the bright lights blaring in my eyes.

Seconds after I lift my arms to block the lights, two gigantic arms are around my waist. Rigg lifts me in the air like a doll—he's seriously lucky the blade of my knife is tucked away—and tosses me in the back of his truck, slamming the door closed. I jiggle the door handle, but nothing happens. Stupid child protection locks.

With a growl, I yank out his headrest and jam a bar into the bottom corner of the back window. My fist clenches, ready to strike down and shatter the glass, but Scarlett is suddenly in the back seat, pulling me away from the window and ripping the headrest from my hand. She holds it out to Rigg, who snatches it from her hands with a snarl of his own.

"Let me go!" I yell, squirming in her grip.

Scarlett's scratchy voice is cool and light. "Calm down, Harper."

If it were Rigg holding me, I'd be digging my chewed-up nails into his skin, trying to peel him off me. But I love Scarlett too much to do that to her.

I stop squirming long enough that she finally lets go of me. As much as I want out of the truck, I know I can't get past Rigg and Scarlett. They're the ones who trained me to fight.

"Who was that?" Rigg asks, jamming the headrest back into his seat.

I hold up the tie clip. "A friend of Wyatt Mitchell."

Both Scarlett and Rigg pause, sharing a shocked look before turning their wide eyes to me.

I wring out the bottom of my dress, letting the water fall onto the carpet of the truck. Thank goodness I recently buzzed my head. I just flick my hand over the fuzz, and I'm good to go.

Seeing my knife on the floor, I snatch it up and tuck it back in the sheath strapped to my thigh, so I'm not tempted to use it on anyone.

"What was he doing?" Scarlett asks. She's squirming in the seat next to me, and I know it's bothering her that she didn't notice some random creep lurking around the cemetery. The fog did a fairly decent job of covering him up, though.

I attach the clip to the top of my dress. "Taking pictures of us."

Rigg sits back in his seat, scratching at the scruff on his chin and sighing. "I'll look into it."

I fold my arms. "No, you won't. I will."

He opens his mouth to say something, but Scarlett cuts both of us off. "I'm assuming you'll want to go as soon as possible?"

I nod.

"It usually takes a week to get on the approved visitor list. I'll call the jail and let them know you're coming." Scarlett scrolls through the calendar hovering above her watch. "Both Rigg and I are busy all next week." She lowers her wrist and turns to me. "I know you love to do things alone, but please take someone with you. At least for the ride there. Akiro or Pearl. I can ask Lincoln if you want."

Lincoln's the tech guy at DPS, and while I enjoy his company, he won't be able to help. The guy has no physical training and doesn't quite know how to deal with my explosive personality.

"What about Bo?" I ask. He's a DPS operative, and way more intimidating than Rigg and Scarlett combined. I've never done a one-on-one with him, and I know I could learn a thing or two from the guy.

Scarlett shakes her head. "He has a pressing assignment right now."

"Zia?" I ask. She's the newest DPS operative, hired by Everly after the showdown at the gala. She's a little zesty—according to Pearl—but she's as tough as they come.

Rigg mutters something incoherent under his breath. He's not the biggest fan of Zia, but Everly insisted on her joining our operation. I think she just wanted someone on the inside to spy on us and make sure we're living up to her standards.

"Also busy," Scarlett says, checking the calendar hovering about her watch, her lips twisting in amusement at Rigg.

I mull it over in my head. That's my list of options when it comes to DPS. There are a few other operatives, but they're all on assignment in the east, a new venture we're trying out. We normally stick to the west.

"I'll take Akiro," I finally say. At least the guy's a ninja and knows how to fight.

Scarlett twists one of the many diamond earrings on her ear, reminding me that I'm wearing my mom's angel wing earrings Dad got her for their anniversary.

I hate jewelry, but when Mom gave me the earrings the day before she died, I made Pearl take me to get my ears pierced. Unless something crazy happens, they're staying on until the day I die.

Someone knocks on the back door of the truck. "Can I come in?" Akiro. "It's raining out here!"

Rigg unlocks the truck and Akiro climbs in next to me. Now I'm sandwiched between him and Scarlett. I expect her to go back up front, but no way is she giving me the opportunity to break a window and escape.

Smart lady.

I turn to Akiro. "I should probably go back out there to my dad."

He takes my hand in his. "Forest finally got him to leave. I think your sudden departure snapped him back to reality."

I tense. "Dad didn't go after the guy, too, did he?"

"Nah." Akiro rubs my hand. "Your dad didn't see him. I told your dad you were running from your feelings."

I'm not sure if I should tell Dad that a creepy man was taking our pictures. He has enough to worry about right now.

Rigg enters my address into the system and sets the

truck to autopilot. The man usually loves to drive—he has to be in control—but even from the back seat, I can hear the wheels grinding in his head. He's probably dying to know what Wyatt is up to as much as I am.

Akiro clears his throat. "So, are you guys going to update me on who that guy was, or we just going to sit here in surly contemplation?"

I squeeze his hand. "Clear your schedule one week from today. We're going to jail."

CHAPTER THREE

WYATT'S BEING HELD in a maximum-security prison up near San Francisco. Akiro and I hop into my car in the early afternoon and I enter the address into the GPS system, including a pitstop at Canyon Crest High School. Though San Fran is about five hundred miles away, if I use the autopilot lane on the freeway, we can be there in about three and a half hours.

Even after eight months, I'm trying to wrap my head around the fact that I have a car. My whole life, my family has been poor. Most days we were just scraping by, hoping we'd have dinner on the table that night.

Everly had bought the car for Akiro to replace his gas-guzzling dinosaur of a car, but he gave it to me instead. I think he regretted the decision when his car died three months later. Since we're together all the time, in the end, it doesn't matter.

The sun is still occupying the sky, so I turn the windshield to visor mode, blocking any sun from getting frisky with our eyes. Thank goodness the storm has passed.

I wanted to leave early in the morning, but Pearl had some function at school, even though it's summer. The girl takes her student body president role way too seriously.

I hadn't planned on Pearl coming with us, but when Dad found out I was going to San Fran, he insisted we get a hotel for the night so we wouldn't be on the road after ten with all the ruffians. Then he decided he didn't want me and Akiro being in a hotel room alone, so he forced me to invite Pearl.

When I told Akiro she was coming, he made this squished, pained face like he was going to break down crying. Now that we're on the way, though, he's just excited to be going, bouncing in the passenger seat like me at a knife sale.

As soon as we pull up in front of the school, Pearl skips toward the back seat, opens the door and slides in, her blonde hair in a perfect bun atop her head. A pink paisley ribbon is tied around it, the ends hanging down to her slender neck.

I run a hand over my buzzed hair. Pearl kept arguing with me on how I needed to style my hair for the funeral, so I shaved my head. Problem solved. Not sure if Pearl's forgiven me for it yet, and I really don't care. It's just hair.

Pearl pulls a mirror from her bag and reapplies her ultra-shiny lip gloss. "Thanks for waiting for me. I wanted to make sure everything is in order for Homecoming."

"It's three months away," I say.

Pearl purses her lips in frustration. "I know. We're so behind this year. Life has just been crazy with the new job and everything else ..." She trails off, and I wait for her to expand, but she doesn't.

I pull my legs into my chest, turning to face Akiro. He has his hair in two spikes today, side by side on his head. I reach forward and set my hand between the two spikes. "You could totally use this as a taco holder."

Akiro grins, splitting his face wide. "That would be so freaking awesome." He adjusts his shirt that says, *I study between ninja sessions*, so the collar hangs better around his neck. The shirt has a couple of holes in it, but he knows it's my favorite shirt of his, so he wears it all the time. I could probably make him a new one. It's an easy enough design.

He points to his hair. "It was actually my uncle's idea, going with the two spikes."

His Uncle Hitoshi recently came here from Japan. They haven't said how he got here—the current president, Gilford Poulson, shut down all international travel when he was sworn in after the War of 2098. But given that DPS caught Akiro and his dad smuggling in people from Japan on a ship not too long ago, it's easy to put two and two together.

I thought about bringing it up to Rigg and Scarlett but decided to keep the information to myself for now. I mean,

16

DPS hasn't picked up on any potential threat, so, no harm, no foul, right?

Pearl sets her mirror and lip gloss back in her bag before she leans forward. "I'm so excited we get to stay the night in San Fran! It's been forever since I've been there."

"This will be my first time," I say.

Pearl's jaw drops. "You've *never* been? Seriously?"

I roll my eyes at her. "Yeah, my family couldn't afford food sometimes, but we went on all these extravagant vacations around the country."

She answers with an eye roll before her smile splatters on her face. "Where should we go tomorrow? We could see the Golden Gate bridge! I've been dying to see it since they rebuilt it."

Akiro cups his hands over his mouth. "I want some Ghirardelli chocolate!"

The sound of fist meeting flesh echoes around the car, my ringtone for Scarlett. I can't help but grin. I hit answer on the screen and suddenly her bright face is hovering between me and Akiro, the 3D image incredibly lifelike.

"You kids aren't into any trouble, are you?" she asks. She spits some sunflower shells into a cup that disappears from the projection when she lowers it.

"Not yet," I say.

She winks. "Good. Listen, semi-bad news. The prison called and said you can't come tonight. But you can first thing in the morning. I have you scheduled at eight."

Akiro groans. "Eight! That's so early!"

I reach through Scarlett's projection and shove him on the arm. "You don't have to come with me. You two just sleep in."

Pearl shifts uncomfortably in the back seat while she clutches at the pearls around her neck. "Yeah, so not staying in a hotel room alone with your boyfriend for hours, Harper."

Akiro wipes at his shoulder. "I know it's hard to fight off the temptations, Pearl, but you're just going to have to resist my charm."

Pearl, Scarlett, and I all roll our eyes at the same time.

Scarlett turns her attention to me. "Have everything you need?"

I nod. "Lincoln helped me pack all the tech. I'll record everything, I promise."

"Good." She scratches at an eyebrow. "Akiro, Pearl, will you do me a favor?"

"Sure!" Pearl says. "Name it!"

The girl is too happy for her own good.

Scarlett scrunches her nose, holding back a smile. "Make sure Harper has some fun this weekend. Nothing too crazy where you get arrested, but she needs to loosen up and be a teenager for once in her life."

"Hey, I can have fun," I say. When they all stare at me incredulously, I huff. "I can!" Okay, so my life revolves around my family, work, and Akiro. I don't have time for anything else.

"Harper, you know I love you," Scarlett says in her

gentle tone, "and I know you just lost your mother, but she'd want you to enjoy your trip. She'd want you to create a bunch of memories, take a ton of pictures and videos, and then report back to her about everything."

Scarlett and Akiro have been hung up on me visiting my mom's grave as much as possible now that she's buried. They said it will be therapeutic to talk to her. I think I'll just look like a crazy person talking to a projected stone, but whatever.

Frustration boils up inside, thinking about my mother, so I quickly shut it down and move on. Now isn't the time for a break-down.

My only goal for the weekend is to find out what Wyatt is up to. But I know that sometimes you just have to say what people want to hear. "Well, Pearl does want to go see the Golden Gate Bridge."

Pearl squeals in the back. "We're going to have so much fun!"

Scarlett arches an eyebrow. "That wasn't really what I had in mind for something wild, but if it gets you out of the hotel and into fresh air, then I'm all for it."

I clap my hands together, remembering something. "My history teacher last year talked about some island there in San Fran. Used to house Alcatraz prison. Everything's been burned to ashes, but it's supposed to be way haunted. Like you can see the ghosts of old prisoners walking around. People have gone missing from the island, too!"

The smiles on Akiro and Pearl's faces are strained. They both laugh uneasily.

"Or, we could go to the Golden Gate Bridge," Pearl says through her strained smile.

I wave a hand. "There's time for both. We can stay until Sunday. I mean, none of us have to be back until Monday, right?" I've been itching to get back to work, but Rigg and Scarlett forced me to take this week off. Monday, though, my life will finally go back to normal. Somewhat.

They share a look, and I try not to read too much into it. It's their, 'how do we put Harper down gently?' look. I really should have picked creepier friends.

Scarlett's eyes light up. "If I didn't have to work, I'd join you for that."

See, that's why I love Scarlett so much. She gets me.

Scarlett spits some more shells into her cup. "Oh, and Pearl, love your mockup for the new DPS jackets. They're brilliant."

Pearl shimmies, her infamous dance when she's excited. "Thank you!"

Scarlett waves her fingers at us. "Take videos. Have fun. Don't get arrested. Got it?"

We all nod at her before her projection disappears and the call ends.

A couple of months after the attack at Everly's gala, Pearl randomly went off one day, telling me how impractical our gala outfits had been. She said we needed to look glamorous yet be able to fight at the same time. She rattled off about different materials, flexibility, wigs, and a whole bunch of other crap I don't care about. But it did tell me she'd be a wonderful asset for DPS.

She spent days working on the perfect bullet-proof dress, covered with sequins and still giving me the ability to scale a wall in the thing. After showing it to Rigg and Scarlett—complete with a demonstration of me beheading a dummy without wrinkling or tearing the dress—it didn't take long to convince them to hire her.

Pearl immediately accepted the job. While she'd been nervous at the gala, the whole thing had given her a rush she'd never felt before. And, like Lincoln, she prefers being behind-the-scenes, which works out perfectly.

It meant giving up being a ballerina, but that had always been her mom's dream, not Pearl's. I do catch her doing pirouettes around Headquarters now and again, though.

Pearl's eyes gleam, and I really don't like the smile on her face. "We should go dancing tonight! There are so many fun clubs in San Fran."

I point to my tattered shirt, ripped jeans, and duct-taped shoes. "Do I look like someone who likes to dance?" Yeah, I can afford new clothes now with my higher pay, but I didn't feel right in them. No matter what, I don't want to lose the side of me that shaped me into the woman I am today.

Pearl shimmies again, and my stomach clenches. "I may have brought you an outfit to wear."

I throw my head back, groaning. "You know I hate dresses."

She puts her hands on her hips. "Who said anything about a dress? Did you forget that I know you, Harper?" She grins. "This is going to be the best night ever!"

CHAPTER FOUR_

I HAVE to give credit to Pearl. The outfit she brought me is spot on, fitting my personality better than anything else she's thrown together. The black, shiny slacks have rips and tears, but is somehow done in a classy way. She took a red dress shirt and ripped off the sleeves, cinching the ends so they made a little ruffle. She made a skinny, straight tie from the same material as the pants, tying it loosely around my neck.

With a wicked grin, she clips the gold and diamond tie clip I took from the creepy picture-taking dude onto my tie. "Perfection."

Akiro comes out from the bathroom in the hotel room, whistling and wriggling his thick eyebrows when he sees me. He has on pants similar to mine, a red tee, and a black leather jacket. He snaps a pic of the two of us and then sends it to his uncle, so he can show off his hair. Akiro and Hitoshi have been thick as thieves since he arrived, hanging out often. I think Hitoshi is trying to catch up for all the years he missed of Akiro's childhood.

Akiro's hair is in three spikes. He points to them. "I can hold two tacos tonight." He wraps his lanky arms around me, pulling me tight against his chest. "One for you, and one for me."

Pearl clears her throat. "You two know I'm here, right?"

We turn to face her, still holding each other close. She has her hands on her hips, accentuating her tall, skinny frame. She's wearing a silky, white dress that matches the pearls around her neck and hanging from her ears. She's ditched her combat boots—she started wearing them in honor of her brother who passed away—for a set of heels that look extremely uncomfortable.

"Why can't *I* have a taco?" she asks.

Akiro kisses the top of my head and then releases me. "You can have a taco, Pearl."

"I didn't realize you like tacos so much." I slip on my black sneakers—sans duct tape. Going fancy tonight.

She smooths out her dress. "I don't really want a taco. I just don't want the two of you to be all over each other tonight and completely ignore me."

Akiro throws his head back, laughing. He cups his fist over his mouth, his shoulders bouncing up and down in his laughter.

"When has that ever happened?" I ask. I punch Akiro in the stomach, so he'll stop laughing.

24

He doubles over, holding his stomach. His words come out in a grunt. "Harper really isn't the cuddly type. Or the PDA type."

I glare at him. "Hey, I don't punch just anyone in the stomach. It's normally someone I care a lot about."

He grins widely through his grimace. "Such a romantic, my Harper."

Taking a fistful of his shirt, I yank his lips toward mine, giving him a nice, hard kiss. When I finally release him, he's still grinning.

"And that is what I *like* about you," he says.

Akiro knows that if he uses the other "l" word, he'll be in big trouble.

Pearl bounces on her toes, her bubbly nature back. "Okay, let's go find someone for *me* to kiss."

I hold open the door to the hotel room and we all step outside.

"What's your type?" I ask as I swipe my hand in front of the elevator pad, letting it know someone wants a ride.

Pearl twists her lips to the side. "Kind. Funny. Tall so I can gaze up at him. Blue eyes. Close with his family. Dreamy. Goal-oriented." She shrugs. "The usual things."

The elevator doors ping open and we step inside.

"You know you can't bring the guy back with you to San Diego, right?" Akiro asks, leaning up against the elevator wall.

I lean against him sideways, facing Pearl. "How are we supposed to know if he's close with his family? You really want us to ask him that?" If Akiro is surprised by my close-ness, he doesn't show it. Smart guy.

"He'll say yes no matter what," Akiro says, placing a hand gently on my back, "if he wants to hook up with you."

Pearl puts her back to the elevator doors, stepping out backwards when they ping open. She throws her arms wide. "I'm good at reading people. I'll be able to answer all those questions within minutes of meeting him."

As we follow her out, a tall, gangly guy with a bandaged nose and a small cut on his neck bumps into Pearl, muttering indecipherable words as he slips past us to get inside the elevator.

"Rude," Pearl says, glaring at him.

Akiro is trying to calm Pearl down, but my eyes are only on the guy. It's the same guy from the cemetery. The creepy one with the 3D camera.

As the elevator doors start to slide closed, he looks up at me, his bruised eyes going wide. At the very last second, I slink into the elevator with him, the doors closing behind me, trapping me alone with the guy.

I'm more worried for him than I am for me, especially with the anger raging inside me at the thought of this jerk taking pictures of my mom's coffin.

He immediately throws up his arms in surrender. "Please don't punch me again."

I step close, staring up at him. "Are you following me?"

He swallows, his large Adam's apple bobbing. "If I

were, I wouldn't make it so obvious." Sweat slides from his forehead, careening down his cheeks like a faucet has been turned on. The guy must have some weird disorder or something for it to be this excessive. He wipes some away, flinging it in my eyes.

Blinking the sting away, I step back, creating a distance from the sweat waterfall happening before me. "Seriously, if Wyatt hired you, he picked a terrible person for the job. You're sweating more than my uncle at Thanksgiving dinner."

The guy runs his lanky fingers through his damp hair. "I'm just a photographer, that's it. He asked me to take pictures of the funeral, so I did."

"Have you delivered anything yet?" I ask.

The guy shakes his head. "I'm seeing him tomorrow."

If I had sleeves to roll up, this is the part when I would do it. Instead, I space my feet shoulder width apart, squaring myself. "You're not going to see him and you're not giving him any footage of my mom's funeral, understand?"

"Listen, kid—"

With a growl, I sweep out my leg, knocking the guy from his feet, as I reach down and retrieve my knife strapped to my ankle, flipping open the blade. The man lands with a thud on his back, gasping for air.

Leaning in, I press the blade to his neck as I drive my knee into his chest. My hand twitches, wanting to hurt this guy who took advantage of my grieving family.

The elevator doors open behind me, and there's a sharp gasp. I turn to see an elderly couple about to get on the elevator, their jaws dropped in shock. Their gaze passes between me, the guy, and the knife I have against his throat, and they take a few noticeable steps back.

Crap. I'm usually not this careless in public, letting regular citizens seeing me threaten people. Rigg will kill me if he finds out.

"This elevator is full," I say, moving away from the guy so I can slam my hand over the button that closes the door. Then I lock it in place, so we're stuck in an unmoving elevator.

The guy is trying to get back on his feet, so I pounce on top of him, holding my knife toward his face, but he throws his arms up to protect himself, whimpering like a puppy the whole time.

"Okay! I won't give him the images!"

With a sigh, I stand and let the guy scramble away from me. Why would Wyatt hire such an idiot? I mean, he knows what I'm capable of, yet he still hired a pansy.

I can't shake the thought that he did it on purpose. Like Wyatt *wanted* me to come to him. It piques my curiosity that much more.

I hit the button so the elevator will move again. The guy is backed into the corner, shaking in fear. I point the knife at him. "Delete *everything* from my mom's funeral." I wait for him to nod before I continue. "I never want to see your face again."

"Feeling is mutual," he squeaks out.

When the elevator doors open, he hightails it out, squealing like an injured animal.

Both Akiro and Pearl are glaring at me, arms folded, shaking their heads. I flip my knife closed, then strap it back to my ankle.

"What did you do to the poor guy?" Pearl asks.

Straightening out my tie, I join them in the lobby. "A small threat. No big deal."

Akiro clucks his tongue. "Pretty sure the guy peed himself."

I snort. "Wouldn't be the first time I caused that reaction out of someone."

Waiting until morning to talk to Wyatt is going to kill me. Ignoring Pearl's wishes, I make-out with Akiro all night on the dance floor, trying to focus my mind somewhere else. He pauses at one point, I know curious as to why I'm being so affectionate lately, but the glare in my eyes must do the trick, because he just shrugs and goes back to kissing me. I mean, the guy really can't complain about all the action he's been getting.

There's just so much pent up energy inside of me that I don't know what to do with it all. For the time being, it's either kiss my boyfriend, or beat the crap out of someone.

Thankfully for everyone around me, Akiro is an amazing kisser.

CHAPTER FIVE_

When I sneak out in the morning, Akiro and Pearl are both dead asleep in the hotel room. Neither of them stir as I get ready, and it isn't like I'm in any way quiet.

On the rails to the prison, I call Dad, accepting the option of a projected screen. In addition to his voice coming through my earpiece, I use a noise-canceling filter that covers the perimeter around me so no one can hear our conversation. They'll just see my mouth moving. The app also distorts the image, so they won't be able to see who I'm talking to. Only I can make out Dad's features. Lincoln just invented the app, and I absolutely love it.

Dad's sleepy face greets me. "Morning, Harper."

Casper, our Persian cat I obtained during an investigation last year, is sprawled out on Dad's chest, snoring. The poor guy has been missing Mom something fierce, just like the rest of us.

"Just wanted to check in," I say.

Casper stirs at my voice, looks up, blinks at my projection, stands, turns in a circle—three times—then cozies back up on Dad's chest.

The puffs around Dad's eyes are larger than normal. He must have cried all night long. I hate that I wasn't there for him. At least Forest is still there. Otherwise, I wouldn't have left.

Dad blinks a few times, then rubs his eye with his hand. "Are you wearing a wig?"

I adjust it on my head. "How about we not talk about that?" Pearl thought it was a good idea to appear innocent while at the prison, not like I was up to no good. My goal is to make myself the least memorable as I can to everyone. The brown hair goes to my shoulders, a small curl on the bottom. "I ran into the creepy cemetery guy at the hotel last night."

Dad sits up, ignoring Casper's growl. "Please tell me he's still alive."

I roll my eyes. "I didn't kill the guy, Dad. I didn't even get to stab or punch him. The guy cowered like Casper when he sees a vacuum."

Dad chuckles. "You do have that effect on people." He yawns, covering his mouth with his hand. "Get anything out of him?"

"Just that Wyatt hired him."

Dad scratches at the scruff growing on his face. He hasn't shaved since the night Mom passed. "Why would he hire such an amateur?"

"I have no idea." I shift in my seat. "I can't help but think he *wants* me to go to him."

Dad knows what I do for a living. He used to work security himself for the president years ago. I had to hide my job from him and Mom for so long, it's nice having him know now. I hate keeping things from them.

"Wouldn't surprise me," Dad says. "Fits his profile. You going to record everything?"

I nod. "DPS gave me all the equipment I'll need."

"Any trace of you visiting?"

"Nope. I'll install a Trojan horse when I get there that will wipe me from the prison's feed."

Dad nods. "Good." He leans forward. "Analyze everything, Harper. Not just his words, but the way he says them. His mannerisms. His reactions."

"Will do."

"Have you covered up your tattoo?"

I take off my watch so I can show him the inside of my wrist. I snuck into Pearl's makeup bag and stole some concealer to completely cover my tattoo. It's an infinity symbol, blue on one side, red baseball stitching on the other, the word 'Cubs' along it. Dad grew up in Chicago and passed his love for the Cubs on to me.

"Good." He sighs, running his hand along his neck. "And please don't do anything stupid."

I put a hand to my chest. "I'm highly offended. When have I ever done anything stupid?"

He quirks a bushy, gray eyebrow. "Is that a rhetorical question?"

"I'll be on my best behavior, promise," I say, putting my watch back on.

He squints his eyes at me before he finally leans back, scratching Casper behind the ear. "I better not see anything on the news about a prison riot or an inmate being shivved by a visitor."

I go to twist one of Mom's angel wing earrings on my ear, but then remember I left them back at the hotel. I hate not wearing them, but the prison would do a thorough scan of them, plus they're memorable. I don't want to risk losing them. "Can't shiv him. There will be glass separating us."

"Please don't take that as a challenge, either," Dad says.

The man knows me too well.

"Love you, Dad," I say.

He smiles softly. "Love you, too, Harper. Call me when you're done."

A couple of minutes later, my watch vibrates, a projected preview of Rigg hovering over my wrist. He's calling, and wants to video chat, which is unlike him. So, it's either really good news, or really bad news. With my recent record, I'm banking on the latter.

Steeling myself, I accept the call.

Rigg is so ticked off, I reel back, even though it's just a

projection of him, not the real thing. "You attacked a guy in an elevator?"

I swallow. "It was the guy from the cemetery."

"You drew a weapon on him with innocents around!"

Even though I have the new app, I glance around the rails out of habit to see if anyone is listening, but everyone is preoccupied with videos or music.

"I'm sorry," I say. "I got caught up in the moment and wanted to see why he was there."

Rigg takes a deep breath, briefly closing his eyes, trying to pull himself together. When he opens his eyes back up, the anger hasn't melted even a little bit. "You're smarter than this, Harper. Act like it."

"Yes, sir," I say, unable to hide the annoyance in my voice. I mean, no one got hurt, and the couple was really old. They'll probably forget all about it in a day or two with their fading memories, right? "How did you find out?"

"The couple reported it to management," Rigg says. "They threatened to involve the police. I had to talk them down."

That means DPS has been monitoring everything from our trip. I shouldn't be surprised, but I am. I thought we had more trust than that.

"I want a full write-up, plus a video confession, of everything that happened in my inbox by tomorrow morning," Rigg says, his jaw clenched tight.

"Yes, sir."

"Use your head next time." With that, he ends the call.

Seconds later, a message scrolls above my watch in a slanted black font. It's from Bo, another DPS operative. With how guarded he is, I've started to call him The Brick. Doing a one-on-one mission with him is on my bucket list. I bet the number of things I could learn from him would be mind-blowing.

> Bo: *You got in trouble because you were caught. I can show you how to threaten someone with a knife without anyone else noticing. Come find me when you're back from San Fran.*

My hearts actually skips a beat in excitement. Bo wants to train me? It's so out of character for him, but people have been doing all sorts of weird things for me since Mom died. Normally, I'd tell him to shove his pity where the sun don't shine.

But there's no way I'm passing up on this golden opportunity to work with The Brick.

CHAPTER SIX_

CALLOWAY PENITENTIARY in San Francisco is state-of-the-art, the high-rise almost ninety floors. Prisoners are housed starting at the twentieth floor, so if they want to escape, they'll have to jump from a window. Two problems with that. One, they'll die from the fall. Two, there are hardly any windows in the gray slab, and of the ones that do exist, you have to be smaller than me to squeeze through. Needless to say, no one has ever escaped the prison.

Before I enter the building, I install Lincoln's Trojan horse that will easily override the prison's system. They probably think it can't be done, but they've never met Lincoln or anyone that works at DPS. We only hire the best of the best.

The Trojan horse will wipe me from any camera feed in the building, making it seem like I never even stepped foot inside. After I leave, my name will be wiped from the visitor's log, leaving no trace, hence my need for making my appearance as bland as possible. I can't be memorable to the staff.

The visitor's entrance is on the east side, the huge iron doors practically impenetrable. They make me enter a vacuum-sealed room, cleansing me of any bacteria I might bring in with me. They need one of these babies at my high school. Bonus points if it could cleanse people of their stupidity as well.

Then they do a scan of my body, making sure I don't have any weapons stuffed in any crevice. Wyatt's tie clip I brought with me is put inside a metal box where they do a thorough scan.

The guard hands me back the tie clip, satisfied it can't be used as a weapon of any kind. Another person underestimating my abilities. My fist clenches around the clip, and for the tiniest of seconds, I want to jam it in the guy's eye and prove him wrong.

Surprised, I shake the thought from my head, loosening my grip on the clip. I need to get to the workout room in DPS Headquarters as soon as possible and work off this aggression before someone gets seriously injured.

As I sit in the waiting room, trying to calm myself to a reasonable level, projected ads float about, their respective businesses seeking out potential clients. A round disc stops near me, the 3D image being projected upward. A lady with a beehive hairdo smiles at me.

"Get something special for your inmate," she says in a way too sultry voice. *"We have a full catalog where you can find the perfect lingerie to suit your personality."*

I gag and then flip off the projection. With a scowl, the ad moves on to a lady sitting near me, who perks at the mention of lingerie.

Conjugal visits aren't allowed at Calloway. You can, however, wear practically anything you want so your significant other can ogle you from the other side of the glass. One of the many things wrong with this world, if you ask me.

A minute before my scheduled visitor's time, I start the recorder on my watch. Even though the prison did a security scan of it, the software on it isn't detectible. It's not necessarily illegal to record your conversations, but you do have to have the permission of the other party. No way Wyatt would allow that.

"Harper Chandler?" a guard says with an accent that tells me she grew up on the east coast. She must be one of the few that escaped to the west after the war.

When I stand, she motions for me to follow her. As we walk down the hall, she's scrolling through her datapad, information about me displaying on the projection above it. I hold in a laugh at the picture. Scarlett thought it was a good idea to have a picture of me that seems innocent, instead of my usual rough-around-the-edges self. Pearl had dressed me in a pastel dress she owns and put on the brown wig I'm currently wearing to take the picture.

She wanted me to wear a dress today, but I wanted to wear a dress shirt and tie so I could wear Wyatt's tie clip. She did talk me into a skirt, though, but only because there are shorts underneath. If a fight were to break out, I can rip off the skirt layer, making it easier for me to maneuver, but also so I can use the skirt as a weapon. Could come in handy to have the option of strangling Wyatt.

"So, you're Wyatt's niece?" the guard asks as we step into the elevator.

"Yep." I clasp my hands behind me and swivel my hips back and forth. "Uncle W is the best. I just hate that I haven't been able to visit him before now."

The elevator shoots up, and six seconds later, the doors are opening for the fiftieth floor. Wyatt made it to floor fifty. That means they consider him middle-of-the-pack when it comes to his threat level.

The man broke into my house, beat my mom, took me hostage, left me to die, plotted to assassinate Everly at her own gala, and blew a guy to pieces at said gala, yet, somehow, that's only a middle-of-the-pack threat.

Makes me wary of all the prisoners above me.

The guard escorts me to a concrete room at the end of the hall. The only thing in the room is a glass wall dividing it in two. No chairs. No tables. Nothing.

"You have thirty minutes," the guard says, standing in the doorway.

A buzzer on the other side of the room catches my attention. A door opens, and Wyatt steps inside, wearing a hideous fuchsia jumpsuit that does nothing for his pale complexion. He's shackled on the wrists and ankles, and the beeping red light on the chains tells me they're wired somehow, probably to shock him if he steps out of line. I wonder if I can make that happen and add some fun to this crappy situation.

The next thing I notice is that his hair is buzzed short, just like mine. I'm suddenly happy to be wearing a wig.

The door slides closed behind him and he runs his tongue across his sharp canine, his gaunt face shocking to see. "Harper Chandler." His lips tug into a smirk. "Miss me?"

CHAPTER SEVEN_

I THROW MY ARMS WIDE, smiling like the most ecstatic girl in the world. "Uncle W! You look …" I stare at his once buff body, noting how scrawny he's become. "Well, I'm going to be honest. You look absolutely terrible. Do they feed you in this joint?"

He grunts. "I have a new-found appreciation for Everly's cook."

"Probably should have never plotted to kill her and this"—I sweep my arms around the cold, concrete room —"would have never happened. Probably. I mean there were *a lot* of other bad things you did. But it started with Everly."

It's weird seeing Wyatt so skinny, no three-piece suit with that little handkerchief in the pocket, no fancy tie-clip, and no e-cig to be found. He used to be a man standing in a cloud of smoke.

He eyes my hair, then my clothes. "What's with the wig and skirt?"

I nod at his outfit. "What's with the fuchsia jumpsuit?"

His eyes narrow. "Didn't really have a say in my wardrobe."

"Same."

Wyatt saunters closer—favoring his left leg—the chains of his shackles clinking against the cement floor. "How's dear ol' Mom doing?"

I want to remain calm, and it takes everything in my power to not throw myself at the glass and yell every swear word I know at the guy. I clasp my clenched fists behind my back, trying to keep a passive face. "I didn't know you have a thing for dead ladies. Weird fetish, man."

The arrogance on his face falters for a moment before it comes settling back. "I had to keep tabs on the girl that ruined my life."

Placing my hand against my stomach, I chuckle. "Oh, Uncle W. You did this to yourself." I point to his left leg. "Noticed you're limping. Did it not heal properly?" I shot him in the leg during my investigation for Everly. He was arrested shortly after, so he probably never got the best medical treatment for it.

"It's fine." His wild, brown eyes slide down to the tie clip and he bares his fangs. "What did you do with Rodger?"

I glance down at the clip, straightening my tie. "Nothing, really. The guy is a coward."

"That was his payment."

I feign innocence, purposely doing a horrible job. "Oops." I stuff my hands in the pockets of my skirt. "I'm a little put-off that you haven't asked about Peaches."

Peaches is his fake toy poodle I used as an excuse to break into Wyatt's apartment last year. Same night I shot him. A truly memorable night. I ended up naming my car after good ol' Peaches.

I'm only bringing it up to see Wyatt squirm in his ugly jumpsuit. He hates the fact that I outsmarted him. I've added it to my list of totally awesome accomplishments. Gotta pad that resume.

"Why am I here, Wyatt? I know I'm charming, but I have a feeling you didn't miss me."

He takes another step closer, covering up his annoyance. "I thought we could help each other out."

I scratch at the back of my wig, wishing I could take it off. Then I remember Wyatt and I have matching haircuts and now I want to grow my hair back out. "Uh, you're in a prison and not getting out any time soon, plus I don't need anything from you." I shrug. "Also, I hate you."

Wyatt laughs, low and gruff. He holds up a shackled hand, waving a finger at me. "You see, you do need my help. In fact, you're going to *want* it."

I can't help but snort. "Why on this terrorist-infested earth would I *want* your help?"

He snaps his fingers. "You just answered your own

question."

Going over to the glass wall, I lean against it, crossing my feet at my ankles. They could have at least provided *me* a chair. Although, I don't like the idea of Wyatt being able to tower over me like that. They should give me a stool. One that I can raise as high as I want. "I don't have time for games. Just get to the point."

"How's everything going with Akiro?"

I scrunch my eyebrows together. "Ugh. Is this another weird fetish? High school relationships?"

With a smile, Wyatt leans against the glass, the skin on his arm squished. "Heard his uncle recently moved here."

It takes everything in me to hold back the surprise. "How would you hear anything? You're not allowed communication from the outside."

"You're not the only one with tricks up your sleeves, Harper."

I arch an eyebrow. "You know they can hear you, right? They record all visits."

He taps a finger against the glass. "We both know DPS did something to shut it down. The only recording is your personal one." He cracks his knuckles, one by one. "And, I'll bet my entire tie clip collection that there will be no record of you coming here today once you leave."

I'm squirming on the inside, but I stay cool on the outside. He's already dangled a couple of things in front of me: terrorists and Akiro's uncle. I finger the clip on my tie. "Time's running out. I have to leave soon."

"You just barely got here."

The man must be really craving attention to drag out a conversation with me. I wonder if he gets to talk to anyone here, or if he's all alone?

I push away from the wall, heading toward the door. I don't want to leave, but I want the man to get to the point. "Want me to tell Everly you say hi?"

"How much do you know about Hitoshi Fukunaga?" Wyatt asks, all casual and smooth.

With my back to him, I take a few deeps breaths, wanting to keep my cool. I need to find out who's feeding Wyatt information. I bet Scarlett or Rigg can help me find out.

I turn back around, resting my weight on my left foot. "He's Tomi's brother, loves sushi, and has an excellent sense of humor. Why? I don't think he's interested in guys, especially ones who are incarcerated, but I can ask."

Wyatt pounds a fist against the glass and then closes his eyes, breathing deeply. "I forgot how annoying you are."

"Why do you care about Hitoshi?"

He opens his eyes, glaring at me. "Let's just say, he's not the man you think he is."

My curiosity is totally piqued, and I have to bottle it in. "Was he adopted or something? Different father?" I clap my hands. "They aren't actually brothers, but have been best friends for so long, they *feel* like brothers."

"He's not as innocent as his brother."

"What do you want me to do about it?"

Wyatt pushes away from the glass and faces me, squaring his shoulders. "I have information for DPS that could stop a lot of people from getting killed."

"And I'm supposed to believe you? You're a terrorist yourself."

"I'm not a terrorist!" Veins are popping out of his neck. When he was beefy, the look intimidated me. Now, I'm doing everything in my power not to laugh. It's actually kind of adorable, in a pathetic sort of way. "I did what I had to do." His chest heaves in and out.

I hold up my palms. "Might want to calm down there, Uncle W. You don't want to have a heart attack, do you?"

He places his forehead against the glass. "Something big is about to happen, Harper, and you can stop it."

"If there is, DPS will pick up on it. It's what we do."

He shakes his head, his forehead sweeping back and forth on the glass. "DPS *might* pick up that something is off, but you won't be able to piece everything together before the attack. Not without my help."

I take a step forward. "Let's play your game for a second. Let's say there is some crazy attack going down, and we would need your help for some odd reason, why would you help? What do you get out of it?"

A grin breaks out on his face, his tongue running across his canine before he speaks. "You're going to break me out of prison."

CHAPTER EIGHT_

WE STARE at each other for a few seconds before I burst out laughing, clapping my hands together. Tears trickle down my cheeks as I wheeze for air, my stomach muscles clenching tight. With my eyes watering, I can't see Wyatt, but I know he can't be liking my reaction.

The man has lost his mind. I guess months of solitude and lack of nutrition will do that to someone. Why would I *ever* help him break out of prison? *How* would I even do it?

Bending over, I place my hands on my knees, trying to calm my laughter. It feels good to laugh. I haven't laughed like this in the longest time.

I can't wait to tell Mom and Dad about this.

My laughter abruptly stops.

I can't tell Mom. She's dead.

Standing straight, I wipe the rest of the tears from my eyes, willing myself to not break down.

"Are you done?" Wyatt asks, annoyance written all over him. He's back to leaning against the glass, looking at his short nails.

"Need some polish? I can see if I can smuggle you some in."

His eyes slide to mine. "DPS has the power to break me out."

I shake my head. "I'm not entirely certain they can, and even if they could, they wouldn't."

"Not even to save thousands of lives?"

That actually catches my attention. "Thousands?"

"Something big will happen within the next two weeks. Something that will kill *tens of thousands* of Americans. Including those you love." He points at me. "You can stop it."

The man is really grating on my nerves by dragging this out. He's lucky the glass is separating us, otherwise I'd be strangling the man with my skirt. "What do you know?"

He tsks. "I'm not telling you anything until you get me out of here."

"Like I said, that's not happening."

He pushes away from the wall so we are standing face to face, only the piece of glass keeping us apart. "You're willing to let that many people die because you're so stubborn?"

"I'm not stupid. Letting you out of here will be a huge mistake."

"You want all those lives on your conscience? Wasn't losing one parent enough for you?"

I slap my palm against the glass. "How can I even trust that you'll tell us anything if we got you out of here?"

He holds up his arm like he's swearing an oath, his other hand up next to it, thanks to the shackles. "You have my word. I'll tell you everything you need to know to stop the attack in time." He nods at me. "Now you promise to get me transport out of the U.S."

"You're joking, right?"

"That's all I'm asking in return. Safe passage for me and a guest out of this rotten country."

I quirk an eyebrow. "A guest? Who in the world would you invite to leave the country with you?" I laugh. "Who'd even accept the invite?"

"That's none of your concern."

I'm very curious to find out who it is, but I know he won't tell me. Not yet. "Why me, Wyatt? Why not ask Scarlett or Rigg?"

He lowers his arms, clasping his hands together. "As much as it pains me to admit, you're smart, Harper. You think in a way that no one else at DPS thinks. You're willing to sacrifice yourself for others."

"Everyone at DPS is like that."

He shakes his head. "No. Not like you. You have a fire and dedication that the others lack. They're just going through the motions, doing what they have to. Every move you make is intentional, calculated. There's a purpose to every choice you make in your life." His lips twitch. "You're a lot like me."

I scoff, taking a step back. "I've never been so insulted in my life."

He squeezes his eyes closed like he's trying to calm himself before he opens them back up and sighs. "Here's the thing, Harper. In less than two weeks, an attack you can't even fathom is going to happen. I'm being nice and throwing you a nugget of information here. Hitoshi Fuku-naga has been corresponding with some crime bosses in Japan." He takes a step back. "Do what you do best, look into him, and you'll find that I'm right. Then, you and DPS are going to break me out of here, and we will stop the son of a terrorist together."

I snort. That's my phrase and he knows it. "You better not be wasting my time."

"Trust me, I wouldn't have reached out if I didn't have to. You're one of the last people I wanted to see, and that I want to work with. But you're the only one who can help me, and I'm the only one who can help you. When you find out I'm right about Hitoshi, you'll be back here. Mark my word." He checks his nails, trying to appear casual. "Have you heard of Alcatraz?"

His question takes me aback. Why would he bring that up? "Yes."

He lowers his shackled hands, clasping them. "Might want to check it out before you go. Could find something useful in those haunted grounds."

"Useful, how?"

"Guess you'll have to figure that out. I think I've given you more than enough." He backs toward the door he came in. "Be seeing you soon, Harper."

"Wouldn't count on it, Uncle W."

I turn around and leave the room.

I have no idea if Wyatt is just playing a game with me, but I'm not sure why he would want to. I mean, he could be really bored in prison. What else is there to do? But, what if he's right? What if tens of thousands of Americans are in danger? Including my friends and family? It's my job to save them.

First things first, I need to do a little investigation on my boyfriend's uncle, the same man that Akiro idolizes. I really hope Wyatt is wrong.

CHAPTER NINE_

I'm GREAT AT LYING. I've been doing it since I could talk. But I only do it when it's truly necessary. Like when a convicted criminal tells you that your boyfriend's uncle could possibly be a terrorist.

No way I'm telling that to Akiro. Not until I have solid proof. There's always the chance that Wyatt is playing me. I have to approach this whole thing with that in mind. But I also can't ignore it. My job is assessing every threat, even if it seems minuscule or farfetched. I mean, Rigg once had me look into this sweet, old granny. Loved to bake cookies for her grandkids and knit them sweaters. When I broke into her house, I found an arsenal in the basement. Guns and ammo aplenty. Turned out she was planning an attack at her old workplace, seeking revenge on a power-hungry boss. Don't mess with granny, man.

It's also my job to keep everything close to the vest. So,

when Akiro and Pearl want me to spill every detail of the meeting, I don't reveal much.

We're sitting in a packed café near the bay. Chatter from the patrons buzzes through the air as tall robotic trays zoom around, delivering food to the guests. One pauses at our table and mechanical arms come out from either side, snatch two glasses of Dr Pepper from the tray, then reach out to me and Akiro. As soon as we take our drinks, the arms snap back inside, and the tray moves on to the next table.

I stuff my face with a massive club sandwich just so I don't have to speak. All I've told Akiro and Pearl is Wyatt thinks he knows about a terrorist attack going down.

Akiro doesn't work for DPS like Pearl and I do. The details of my visit with Wyatt, and his stupid demand to break him out of prison, is going to be kept under lock and key until I can talk to Rigg and Scarlett. I don't even want to tell Pearl. There are a lot of things that go down at DPS that I don't know about. You're only read into the missions you're working on. Lessens the chance of information falling into the wrong hands.

Akiro twirls a fry around in the ketchup splattered on his plate. "There's got to be more to it than that."

Pearl nods as she pokes at her kale salad. "How would Wyatt even know about it? He doesn't have access to anyone on the outside."

Akiro quirks an eyebrow. "Unless he does. Maybe he

paid off a guard with one of those fancy tie clips." He uses a fry to point at the one on my tie.

Grabbing a napkin, I wipe off the mayo spread across my mouth. "I think he's just bored. He hasn't talked to anyone for months. I was just an easy target because he knew he could piss me off in the process."

Pearl grins. "At least we got a fun trip out of the whole ordeal."

This is the part I'm not sure they'll agree to, but I'm going with or without them. "Speaking of fun trips, I want to go to Alcatraz Island tonight."

Pearl stacks some kale on her fork. "I know I can't talk you out of it, or anything, really, but what about tomorrow? During the day? You know, when there's sunlight and less chances of us running into ghosts."

Akiro drapes his arm behind me on the bench. "I didn't know you were a believer, Pearl."

She dabs gently at her lips with her napkin. "I like to keep an open mind." She sets the napkin on the table next to her plate. "You're Christian, Akiro. Do you believe in ghosts?"

He runs his fingers long my neck, gently tickling my skin. I love when he does that. I'll never tell him that, but he's good at reading cues.

"I do," he says. "I think we're surrounded by them."

They both turn to me and I try not to squirm. My family never really talked about religion growing up. Mom and Dad never said they believed, but they never said they didn't. Now that Mom is gone, a deep part of me wants to believe that she's still alive in some way and that I can see her again.

But Alcatraz is more along the lines of evil spirits, not the likes of my mom.

"I've seen a lot of evil with my job," I say carefully. "I have no doubt evil stuff went down at Alcatraz, and I wouldn't be surprised if some souls got trapped there."

Pearl folds her arms close to her chest. "And you want to go hang out with them tonight? That sounds appealing to you?"

"Learning more about our past is interesting to me," I say.

"That's what history books are for." Pearl opens one on her pink paisley watch, the words hovering above it in a projection. "Right here in the palm of your hand."

Akiro points a finger at her. "That's technically on your wrist."

His watch vibrates from an incoming message, and a smile breaks out on his face. Akiro holds out his arm so Pearl and I can see the projected picture his uncle sent him. Hitoshi is trying—and failing miserably—to stuff his face with a triple cheeseburger, pink sauce oozing out and falling down his chin. Akiro has been introducing him to all things American since he arrived.

Normally, I'd laugh at the image, which is exactly what Akiro and Pearl are doing. But my stomach clenches. Hitoshi can't be a terrorist. It would break Akiro's heart.

Our projected waitress hovers over to our table, smiling at us. "Anything else I can get you?"

"Just the checks," I say.

"Separate?" the waitress asks.

Akiro starts to say one check, but I elbow him in the stomach and Pearl shoots him daggers with her eyes from across the table. His voice comes out in a squeak. "Yep. Three checks, please."

Robotic arms come from the wall, removing our empty plates from our table. Seconds later, each of our watches ping, our checks hovering in red. I tap the checkmark to accept, and the image turns to green, letting me know the money has been pulled from my account.

Akiro accepts his check as well, the projection switching to green. "Did you know they used to have tips in America?"

"Tips?" I ask. Eating out is something I'm still getting used to. As a family, we try to eat at home as much as we can, sticking to our cheap meals we're accustomed to. It'll be interesting to see what happens now that Mom is gone.

"Yeah," Pearl says, adjusting the bun on top of her head. "People actually worked at restaurants." She shrugs. "I mean, besides the cooks. So, customers would give them a couple extra dollars for waiting on them."

I snort. "Sounds like an awful job. Having to deal with people."

We slink out of the booth and head toward the exit.

"Have a great rest of your day," our projected waitress says as we pass her.

The exit automatically opens when we approach, and we step out into the warm day in San Fran.

"Can we at least go to the Golden Gate bridge first?" Pearl asks with her fingers clasped together.

I bump her arm. "It's already routed in my vehicle."

With a squeal, she jumps up and down.

Now, I just have to pretend to be having fun until we can get to Alcatraz Island and find out what Wyatt is talking about.

CHAPTER TEN_

It somehow dropped about twenty degrees from the time we went back to the hotel to change and the time we came back out, ready to head to Alcatraz. I've always heard the weather near the bay can change dramatically in mere moments, but to witness it is something else.

Before we leave, I shoot off my 'incident report' to Rigg, breaking down everything that happened in the elevator in written and verbal form. I still don't see what the big deal is, but whatever. If he wants to read a totally boring report and then listen to my snarky voice, then he can have at it.

Pearl decides to wear a neon pink outfit, like it might scare away any ghosts. Honestly, it's almost scaring me away, it's so blinding. She's basically wearing a beacon that says, "Hey, please haunt me!"

She at least has black pants to tone down the bright

pink blouse, jacket, combat boots, earrings, and lipstick. Okay, it's doing nothing to tone it down.

I slip into the gray jacket Everly got for me last year when I worked for her. It was the first present I'd gotten in a long time, and I've taken better care of it than I have anything else I own.

Well, aside from Mom's earrings I'm currently wearing.

I tug a beanie over my buzzed haircut, hoping for some warmth while out in the night. Akiro has gone full black, like the true ninja he is. We tell Pearl she can stay at the hotel, but she insists on coming.

"I'll never forgive myself if something happens to you," Pearl says as we hop on the ferry that will take us to the island.

Besides us, there's a large group going on a ghost tour. Their guide tries to talk us into joining them for only ninety-nine dollars each, and before I can tell him where he can shove that ninety-nine dollars, Pearl politely declines while Akiro steers me away from the group.

Akiro holds up a palm. "I'm sorry, are you saying that you're here to be *our* guard?"

Pearl lifts her chin as she leans against the rail. "Scarlett has been training me recently, so I have some skills as well."

Akiro chokes on a laugh. "That's true, but that doesn't change the fact that I'm a ninja and Harper is, well, Harper."

Pearl throws out her arms. "I don't like to be left out, okay?"

"Shocker," I say under my breath with probably a little too much venom.

By the frown lines on her forehead, Pearl heard me. I shift my focus so I don't say anything else stupid.

A guy in the tour group catches my eye. There's something off about him. I can't point to a specific thing, but my bad guy radar is pretty much blaring. I gotta keep a close eye on him. He's chatting with a small group of people, seemingly harmless. I think it's just the way he carries his stocky build.

When we step off the ferry and separate from the tour group—once again declining the guide's crappy offer—Pearl switches on the flashlight on her watch, practically illuminating the entire island.

"Love the upgraded watch Lincoln gave me," she says, grinning. I can see every single detail on her face, thanks to the high beams. "The flashlight has a half-mile radius."

"Oh, good," Akiro says, shoving his hands in his jacket pockets. "That way the ghosts can't miss us."

All the color drains from Pearl's face. "I thought the light would scare them off!"

I pat her on the shoulder. "Some ghosts like the spotlight. Better watch your back." I hop onto a boulder, surveying the scene before us. Remains from Alcatraz Prison cover the island, making everything a haphazard mess. "Rumor has it, if you wander the ruins, dead inmates will speak to you, asking for help." I hop onto another boulder. "Some try to lure you underground."

Pearl lets out a small cry. I spin around to see her teetering on a rock, holding a baton in one hand. Akiro takes her hand and helps her gain her balance.

"You brought a baton with you?" I ask, gripping the strap of the messenger bag,

She swings it out in front of her, attacking the air. "I want to be able to protect myself."

"Should have brought holy water," Akiro says. "That baton will do nothing to a ghost."

Pearl swallows, her flashlight illuminating her face well. "I didn't think about that." She doesn't put her baton away. I guess just the thought of it is some sort of comfort.

I bounce through the building remains, grateful I wore my work boots. They're thick and sturdy, the light material molded to my feet. I might work for DPS the rest of my life just for the wardrobe they provide.

Before I became a full-time operative, I could only wear my gear on work-sanctioned missions. But now that I can be called upon at a moment's notice, I'm allowed to have DPS gear on me at all times. It's been pretty much amazing.

"There's supposed to be a secret underground facility," I say, kicking at some small pieces of concrete.

Akiro steps up beside me. "Let me guess. You want to

find it, break-in, and basically scar Pearl and me for the rest of our lives?"

I smile at him. "Hey, Scarlett told you to make sure I have fun on this trip. This is my idea of fun."

"You're so weird," he says under his breath, "in the sexiest way possible."

I push up on my tiptoes, kissing him hard on the lips. "Thank you."

"Did you hear that?" Pearl asks, panic in her voice. She's frantically sweeping the area, her flashlight showing no one near us.

"Hear what?" Akiro asks.

Pearl hurries over to us, huddling close. "It was a weird clacking noise, like someone was snapping their teeth together." She swallows. "I think there might be a ghost nearby."

I'm about to tell her there aren't any ghosts, when I remember a story Uncle Forest used to tell me as a kid, and I decide to have some fun with Pearl. "Oh, it might be Rufus McCain!"

Both Akiro and Pearl turn to me with raised eyebrows.

"Rufus tried to escape with Henri Young, but they were captured and sent to solitary for twenty-two months." I'm bouncing on the balls of my feet. "After they were released, Henri stabbed Rufus with a sharpened spoon. They claim Rufus haunts the place, clacking his teeth when someone is nearby, hoping the person is Henri so he can devour him."

Pearl folds her arms close to her. "Okay, you're way too excited about this."

Akiro eyes me, and when Pearl looks the other way, I wink at him. A smirk pulls at his lips for the briefest of seconds, and I know he's on board with scaring Pearl.

"Shh!" I hold up my finger, listening to the night. Waves slap against the shore, the smell of the ocean in the air. I close my eyes, trying to concentrate. Behind me, a pebble skids down a rock, landing with a quiet *thunk* against the debris. Wind brushes my cheeks, the breeze cool.

I suddenly open my eyes, and turn to the right, like I heard something.

"Please tell me you heard that," Akiro whispers right behind me, the tremble in his voice a nice touch.

I start toward the area, careful of every step.

"Someone is *hungry*," I sing under my breath.

"Shouldn't we be going the *other* way?" Pearl asks. She's suddenly at my side, clasping my arm. "Maybe it's just a sound system. All part of that tour group. You know, really creating an experience for them?"

With my watch, I scan for any tech equipment in the area and show Pearl the results. Nothing.

"Or, there really is a ghost," Pearl whimpers. "They'll go for me first!"

"Why you?" Akiro asks from the other side of me.

"Harper is way too salty," she says, "and you're way too sweet. I'm the perfect blend!"

Akiro scoffs. "Hey, I can be salty."

My foot sinks through the rocks and concrete, pushing against squeaking metal. I press against it. "I think there's something down here." Falling to my knees, I yank off my owl fingerless gloves, stuff them in my messenger bag, and pull out a pair of DPS gloves. After I tug them on, I start brushing away all the debris.

Akiro is quickly at my side, snatching another pair of gloves from my bag before helping me clear the area.

Pearl bounces near us. "This is a really bad idea."

Akiro and I work swiftly until a metal hatch is revealed. We both grin widely at each other.

"Well, even though you found it," Pearl says, "it's probably rusted shut. We should just leave. Like, right now."

Together, Akiro and I yank on the handle. It doesn't budge.

"See!" Pearl is giddy with excitement and relief. "Nothing we can do."

I rifle through my bag, seeing if I can find anything useful, but then remember I can't use anything obvious. I don't want anyone to know we were here, which means anything I have is out.

Closing my bag, I glance around, until I see a small chalk mark on a boulder next to me. I trail my finger in front of it, not actually touching the rock.

"Oh," Akiro says from over my shoulder, "do you think this is a drop point of some kind?"

Pearl squats next to us. "This would be the perfect place for one."

My skin itches. Is Wyatt right about people meeting up here to exchange information? I scan the area, running my fingers along the bottom of the boulder until I brush against some sort of envelope.

I dig in the dirt underneath the envelope until I can free it. I look up at Pearl. "Keep an eye out."

With a nod, she goes into training mode, turning her back to us and shining her light that way. I like this new Pearl. No questions, just actions. When it comes to ghosts, she's a scaredy-cat, but with real-life threats, the girl can hold her own.

"What do you think it is?" Akiro asks.

I shrug, not wanting to mention Wyatt or Akiro's uncle. "Only one way to find out." I carefully open the envelope and pull out some papers. They're covered in letters and numbers, nothing making sense.

Akiro grunts. "Secret code. I *hate* those."

With my watch, I quickly scan each paper front and back, making sure I get a good image of every inch of the papers. Being careful not to bend them, I slip the papers back in the envelope and seal it closed.

The light from Pearl's watch flickers until it turns off, leaving us in darkness.

Pearl swears under her breath, very uncommon for her. Both Akiro and I snicker.

"I thought I charged this," Pearl says.

She makes a few unladylike grunts before the light flicks back on, revealing the shady man from the ferry standing there.

He's glaring at us, holding a gun at his side. "Don't move."

CHAPTER ELEVEN_

My MIND SORTS through all the intel it gathers, analyzing everything in a matter of seconds. His finger is casually along the barrel, telling me he's trained. There's a slight bulge under his jacket—bulletproof vest. His middle finger on his free hand is tapping against his palm. Could be a nervous tick, or he's sending a secret code somehow, but I don't see any cameras anywhere. Maybe there's something up his sleeve he wants to get, like a blade of some sort.

He's tall and thick, his muscles more intimidating than Rigg's or Bo's. His hair is long, black, and curly with enough volume to make any girl jealous. By his face, I'm guessing he's Polynesian, which is uncommon since the war. Most went back to the comfort and safety of their islands.

The bad thing about this guy, though? His angry eyes tell me he's willing to do anything to protect himself and whatever secret he's hiding.

I need to downplay the situation before someone gets hurt.

I plaster an innocent smile on my face. "Sorry, mister, we didn't think this area was off limits."

His thick lips twitch, like he's surprised by my words. It takes him a second to respond. "It's not, but you're not supposed to disturb the earth."

Taking Pearl's wrist, I move it, shining the light around. "I don't see a sign."

"It was one of the rules the tour guide gave you," the man says, his finger ticking against the barrel of his gun. The man *wants* to shoot, like it's a favorite hobby of his. But he obviously doesn't want to create a scene if he doesn't have to, and, for all he knows, we're just kids poking our noses where they don't belong. So, like every kid out there.

Akiro shoves his hands in his pockets, going up on his tiptoes for a second. "Oh, we're not part of the tour group. We're just here on our own."

"Doing research for a school project." Pearl sways her hips side to side like an innocent schoolgirl.

Akiro's focus goes to the gun, his eyes going wide. "Are you a security guard or something?"

Pearl's gaze lands on the gun and she squeaks, grabbing my arm. "Is that a gun?"

I brace myself to move, knowing they might be pushing it a little too far and I'll need to take action, but the man seems to be buying the innocent act.

He tucks the gun back in its holster. "That's right. I'm a security guard." He's totally not. "While we let people visit the island, we like to protect the sanctity of it." He nods at the envelope still in my hand. "Where did you find that?"

I point to the boulder. "Under there. I thought it was part of the tour." I shrug. "Thought it would be funny to move it somewhere else and then watch the guide panic when they don't find it here."

"Have you opened it?" he asks, a weird edge to his voice. It's important to him.

I hold it up, waving it around. "No. Should I?"

His eyes narrow on the folder, like he'll actually be able to tell if the seal has been broken from where he stands. "You should probably just put it back where you found it. Don't want to ruin anything for those who actually paid for a tour."

Stepping back, I crouch and slip the folder back in the gap under the boulder. Akiro helps me put the dirt back around it, just like we found it.

When I stand, I brush off my gloved hands. "Sorry about that. Didn't think it would be a big deal."

"Guess we should be heading back," Pearl says, taking my hand.

I almost drop it because I don't do handholding, but then I notice the sweat on her brow, and I know she's freaked out.

The man holds up his palm. "I'll need to check your watches before you go."

"What? Why?" I ask. No way he's getting his grubby hands on my watch.

He smiles, but it doesn't touch his eyes. "I need to make sure you didn't take any images or anything."

Pearl's grip is getting tighter, and she's dang lucky I can take it.

"I didn't even get the thing open," I say. "You think I took a photo of some old envelope? Listen, I'm not one of those girls who takes pictures of every single thing that happens in her life."

The man nods at Pearl. "You might not, but she definitely does."

"Hey!" Pearl puts her other hand on her hip. "I am *not* one of those girls, I'll have you know." She points at Akiro. "He takes more photos than the two of us combined."

Akiro chuckles. "That's true."

The man takes a step closer to Akiro. "Show me your feed from the last hour."

With a shrug, Akiro pulls it up, scrolling through the feed hovering above his watch. It's just a bunch of photos of the three of us, our dinner, being out on the ferry, and that's it. There's a candid one of me that catches me by surprise. He caught me in a moment when I'm smiling at something Pearl said, and if one didn't know me any better, you'd think I was happy.

"That's a really good picture of you, Har ..." Pearl's eyes flick to the man and she clears her throat. "Harriet."

Not the best cover up.

The man motions to Pearl's watch. "Now yours."

She shows him all the footage, taking her sweet precious time, going into excruciating detail about every single photo like the man actually cares. I know she's stalling, trying to give me time to do something with my photos, but there's no way I'm deleting them. They're obviously super important, otherwise we wouldn't be in this mess. I could transfer them to DPS, but the man's attention keeps flicking back and forth between Pearl and me. He's waiting for me to do something out of line.

The problem with my I-don't-give-a-crap attitude is that people usually assume I'm up to something, and they're usually always right. But something is different with this guy. It's like he's *expecting* me to make a move.

I'm great at the art of deflection, but so is this guy. No matter what I try, he'll be suspicious. I hate that he's so skilled. It means everything is as big as what Wyatt is claiming. It also means, as much as I want to, I can't snap a photo of the guy. He'd definitely notice.

When Pearl finally finishes, the guy looks at me, his hand resting above his gun. "Just show me your footage, and you kids can go."

"Listen, buddy," I say, "you have no right to see anything on my watch."

He arches an eyebrow. "If you have nothing to hide, then what's the big deal?"

I tilt my chin up. "Who says I have nothing to hide?"

Akiro sucks in a sharp breath. "Why did you just say that?"

The man takes a step toward us, closing the distance, his voice turning dark. "So, you did look inside the envelope."

I roll my eyes. "No, I didn't. But I have *other* things on here that I don't want you to see."

"Like what?" he asks.

I point my thumb at Akiro. "Photos of us without clothes on, okay, perv? No way I'm showing you those."

"Eww," Pearl says under her breath.

Akiro speaks so quiet, I hope only I can hear him. "When were we ever ... undressed ... together? Did I miss something? Did you do something to me while I was asleep, because that's so messed up. You can't just take advantage of my sexy bod like that, Har ... Harriet."

The man checks his watch. "I'm done playing games. I'd say sorry for what I'm about to do, but I'm not."

I see the taser coming before it has a chance to hit. Rolling into a dive, I move toward the man, knocking him from his feet. But not before his tasers have Pearl and Akiro on the ground, shaking violently, the sight causing anger to roar inside me.

As the man hurries back onto his feet, scrambling to get a grip on his taser, I yank off my messenger bag. I sling the strap around the man's thick neck, using it to help me catapult onto his back and choke him. Seconds later, the pulses from the taser strike my side, electrocuting my body. Everything screams in agony.

Time seems to slow, dragging the horrible ordeal out. I can't get a bearing on my surroundings to try to figure out what's going on with Akiro and Pearl.

The next thing I know, I'm falling into a hole. Since the taser wires are still attached to me, I barely notice my collision with the ground. The shooting pain is almost unbearable, and I welcome it, because, for the time being, the discomfort is distracting the agony stewing in my heart.

The electrifying current suddenly cuts off. I'm lying on my back, staring up at the man, who's holding the hatch that he somehow opened, getting ready to close it.

He tosses my bag down in the hole. "You kids should have stayed home tonight."

"You know people will be looking for us, right?" Pearl shouts from somewhere next to me. So they were tossed down here as well.

He grins. "You'll be dead by the time anyone finds you, and by then, everything will have happened." His gaze locks with mine. "The U.S. will have bigger problems on their hands than three dead teens." He stands. "Oh, and don't bother trying to send any messages. Nothing works down there. Sorry it had to end this way." His eyes find their way back to mine, and everything comes together in a flash.

He knows who I am and why I'm here. Wyatt probably set the whole thing up, and I walked right into their trap.

The hatch suddenly closes with a loud bang, cloaking us in darkness.

CHAPTER TWELVE_

I LIE SILENTLY on the ground, wishing for the physical pain to take over and drown out all the questions zipping through my mind. Instead, I push all thoughts of Wyatt aside and take a way too big gulp of the dank air, instantly regretting it. The smell of rotted flesh mixes with the thick air, making me gag. What is this place?

"I think I'm going to be sick," Akiro says, dry-heaving.

"We really don't need that smell on top of this." Pearl's standing next to me, pounding on her watch, the flashlight going in and out.

Akiro opens my messenger bag and rifles through it until he finds some tissues. He stuffs them up his nose, then smacks his mouth together. "Oh, I can still taste it." He turns on the flashlight on his watch. "Pearl, just shut yours off. Save what battery you have." He scrolls through his homepage. "No connection, just like he said." With a groan, he gets to his feet and shines his flashlight around.

I'm still staring at the closed hatch, wondering what on earth the man is up to. I have this sinking feeling that this terrorist attack is like nothing we've seen before, and if we don't get out of this hole, no one will warn DPS.

"Well, the tunnel goes both ways," Akiro says. "Which way should we try first?"

Pearl pushes to her feet, giving up on her watch. "Do you think either way will actually lead anywhere?"

"Well, they have to go somewhere," Akiro says.

"What if it's to another hatch that's rusted shut like this one?" Pearl asks.

Akiro scoffs. "Well, that guy got it open. We should be able to as well."

"He had some sort of tool to help him," Pearl says, panic in her voice.

Akiro is straining his neck, looking up at the hatch. "There isn't even a ladder. Even if we got on each other's shoulders, I don't think we'd reach the top."

Pearl looks down at me, her lips pursed together. "Harper? Are you okay? It's kind of freaking me out that you aren't talking."

With a sigh, I get to my feet, brushing off my pants and jacket. "I'm not dying down here."

Akiro claps his hands together. "Well, that's good to hear."

I shove his arm. "We need to find a way out. That's our number one priority."

Pearl balls the cuff of her sweater in her hand and

places it over her nose. "I think having air is a top priority. I have a feeling we're going to run out of it, fast."

Akiro nods, the tissues sticking out of his nose bouncing with the movement. "Yeah, there's no air flow, it seems. Our time is limited."

I pull up my watch, entering my code for emergency use. Once the screen turns green, I send DPS a message, letting them know where we are.

"Wait, how is your watch working?" Akiro asks in awe.

I look up at him. "DPS, remember? This questionable underground dungeon has nothing on us." I rub my forehead. "Problem is, it will take them hours to get here, and by then, we could be dead."

Pearl takes big breaths, raising and lowering her hands with each one. "Well, that can't happen. I'm student body president, and nominated for Homecoming Court, so let's get this figured out."

"Yes," I say dryly, "because that's the most important thing. Forget about a possible terrorist attack, we need to make sure you're alive and well for Homecoming."

Pearl blushes. "Sorry. It just means a lot to my mom."

"Well, if we don't stop the attack," I say, "there will be no Homecoming."

Akiro pouts. "Man! I got us matching tuxes." He places his hand over his mouth. "That was supposed to be a surprise."

I arch an eyebrow. "You already got our outfits?"

"Why did you get her a tux?" Pearl asks, completely offended.

Akiro tilts his head to the side. "You yourself got her a shirt and tie to wear last night. Why would Homecoming be any different?"

"Because it's *Homecoming*," Pearl says with a hand on her hip. "It's not just any old night at a club. Special occasions call for special outfits."

"It *is* a special outfit," Akiro says. They're talking over me like I'm not standing right here. He lifts his chin. "I'll have you know that hers is very feminine, will accentuate her smokin' hot body, but still be comfortable to beat someone up in."

"Why would she want to beat someone up at Homecoming?" Pearl asks.

Akiro shakes his head. "Honestly. It's like you don't even know her."

I place a hand on both their arms, bringing their attention to me. "Trapped. It smells worse than a morgue down here. We can talk about this later." Reaching up, I kiss Akiro on the cheek. "I *like* you."

"I *like* you, too," he says.

I pull a scanner up on my watch, getting a feel for the area. Green lights stretch out from above the screen, disappearing down the tunnel. Two feeds hover above my watch, revealing what's down each way.

"That's so cool!" Akiro says. "Man, why can't I work for DPS?"

"Only the best of the best work there," Pearl says, a little too snotty for her own good.

Down the left-hand side, the tunnel ends, running into a dirt wall. I shut off that feed, focusing on the right. "You know you have to bring something unique to the table. Something they don't already have."

"I'm a freaking ninja," he says.

"Technically," I say, "so am I. I'm good at staying hidden. You gotta find something else."

As Akiro mutters under his breath, we take off toward the right, watching the feed above my watch. So far, the tunnel has just stretched on and on, no end in sight. A few times, something crunches under my feet, but there's no way I'm looking down. I'm about ninety-nine percent certain it's bones.

I'm going to kill Wyatt. I should have the first time I had a chance. The man really is the bane of my existence.

Soon, we enter a small cavern. I look up to see a ladder hanging down, heading up to another hatch.

"That's so high up," Pearl says, straining her neck to look. "How can we reach it?"

"Even if we did reach it," Akiro says, looking up as well, "that hatch has to be rusted shut just like the other one."

Pearl looks at me. "Could you tell what the guy used to open it?"

I shrug. "I was too busy squirming on the ground thanks to the taser to really notice." I open my messenger bag and see what DPS products I have with me. I brought more than usual since Wyatt is the reason I'm here and I can't trust the man, but I still have a limited supply.

I pull out the obliterator Scarlett created. I used it last year to break into Mr. Fukunaga's tax firm by putting it over the doorknob and obliterating it. Worked like a charm. Problem is, the chemicals that dissolve the metal are inside the round-shaped cup. Can't really fit that around the hatch.

Putting aside my better judgment, I glance around the floor, looking for a rock. I was right about the bones. They're everywhere. And not just animal bones.

"I really want out of this place," Pearl whispers.

"Are you sure?" I ask. "You could redecorate the place. Just think what a pop of pink could do to the ambiance."

"I'd actually rather be at home than this place," Pearl mutters to herself, but it carries in the cave.

"Why don't you want to be at home?" Akiro asks.

Pearl's face goes red. "What? Oh, no, I mean ..." She bites the corner of her bottom lip, thinking, before she speaks again. "I think it's just the lack of oxygen getting to me."

She really needs to work on her lying. I could teach her a thing or two. And while a part of me is intrigued by what's going on, we really need to get out of this tunnel.

In the corner, I see a large rock perched against the wall. Thanking the stars that I'm wearing my thick DPS gloves, I pick it up and put it in my bag, along with the obliterator.

I eye Akiro's arms. "Okay, you're going to toss me as high as you can in the air so I can reach the ladder."

Akiro rolls up his sleeves, all business. Too bad he looks so silly with the tissues hanging out from his nose.

"Are you guys having a hard time breathing?" Pearl asks, wheezing, her shaking hand pressed against her forehead. She looks like she wants to sit down, but like me, she's disgusted by what's on the ground.

I tap her arm. "You're just panicking. Take deep breaths. We'll be out of here in a few minutes. I promise."

She nods. "I'm so glad you're here, Harper. Otherwise, we'd be so screwed."

"Uh, thanks," Akiro says. Then he shrugs. "Nah, she's right. We'd be dead." He cups his hands together and holds them out in front of himself. "Ready when you are."

I back up, giving myself some running space. It's a long way up, but I think we can pull it off. After I stretch out my neck, cracking the bones, I take a deep breath and run at Akiro, jumping when I'm almost to him.

The second my foot connects with his hands, he hoists me high into the air, and I go flying, even if only for a few seconds. I stretch out, wishing I were taller, but nothing I can do about that right now. Or ever. My fingers wrap around the last rung on the ladder, holding me in air. I quickly throw up my other arm and grab the next rung before my fingers can slip off the first one.

Using all my upper-body strength, I pull myself up, climbing the ladder one rung at a time. When I reach the top, I wrap my legs around the rungs as I pull the obliterator and rock out of my bag.

I place the obliterator against the hatch. With my other hand, I slam the rock against it and hold it in place. The metal sizzles on contact. I move the obliterator around in circles, letting the chemicals eat through the metal of the hatch.

Remnants of hatch shower around me. Akiro and Pearl are coughing down below, but they aren't getting the brunt of it like I am. I need a face mask. I have to lower my head, not looking where I'm placing the obliterator, so the metal remnants can't get in my eyes.

Fresh air bleeds through the holes, and if anything, I bought us some more time down here. But I'd really like to get out.

When my metal shower starts to dwindle, I lower my arms and risk a peek at the hatch. There's a hole big enough for us to get through. I toss the obliterator through the hole, hoping it lands somewhere nearby where I can find it. DPS doesn't like their equipment being left behind, even if it's been destroyed.

I'm going to have to apologize to Scarlett for ruining it. I'm sure she'll understand, though.

I climb back down the rungs, pull out a rope from my bag and tie it to the bottom rung so Pearl and Akiro can climb up.

I'm out the hole first, taking a huge gulp of fresh air, and it's magical.

I have my head thrown back, inhaling all the air I can get as Pearl and Akiro climb out, both gasping for clean air as well.

CHAPTER THIRTEEN_

THE FERRY—AND the jerk who locked us underground—has already left, leaving us alone on the island. The night has only grown colder, but I'll take it over being down in the dank tunnel about to die.

As we wait, Pearl and Akiro practice hand-to-hand combat, but my mind is catapulting all over the place, thinking about Wyatt. Is there really going to be an attack, or did he set this whole thing up to toy with me, and possibly kill me? I snort. No way. If Wyatt wanted to kill me, he wouldn't let someone else get the glory of doing so. That man trapping us in the tunnel was most likely a spur of the moment decision. Wyatt will probably be ticked when he finds out. This guy almost stole his thunder. Luckily for Wyatt—and me—I survived.

Now that I think about it, it seemed like the guy knew me, but was surprised I was here. Maybe Wyatt didn't tell him we were coming. Maybe he didn't have time, though. Wyatt could have just known a drop was going down tonight and he hoped we'd get there before the guy, snap some pics, and then leave without the guy ever knowing we were there.

Wyatt always has an agenda, so there has to be some truth to what he said. Those coded pages have to be real. He wanted me to find them, decode them, and realize he's telling the truth. Otherwise, he'll be stuck in Calloway for the rest of his miserable life.

A half hour later, air lightly whirls around us. I glance up to see a jet slowly descending, practically silent. No lights are coming from it, making it difficult to see.

"Seriously?" Akiro squeals like an excited kid. "You guys have a jet?"

"More than one, actually," I say.

After I helped Everly out with an attack last year and saved her life, she dumped a ton of money into DPS, realizing the importance of our operation. Some of the equipment we'd been able to create has been freaking mind-blowing.

The door to the jet opens, creating an illuminated walkway for us to ascend. The three of us hurry on, the door closing instantly behind us with only a faint *whoosh*.

Warm, fresh air greets us inside, warming me up like a blanket.

Wait, no, that's an actual blanket being wrapped

around me. I look up to see Scarlett smiling down at me before she pulls me into a hug.

"How's my favorite girl?" she asks in her scratchy tone.

"Glad I'm not trapped underground with a bunch of human bones," I say.

"Should have known you'd get yourself out," she says, rubbing my back.

Pearl plops down on a couch against a wall in the main area, takes off her pink combat boots, and tosses them to the side, putting herself right at home. Rigg was against all the cushy furniture, but Everly insisted, in case she were ever on the jet.

Up front, the wide cockpit doors slide open and Lincoln walks out, holding a couple of mugs. He offers Pearl a steaming cup of hot chocolate, which she happily accepts, doing her infamous shimmy.

Lincoln's brown hair is sprayed out all the way around his head, like a static electricity bomb went off. His blue oval glasses sit high on the bridge of his nose. The blue of his button-down shirt matches his glasses, his thick green paisley tie matching the green of his leather belt. Lincoln is all about coordinating.

Akiro takes a seat in a cushy recliner, kicking off his boots in the process. Lincoln brings him a cup of hot chocolate as well, little marshmallows floating on top.

Lincoln smiles over at me. "Want a cup?"

"Did you seriously just ask me that?" I ask.

When he comes back with a fresh cup for me—marsh-mallows on top—I give him a side fist bump. Lincoln doesn't do skin to skin contact with people, but he'll side bump my fist because I'm always wearing gloves.

Rigg steps out from the cockpit and approaches the glass table in the center of the room. A projection hovers above the table, the computer sorting through a bunch of information.

Rigg's wearing his typical muscle tank and sweatpants, his goatee freshly groomed. The lights reflect off his bald head.

He looks over at Lincoln. "Linc, why don't you show Akiro the cockpit?"

Akiro beams. "Can I fly the jet?"

Lincoln laughs, touching the bottom of his glasses with the top of his index finger. "I'll show you the ropes."

With a howl of excitement, Akiro leaps from the recliner, ignoring the hot chocolate swishing out of the cup and falling down his hand. He and Lincoln head into the cockpit, the door hissing closed behind them.

Rigg motions for me to join him. Scarlett comes up next to me, so we're all standing around the table.

"Start with your visit to see Wyatt," Rigg says in his gruff voice.

"You weren't watching it live?" I ask.

"We've been busy with some attacks going on in the east," Scarlett says. "We'll watch it after this."

"Should I stay," Pearl asks, looking way comfy on the couch, "or join them up front?"

"Get over here," Rigg says.

With a reluctant sigh, Pearl gets up from the couch and joins us, setting her hot chocolate on the glass table. She looks longingly at the couch from over her shoulder, probably wishing she could have stayed lounging. She's had quite the night, so I can't blame her.

After setting my mug of hot chocolate on the table, I sync my watch up with the jet's computer, transferring all the images I took so it can sort through it. Hopefully, it will make something of the mess.

I fold my arms. "According to Wyatt, a huge terrorist attack will be happening in the next two weeks. Something *we can't even fathom.*" I do the best impersonation I can, which isn't too shabby. "Hitoshi Fukunaga is involved. Wyatt will help us out if we do something for him."

Scarlett snorts. "And what's that?"

I can't hold back the growl in my voice. "Break him out of prison."

Pearl spits out her current swig of hot chocolate, spraying both the projection and the table. "I'm sorry, what?"

Rigg wipes at some hot chocolate that landed on his cheek, grimacing. "The man's out of his mind."

"Well, we already knew *that.*" I squeeze my eyes shut

for a moment, hating the next words out of my mouth. "But I think we might have to."

"And now *you're* out of your mind." Scarlett tosses some shelled sunflower seeds into her mouth.

"Trust me," I say, "I broke out laughing when he first said it. But after seeing that guy at Alcatraz, I can't shake the feeling that something big is coming."

"If that's true," Rigg says, "then we'll find another way."

Scarlett spits some seeds into a retractable reusable cup I got her for her birthday. "We only have a couple of weeks?"

I nod.

She purses her lips. "Why hasn't DPS picked up anything?"

I squirm uncomfortably. "The system flagged Mr. Fukunaga a long time ago, adding him to our suspected terrorist list, and we never really figured out why. We just assumed it had to do with President Boggs."

Rigg scratches at his goatee, his words coming out in a statement. "But what if it was because of his brother."

Pearl holds up a palm. "We're talking about Akiro's uncle here. I've met the man. He's harmless. And really funny."

I roll my eyes. "Terrorists can have senses of humor, Pearl."

She frowns. "I don't think we should attach that word to him unless we're one-hundred percent certain."

Rigg watches the computer sorting through all the photos I've uploaded. "This coded system looks difficult to hack."

"Which is why we'll need help," I say.

"How can we trust that Wyatt even knows anything about this?" Scarlett asks.

I lean my palms against the table. "He worked for the Fukunaga's. He knows them well. Maybe he saw more behind the scenes than we realize."

"But why would he help?" Pearl asks. "The man is a terrorist himself."

"True," I say, "but he's very self-centered. If it means him escaping this country, he'll probably be willing to do just about anything."

Scarlett spits some more shells into her cup. "He wants to leave the country?"

"Yep," I say. "We break him out, he'll help us stop the terrorist attack, and we provide him with a way out of the country." I can't hold back the chuckle in my tone. "His request to leave the country involves a plus one."

Surprise flashes across Rigg's face for the briefest of seconds. "Who?"

I shake my head. "He wouldn't say. Just that he wants a ticket for two out of here."

Pearl unties the pink ribbon holding the bun on top of her head, letting her blonde hair fall around her shoulders. "So, he can then attempt another terrorist attack?"

"Pearl's right," Rigg says. "Wyatt failed the first time.

He hates to fail. If we let him loose, he's a loaded gun, waiting to go off."

Scarlett sets her cup on the table. "We're talking like we could even get Wyatt out of prison. Calloway at that. It's the most secure prison in the country."

"Yet I walked in today, and there'll be no trace of it." I push back from the table. "If anyone can break him out, we can."

Rigg stares me straight in the eyes, his jaw set. "Tell me your true reading on this, Harper. What's your gut saying?"

Rigg's almost like a second father to me. He pisses me off a lot, but he's pushed me to become the girl I am today. The fact that he trusts me enough to want me to greenlight the project means more than he'll ever know.

I keep eye contact with him. "I hate Wyatt. He's deceitful and cunning. If we break him out, there's a good chance he'll turn on us." I fold my arms. "That being said, I believed him. I think something big is going to happen. My gut is screaming it. I'd rather we run the risk of Wyatt just stringing us along than risk the lives of thousands of people."

Scarlett arches an eyebrow. "Thousands?"

I nod. "That's what he said. Tens of thousands. Including ones we love, so it could be happening close to home." I take a long gulp of my hot chocolate, hoping it will warm me not only from the coldness of being outside, but from everything with Wyatt.

Suddenly the projection goes wonky, everything turning distorted before the images disappear one by one.

Scarlett tries to stop it, her fingers and hands flying all over the projected screen, but it's over and done before she can do anything.

"What was that?" Pearl asks.

"A glitch?" Scarlett's voice has an edge to it, like she doesn't quite believe that. She lowers her hands and sets them on her hips as she studies the screen.

"Or," Rigg says, "the images were coded to delete when they showed up on a server they weren't supposed to."

I check my watch. "All the pictures I took of the pages are gone." I flip through my images folder again, just to double-check, but not a single one remains. "How could they get it off my watch?"

"If they hacked DPS, they'd have access to everything," Scarlett says. "Including your watch." She clasps her hands on top of her head. "This isn't good. If someone is able to hack DPS, we're in for a world of hurt."

"How could they without us detecting it?" I ask.

"That's a good question," Scarlett says.

"I think it's more likely that they self-destructed," Rigg says. "Our system would have been alerted if we were hacked." He rubs his chin. "At least this proves those papers were important." He nods at Scarlett. "Go back through the DPS watch list for the past year. See if there's anyone or anything related to the Fukunaga family, Japan, or imports. I mean, even the tiniest connection."

"On it," she says.

His gaze slides to me. "You're going to have to spy on Hitoshi. Follow him. Find out what he's up to." He looks at Pearl. "This might be a good opportunity for you to do some light fieldwork. You can see how we follow someone without being detected."

"No," Pearl says. "We can't do that to Akiro."

I look at her. "This is the job, Pearl. This is a part of being DPS. Last year, I had to spy on Akiro's dad. I hated every second of it, but if there was a chance he was involved in something shady and I had a chance to stop it? It's a risk we have to take." When her face doesn't soften, I continue. "If you're right about him, and I really hope you are, this will clear his name. Would you rather someone else do it? Another DPS agent prying into their family? You and I will do it right. We'll analyze the crap out of everything and make sure we're one hundred percent certain before we pull the trigger."

Her eyes finally soften, a small frown pulling at her lips. "I hate this part of the job."

"Me, too," I say, "but it's what we signed up for." I go to her, setting my hand on her arm. "Let's do this for Akiro. The sooner we clear Hitoshi's name, the sooner everyone will back off him and we can focus elsewhere."

That completely convinces her, but it sets me on edge. Another Fukunaga family member to spy on. Another person Akiro loves caught in the crosshairs of DPS. I really hope Wyatt is wrong.

"What are you going to do?" Scarlett asks Rigg.

He rubs his eyes with his thumbs. "See if it's even plausible to break Wyatt out of Calloway Penitentiary."

CHAPTER FOURTEEN

WE GET HOME late Saturday night. Rigg sent Zia to our hotel room to get all our stuff. Plus, he wants her to scout out Alcatraz Island and see if she can find anything else. Being the eccentric lady she is, she volunteered to do it. She couldn't wait to check out all the bones in the tunnel.

Akiro and I don't mind waiting until tomorrow to get our stuff back. We desperately want to go home, especially after being stuck in that dank tunnel. Pearl, though, she's hesitant.

"Can I stay at your house?" Pearl asks as we head home.

"Why?" I ask.

Her focus is on the ground. "I just don't want to be alone after what happened."

"Won't your parents be home?"

Her eyes go wide for a second. "Uh, yeah, of course

they'll be there. Forget I said anything." She takes off without looking back.

I know a friend would reach out, ask her what's going on, but I'm too freaking tired and I have my own stuff to worry about.

The second I walk into the house, I head straight for my bedroom in the back, peel off my clothes, and toss them in the hamper. I'd burn them all if the sweater Everly gave me wasn't included in the mix—it means too much. I turn on the water in my shower, letting steam fill the bathroom, immediately calming me.

The hot water sears my skin. At our old apartment, I had no idea what a hot shower was. The hottest we got was lukewarm, and that was on a good day.

I normally wasn't one for wasting water—or anything, really—but I needed to wash everything that happened in the tunnel off me. Who knows how many people died down there? I could have been added to the bone collection, along with Akiro and Pearl.

A smile finds its way onto my face. I bet Pearl's bones are pink.

When my skin starts to wrinkle, I turn off the water and throw on a robe, having a love-hate relationship with my new life. I love all the luxuries, all the things we never had before, but I hate extravagant things. So many people are out there suffering, barely scraping by, and I never want to forget that. I don't want my new life to change me. But I know it will. It's inevitable.

I sneak into the kitchen, being light on my feet. Dad's passed out on the recliner in the front room. He told me to wake him when I got home, but I don't have the heart. He hasn't been sleeping well, so I don't want to disturb what sleep he can get.

Somehow, everything that happened today has worked up quite the appetite. Good thing the fridge is full of leftovers from the funeral. Everyone felt the need to bring us food, and I've never turned down food.

I open one of the storage containers, peering inside. Looks like some sort of potato casserole with an abundance of cheese. Perfection. I scoop a huge helping onto a plate and pop it into the microwave for twenty seconds.

When I open the door, steam and a cheesy smell welcomes me, and I can't wait to get the food into my mouth. After I fish a fork from the drawer, I pad across the concrete floor and sit down at the table like a good little girl.

I usually love to sit on the couch when I eat, but ever since we moved into the new place, Mom insisted we eat at the table like a normal family. I told her countless times that no normal family did that, but she'd just cluck her tongue at me.

I smile at the memory.

I scoop a large bite into my mouth, using my tongue to fling the piping hot potatoes around. Should have waited a minute for it to cool down.

"Harper?" Dad sleepily asks from the front room.

I hear Casper jump down from his lap, the bell on his collar jingling as he shakes his head.

"Hey, Dad," I say once I finish off the bite in my mouth. "I didn't mean to wake you."

He stands, stretching his arms over his head. "You were supposed to wake me." He smooths out his blue cardigan and joins me in the kitchen. I love that he still wears his old, holey cardigan, despite owning new ones. We're so much alike. We'll wear our clothes until they fall apart while we're wearing them. Even then, if we can find a way to patch them back up, we will. Mom always said it makes us look homeless, but we say it makes us resourceful.

Dad takes a seat next to me at the table. "That smells good."

I hop up and dish him his own plate, setting it down in front of him when it's been heated.

He winks at me. "Thanks."

Casper has taken Mom's usual seat, sitting tall and staring over the table at us like he's a human as well. I'm so glad he followed me out of a house I broke into last year for an investigation. The cat has been the missing piece our family needed. Although, I'm sure the guy is just happy to be getting undivided attention. He had around twenty siblings at his last place. Owner was a smidge obsessed with cats. And by smidge, I mean the guy has serious issues.

Dad blows on his food before he takes a bite. "How was the trip?"

"It was ... interesting." I take another bite of my food, contemplating my next words. The more I tell him, the more involved he'll try to be. While I normally wouldn't mind that, he just lost the love of his life. He needs some time. But Dad also has experience that could help me out.

"Interesting how?" he asks.

I set my fork down. "How well do you know Hitoshi Fukunaga?"

He shrugs. "Not well. Tomi didn't talk about him all that much. Hitoshi was born in Japan, so Tomi didn't see him all that often."

Tomi was born in the U.S. His mom had fled Japan and her controlling husband, leaving her four-year-old son there. She was pregnant with Tomi at the time. Akiro says Hitoshi always resented Tomi because of that, but ever since Hitoshi moved here, he's always been so friendly and kind to everyone. He seems genuinely happy to be here. But it could all be an act. He does have a good reason to hate Tomi and the U.S.

I poke at the cheesy potatoes on my plate. "Do you think he's capable of doing something evil?"

Dad's fork pauses mid-air, cheese dripping down the side. "Did Hitoshi show up on the DPS watch list?"

I tilt my head to the side. "Not quite, but Wyatt told us he might be up to something."

Dad pops the fork into his mouth, sliding the food off. His eyes narrow as he thinks.

"Wyatt is convinced a huge terrorist attack is going to happen in the next couple of weeks, which is why he reached out to me."

"And that Hitoshi is involved?"

I nod. "Do you think it's possible?"

He scoops another helping onto his fork. "You know to look into every possibility, whether you want to or not. You can't push intel aside, even if it's from someone you don't trust. What else happened?"

Usually, I keep DPS intel a secret. I'm not supposed to tell anyone about our missions or anything we do. But Dad knows the field. He did top-secret work for the former president, Gladys Boggs. And keeping things from him has never turned out well in the past.

So, I tell him everything Wyatt said and what happened down in the tunnel. Dad listens thoughtfully the whole time, nodding and scratching his chin.

When I finish, he sits back in his chair, folding his arms. "You believe Wyatt?"

I twirl an angel wing earring. "My gut tells me to trust him, as much as it pains me. There was a look of honesty in his eyes that I can't shake."

"What does Wyatt want in return?"

I stare at the plate, unsure how Dad's going to react. I purposely left that part out, because I don't need Dad running interference.

Dad arches an eyebrow, giving me his *Dad* look. "Harper, spill it."

I blow out a deep breath before I speak. "He wants DPS to break him out of prison."

Dad chokes on the food in his mouth, pounding his fist against his chest. It takes him a minute to compose himself. "He *what*?"

"I know, it's crazy," I say.

"That man is out of his mind," Dad mutters.

"Everyone keeps saying that." I fold my arms, resting them on the table. "Thing is, if he's right, we could possibly save tens of thousands of lives."

Dad leans forward as well. "And if he's wrong?"

I sigh. "We could possibly risk tens of thousands of lives. He might be planning his own attack."

Casper's head is moving back and forth between me and Dad, like he's fully listening to the conversation.

Dad taps the table. "Or *he's* behind the threat and needs out of prison to go through with it. Maybe he's casting blame on the Fukunaga family because he knows you've already been wary of them."

I rub my forehead. "Rigg thinks we should treat it as a legit threat."

He slowly nods. "I've been talking with Tomi more recently, maybe I can poke around, see if he knows anything."

"What's going on with the two of you?" I ask.

Dad and Tomi Fukunaga have been hanging out a lot

recently, which Akiro and I have found odd. Dad and Tomi had been out of each other's lives for years. Now, after Tomi showed up on the DPS watch list, he and Dad are talking again.

Dad admitted he knows where President Boggs is. Well, he lied and said he didn't, but I can detect lies, so I know he does.

Dad rubs the back of his neck. "Nothing for you to worry about, I promise. You're going to have to trust us."

Trust. That isn't a word I take lightly. But I do trust my dad, and the more I've gotten to know Mr. Fukunaga, the more I trust him. They aren't terrorists.

Now I have to hope that Hitoshi isn't one as well.

CHAPTER FIFTEEN_

MY HEAD HITS the pillow and I'm seconds away from passing out when my wrist vibrates with an incoming message. Groaning, I lift my arm. It takes my blurry eyes a second to focus, but when they do, I shoot up in bed.

A creepy black font hovers above my watch. A message from Bo, aka The Brick.

Meet @ HQ.

I quickly message back.

Now?

No response. Which is no surprise because the man really limits his words.

Adrenaline takes over and I'm out of the bed in a flash,

quickly dressing into my DPS uniform and hightailing it out of the house.

Headquarters is below an abandoned high school. I enter near the goalpost on the football field, the system scanning my face before allowing me to descend the stairs and go inside.

I find Bo in the workout room. He's tall and strong like Rigg but has hair. Like, an abundance of it. It's tied back in three braids right now, which as much as I want to, I'm not allowed to comment on it. The guy would rip me to shreds.

Like me, he's dressed in his full DPS uniform. He likes to train in it, but he also likes to be able to leave at a moment's notice. It also covers up his million Polynesian tattoos that cover his arms, torso, back, and legs. Bo was one of the few Polynesians that chose to stay and help DPS after the war instead of going back to Tonga, where his parents are from and currently live.

Before I can say something, like ask him why he asked me here in the middle of the freaking night, Bo is at my side, his massive arm around my waist, and something sharp presses into my back.

I try to hide my shock, but I know it's all over my face.

Bo nods at the mirror on the wall and turns us so I can see. "What do you see?"

Yeah, definitely not hiding the surprise lighting up my eyes. It's blinding. "Uh, you with your arm around my waist like we're a couple or something. It's really weirding me out, Bo."

He ignores my comment. "What do you feel?"

"A blade about to pierce my skin." My gaze goes to his hand. I can see his fingers on my waist. "How are you holding the knife?"

"Pinky. Knife is up my sleeve."

When I thought I could learn a thing or two from The Brick, I was right. It's been less than a minute with the guy, and I've been taught something valuable.

His arm drops from around me and he slips out the knife from his sleeve, tossing it to me.

I catch the hilt, turning the straight, flat knife over in my hand. "This weighs next to nothing."

"Imagine we were in a crowded room. No one would have known I had a knife on you. I could have stabbed you and been gone before someone realized you were dead." His face is stoic, making it impossible to read the guy. Hence, The Brick.

I slip the knife up my sleeve, the metal cool against my skin. "That's comforting."

"You need to learn to control your emotions, Harper."

My gaze snaps to his. "I can control my temper."

His hard eyes have me instinctively taking a step back. "You didn't in the elevator."

"That was different," I say. "It was the same guy that took pictures at my mom's *funeral*. He's lucky I left him alive."

"Doesn't matter if the man had killed your mom. You must reel in the anger if you want to survive this business."

I fold my arms, noticing how nicely the knife is still nestled against my skin, not causing any discomfort. I really need to get myself one of these. "Did Rigg put you up to this? You're sounding a lot like him."

"I want you to be prepared for anything that comes your way." Suddenly, another knife is in his hand, but it's already flying toward me, whizzing past my ear, and lodging into the wall behind me before I can react. "Especially if Wyatt gets his way."

"Rigg already told you?"

"He and Scarlett debriefed me the second you got back." He casually walks to the wall, removes his knife and looks it over. "Has Rigg or Scarlett ever mentioned that I worked with Everly before I joined DPS?"

I shake my head. "They don't tell me anything about you."

Bo and I are rarely around each other, and when we are, he never tells me things about himself. In fact, I don't think I've ever heard him talk this much before.

He takes a seat on a bench, leaning his forearms on his legs, twirling the knife with his left hand before switching over to his right. The guy is ambidextrous, adding to his cool factor. "I was part of her security detail. When I got the job with DPS, Paul took over my position."

Paul is a current member of Everly's personal security, or 'the burlesque show' as I like to call them. A bunch of beefy, good-looking guys, who, despite appearances, actually know how to fight. Not as well as me, but they try. It can be adorable at times.

If it were Rigg or Scarlett on the bench, I'd take a seat next to them. Since it's Bo, I lean against the wall, putting a nice buffer between us.

"I used to work closely with Wyatt." His voice holds as much emotion as his face, which is zilch. "The man is as clever as they come, so you always need to be on your guard around him."

"Did you see his betrayal coming?"

His knife switches hands, not skipping a beat in its spinning. "No."

I wait for him to expand, but in true Bo fashion, he doesn't.

"Do you think he's telling the truth?" I ask. "About an attack?"

"Probably." He tosses the spinning knife from hand to hand, the motion smooth and effortless on his part. "Wyatt never does things unless he has to." Back and forth the knife goes, mesmerizing me. "He wouldn't have taken the time to reach out to you if nothing's going on."

"But why wouldn't DPS pick up on it?" I can't tear my gaze from the knife. It's almost like it's performing a dance.

"DPS doesn't pick up on everything." The knife suddenly stops in his right hand and he slips it back up his sleeve. "And some people are smart enough to cover their tracks, making it difficult to detect them."

I shake my head from my trance. "If Wyatt knows you so well, how come he reached out to me and not you?"

Bo stands, the muscles in his firm jaw twitching. "I wouldn't have come if he had. He knows that." His knife is suddenly in his hand again, and he points it at me. "And he knows you can't control your emotions. You were an easy target."

I want to deny it, but I can't. Wyatt knew exactly how to get through to me. No one messes with my family and gets away with it. No one.

Bo moves toward the exit. "Get some rest, Harper. I think we're in for a couple of busy weeks."

"Hey, Bo?"

He looks over his shoulder at me.

"Wyatt wants safe passage from the U.S. for him and one other person. Do you know who that would be?"

Bo shrugs. "If I had to take a guess, probably his daughter." He nods at my sleeve. "Keep the knife." He disappears out the door, leaving me in shock.

Wyatt has a daughter? Where? How old? How has no one mentioned this before?

I place a hand to my head. "Wait. I have a cousin?"

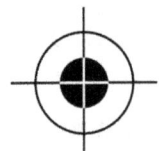

CHAPTER SIXTEEN

Rigg is trying to concoct a plan to break Wyatt out of Calloway. A sentence I never thought I would ever say. I really hate that I even said it now. But we aren't going through with anything until there's more weight behind Wyatt's words beside some guy locking us in a tunnel on Alcatraz.

We're also trying to track down Wyatt's daughter. So far, no luck. All Bo knows is that she should be around fifteen right now. Just a couple of years younger than me. If we find her though, she'd be the perfect leverage to hold over Wyatt.

Until then, Pearl and I are following Hitoshi Fuku-naga around like a bunch of fangirls, creeping on him at his favorite spots, snapping candid photos, all the while trying to stay hidden and not let Akiro know about our "crush."

Let me say, it was Pearl's idea to say we had a crush on

him if Akiro were ever to find us snooping. I argued that *she* could just have the crush, not me, but she said it was more believable if we both did.

In what universe would it be believable that I have a giggly-type crush on an old guy? Honestly. No way Akiro would fall for that. Pearl agreed to that, but said I'd still have to sell the crap out of it if Akiro sees any photos on my watch.

Let's just hope it doesn't come to that, because, gross.

Pearl told Akiro that she needed a girl's night with me. He wouldn't fall for that either. When she wasn't looking, I mouthed, *"She's on her period,"* so Akiro threw his hands into the air and mouthed, *"I'm out."*

So much easier to get him to not want to hang with us.

It's why we're hanging out at a bistro on a Tuesday night, hiding behind some books while we watch Hitoshi have dinner with a friend.

I "borrowed" the books from my old school janitor and apartment night manager, Ike, last year. He still likes to read the physical things for some odd reason.

The thought of him makes me wonder what he's been up to. He cut off contact once he quit both jobs. I kind of miss the man. I could track him down, but usually when someone moves and changes their number, it means they don't want to be contacted. I respect that.

Pearl wanted to get in disguise for our outing, but she's not ready for that level of reconnaissance yet. It's better to start subtle, especially when you're in territory you frequent. The odds of Pearl running into someone she knows is high, because she's friends with *everyone* at school. While they might not recognize her in disguise, she'll certainly recognize them, and I wouldn't put it past her to say hi to them, forgetting she's on a mission.

Pretending like you don't know anyone around you is harder than you think. It takes practice, especially with someone as social as Pearl.

I peer over the book—an intense political thriller according to Ike—looking at Hitoshi and his friend. I've never seen this "friend" before.

Pearl is scrolling through all his correspondence on her phone, the color screen hovering above her watch. "This guy is nowhere."

"Facial recognition didn't ping him, either," I say as I watch them over the book.

From where we sit, Hitoshi and this guy seem to be having a fabulous time. They're all chummy and laughing, like two long lost friends catching up.

Thing is, the words they're saying? They don't make sense. I'm great at reading lips. At first, I worried I lost my touch, because I thought I was reading them wrong. I mean, Hitoshi doesn't even have a bulldog named Duke that he brought back with him from Japan that was just diagnosed with diabetes, not to mention being worried about losing him.

Then I think, they're probably talking in code, just like the papers we found on Alcatraz. The bulldog could be referring to something else. Or someone. Like Wyatt. I mean, the man does have sharp canine teeth.

"Whoever this guy is," Pearl says, her arm pressed up against mine, "he's either meaningless, or the complete opposite and we should be extremely worried about him."

"I'd usually bank on the latter, but I hate thinking that about Hitoshi."

Pearl grunts. "I hate that there isn't a simple solution to this. The fact that the man is nowhere online, and everything they're saying is weird, doesn't help his innocence." She snatches a fry from the plate in front of her and shoves it in her mouth. "Like, at all."

A mechanical arm comes out from the wall and refills our empty glasses with Dr Pepper. I pat it as it goes back into hiding. "Good boy."

Pearl's phone pings, and I look over to see an animation of a puppy hovering above her watch, holding out a bouquet of pink roses. Pearl's blushing as she hurries to close the message. I've never seen her so flustered.

"Who's sending you animations?" I ask.

It's common to send an animation of a cute animal performing some sweet gesture to people you like. Akiro likes to send me ones of cats in little ninja outfits performing stunts.

"No one." Pearl's voice cracks, giving away her lie.

If I wasn't holding the book up to cover my face, I'd fold my arms and glare at her. "Don't lie to me, Pearl."

When she doesn't say anything, I huff. "If you don't tell me, I'll just investigate it and find out myself."

She sticks her tongue out at me. "If you must know, it's a guy named Bellamy—"

I break in. "The guy on the track team?"

Her eyes go wide. "I thought you don't know anyone at school!"

I roll my eyes. "I made it a mission to know all the idiots that go to our school. Now I know everyone, including their deepest, darkest secrets. I just choose not to talk to them or recognize their presence if they're near me." I shrug. "Usually because of their deepest, darkest secret."

Her face goes beet red again. "I don't have a deep, dark secret."

"You still have all your Barbies from when you were a kid, and sometimes you vent to them when you're having a rough day."

If I thought her eyes were wide before, they're practically bulging from her sockets now. "How—"

"This is *me* we're talking about, Pearl. I can find out anything about anyone." Now that I'm a full DPS operative, I have access to everything. I'm not supposed to use the information for personal uses, but I'm stuck inside a building with these people every weekday during the school year. I have to know what I'm up against and rule out any potential threats.

Like Bellamy Calhoun, who has a weird obsession

with clowns. He's got a whole collection at home and sometimes dresses up as one. I pegged him as the kid that could lose it and show up at school one day, dressed as a clown, holding a bazooka, cackling the whole time as he blows the place to smithereens.

I take in Pearl with her pink dress, pearl necklace, and perfect bun with a pink ribbon tied around it. Guess they kind of go together. He likes clowns and dresses like them. She likes Barbies and dresses like them.

She clears her throat. "There's nothing going on with me and Bellamy. He just likes to send me animations now and again."

I arch an eyebrow. "So, if I were to check your phone records, I'd see, what, like three or four animations from him?"

Her gaze goes to the book she's holding, like she's suddenly interested in it. "When's the last time you read a physical book?"

"What's wrong with Bellamy liking you?" I ask. Well, aside from the whole possible killer clown thing.

She bites her lip, and the words come out so quiet, I barely hear them. "He's just not the usual type of guy I date."

"Meaning, your mother wouldn't approve." I nod. "I can see her apprehension, but it's your life, Pearl. Date whoever you want to date."

She frowns. "Why are you apprehensive about him? What's his deepest, darkest secret?"

114

I laugh. "No way I'm telling you that. I don't spill people's secrets. I just use them against them if I have to."

She lifts her chin, trying to appear tough. "I can find out myself, you know. I work for DPS, too."

I take a sip of my soda and then smile at her. "But you won't. That's the difference between you and me. You're too good of a person to invade someone else's life."

I do that for a living, so my guard for that dropped years ago. Pearl's never actually broken into someone's home and rummaged through their stuff. Honestly, she'd be terrible at it. I can see her getting frustrated if the house was a mess, so she'd start cleaning it, leaving it spotless in her wake. I mean, the owners really couldn't complain about that. Who wouldn't want to wake up to a magically clean home? But she'd get caught. We have a ten-minute policy when breaking and entering.

"Oh, they're leaving," Pearl says, looking over her book at Hitoshi and his friend.

"I think we should say hi," I say.

Pearl looks at me like I'm crazy. "Then he'll know we were here!" She waves the book. "All this hiding would be for nothing."

"No, it won't. If he'd seen us earlier, it would have caused him to leave or talk about other things than what he really came here for." I stand, using my watch to pay for my meal. "I want to see his reaction when he sees us here. It will tell us more about this mystery guy."

She reluctantly nods.

"You call his name," I say, adjusting my new knife inside my sleeve as a precaution. Long sleeves in the summer isn't totally practical but having an extra weapon on me is.

"Why?" she asks.

"Because he'd be suspicious of me excitedly saying his name. You, on the other hand, he'd expect that."

"True." She does a dramatic ballet walk toward the door, her arms daintily held out, which looks hilarious in her pink combat boots.

Hitoshi and the guy are still in deep conversation about Hitoshi's imaginary bulldog, Duke.

"Hitoshi!" Pearl says with enough giddiness to make me gag.

He turns to us, the certainty on his face falling for the briefest of moments. He quickly covers it up with a smile. "Pearl. Harper. What are you ladies doing here?"

Pearl links her arm with mine. "Girl's night. We heard this place had the best chicken salad sandwich."

I rub my stomach. "And it does, in case you were wondering." I look at the friend and smile. "Hi, I'm Harper." I point to Hitoshi. "I'm dating his nephew."

The guy—who had been scowling the whole time—suddenly finds a smile, the tension in his shoulders relaxing. "Nice to meet you. I'm Nozomu."

By his accent, he's definitely from Japan, but that doesn't really mean anything bad. Maybe he came over on the same ship as Hitoshi. There's only one way to find out.

I motion between the two of them. "How do you two know each other?"

Nozomu hesitates only a second—actually, probably not even that long—and normal people wouldn't notice. He slaps Hitoshi on the shoulder. "We went to high school together. Just catching up."

"Oh, cool!" Pearl says. "Back in Japan?"

"Yes," Hitoshi says. He looks like his younger brother, with the dark hair and dark eyes. He has more of a hardness to his face, though. When he's smiling, you can't tell, because it matches the contagious Fukunaga smile. It's when he's serious that you can see the roughness behind his eyes.

I never really noticed it until this moment. But I hadn't been looking for it before.

"Are you coming to the family dinner on Thursday?" I ask. I tap Hitoshi's arm. "I'd love to hear stories about this guy from high school."

"Oh, for sure," Pearl says, nodding. "I bet they're hilarious!"

Nozomu points at Hitoshi. "Are you kidding? This guy doesn't know the meaning of fun."

Pearl's smile falters. "Really? He's always cracking jokes and telling us fun stories."

Now it's Nozomu's turn to frown. "Maybe America has changed him for the better." His smile is back. "That's good."

A small vibration comes from Hitoshi's wrist. He's

getting a message, and by the way he tenses, it's certainly not a message he'd want me or Pearl to see. Another thing someone else wouldn't pick up on, but I've been hyper-aware of what's going on around us since the moment we started talking.

Like the set of beefy guys in the back of the bistro, watching the whole exchange between us. They're with Hitoshi. Or Nozomu. Or both.

Either way, we're going to have a tail on our way home, which means we're going to have to lose it. A rush of adrenaline spikes through me, and I can't wait to get into my car and make the guys regret ever following me.

CHAPTER SEVENTEEN

THE GREAT THING about having a car is that I can control my surroundings now. Before, if I knew someone was following me, I'd have to get away on foot, or on the rails. Which, on the rails, there's nothing you can do except sit there at the mercy of the automated driving system.

And, with another person with me, it makes it that much more difficult. Especially when she's new to the whole spy field and has an obsession with wearing bright colors. She's pretty much failing the art of espionage. We'll get her there, though. One drab color at a time.

Usually, I just enter the address into the car's system and let it take me to the location, so I can relax and enjoy the ride. But I need to be able to make last-second maneuvers when possible.

When I first got the car, I made Scarlett give me lessons. She's the only one who could teach me without losing patience and be totally fine with showing me how to safely drive recklessly.

The two beefy guys get into their Versatile, the newest, sleekest car out there in the world. The silent electric car can reach four-hundred miles per hour if the driver wanted to. Obviously, out on the streets, it would be crazy to break two-fifty, since other cars can't keep up. And the turning radius? The thing can flip a U-turn while going two-hundred miles per hour without even making the tires squeal.

I've been able to get my car over three-twenty on the highway, and it rides smooth as butter. But it's no Versatile. So, my biggest play will be getting their car stuck behind me, with the driver unable to scoot around traffic.

Pearl's clutching the grip bar in front of the passenger seat, her face determined like she's helping with the drive by sheer will.

I'm weaving through traffic, not even breaking a sweat.

"I hate to say this," Pearl says, using the reflective mirror on the passenger side to watch the guys tailing us, "but I have a bad feeling about Nozomu. He so didn't go to school with Hitoshi."

I would smile at her, but I gotta keep my eyes on the road. "You're getting better at reading people."

She huffs. "I know, and it really sucks. I kind of miss the days of being completely oblivious of everything around me."

"Why do you think I steer clear of people?" I squeeze

between two trucks before I check the sideview mirror and make a sudden right turn down a quiet street, the car jerking with the motion. "I hate being able to read all their emotions. And teenagers are the worst. Always brooding or getting way too excited about stupid stuff."

"They're still following us," she says, keeping an eye on them through the mirror. She runs her hand over the dashboard. "You need a 'disable bad guys' button on here. Something that throws out spikes or a net or something."

"That's actually not a bad idea." I make another quick right-hand turn, barely avoiding a collision with a fancy sports car. The driver blares his horn, flipping me off. We could be friends.

"What do you think they're planning?" Pearl asks. "A bomb? Mass shooting?"

I tap my fingers against the steering wheel, plotting my next move as I answer her question. "Shootings are rare. Harder for the average person to get their hand on a gun. Plus, you can do a lot more damage with a bomb."

I've already made two aggressive turns, which the guys following us could chalk up to reckless teenage driving. One more, though, they might be suspicious that I know they're following me.

Pearl glances over her shoulder. "There's also poisoning." Her watch pings, and out of the corner of my eye, I see another animation, which looks like two kittens lying down, forming a heart with their bodies.

"Another one from Bell—"

"Don't say his name!" Pearl glances around like her mom might be hiding in the car, eavesdropping on our conversation.

"Fine. I'll call him B. Have you sent B any animations in return?" When she's silent for a good twenty seconds, I chance a glance at her. "How many, Pearl?"

"Just a few," she says quietly. She checks the mirror again. "We really need to lose these guys."

In the back of my mind, I know I should just drive normal and head home. The guys following us wouldn't be suspicious about that, and they can find out where we live easily enough.

But this other part, the part still mourning my mom and a life without her, takes over, wanting to do something completely reckless and free.

I'm stuck on a four-lane road, the two cars in front of me going side-by-side, making it impossible to go around them. That always pisses Rigg off. He'll slam his hand against the steering wheel and swear, like that's going to solve the problem.

I, on the other hand, like taking matters into my own hands. I've come to realize I can't rely on others. People are stupid and self-centered, completely oblivious to the fact that there are other people around them, living their lives.

Well, that and they're probably on auto-pilot, chatting away with other passengers in the car, not noticing the girl driving wildly behind them, flashing her brights at them so they'll get the point and scoot over.

After turning on the police scanner function Scarlett installed in my car's navigation system, I check to make sure there aren't any cops nearby.

It's green for go, baby.

Barely sliding into the oncoming lane, I crane my neck to see if there's anyone coming at me. It's empty. With a smile, I slam on the gas, jerk into oncoming traffic, and floor it around the car in front of me.

"What are you doing?" Pearl shrieks, her hands so tightly wrapped around the grip bar that her knuckles are turning white.

"Losing them," I say, flipping on my blinker and swerving back into my lane.

The odometer creeps over one-twenty, slowly working its way up.

I can feel Pearl staring at me, her tone so incredulous, it's practically dripping from her pores. "Did you seriously just use your blinker?"

I shrug. "That's what they're there for." A car in the right lane drifts into my lane, not using their blinker, and I slam on the brakes. I throw up a hand. "See! You gotta use a blinker, man."

With another check of oncoming traffic, I floor it again, swerving into the lane, pushing my car over one hundred and fifty miles per hour, passing at least three cars on my right.

"Car!" Pearl screams, pointing at the blur headed straight for us, like I can't see it.

Just one more car to get in front of, and I'll be in the clear.

One-eighty. I love this car.

"Harper!" Pearl's scream combines with the blaring horn of the car seconds away from ending our lives.

With inches to spare, I swerve back into my lane, the horn of the oncoming car whooshing by with it.

My heart pounds, blood pulsing loud in my ears. I glance down at the odometer. Two hundred and climbing.

"Red light!" Pearls shouts.

"Will you stop yelling the obvious at me?" I scream back.

"Stop driving like a wild woman and I will!"

A beep sounds from the speakers, and suddenly the steering wheel locks, the computer system taking over.

"*Oncoming east and westbound traffic detected,*" the computers says. "*Auto-pilot initiated.*"

"Can it do that?" Pearl asks, her horrified gaze on the screen between us.

"Apparently." I look down to see the odometer climb. Two-twenty-five. "Uh, shouldn't it be slowing down, not speeding up?"

A strangled cry escapes Pearl's mouth. "We're going to die."

We whiz through the intersection, running the red

light. Both Pearl and I glance over our shoulders just in time to see the east and westbound cars flash by.

The car begins to slow. *"Code OHRP engaged. Destination: Home."*

Pearl noticeably swallows. "What's code OHRP?"

I lick my lips, trying to work moisture back into my mouth. "Not sure."

My car resumes normal speed, taking us in the direction of my house, safely stopping at lights, and using the blinkers.

I try changing course, wanting to drop Pearl off at her home, but I've been locked out. None of my hacking tricks work.

I grunt. "I can't override the system. Guess you're coming to my house."

When I check the rearview mirror, I see the guys stayed with us. They've kept a good distance behind us, doing a professional job of tailing. I'm really impressed. But that means these guys are more of a threat than we realized.

"Didn't lose the stalkers," I say.

Pearl is still in a state of panic, her breathing so fast that her heart is probably pounding. "You know they'll wait outside to see where we go next. We need to talk to DPS about this, and we can't have them following us to Headquarters or a safe house."

"Wanna spend the night?"

"Wha ..." she trails off, shocked by my question.

I smirk. "Everly built my house. Which means there's a secret underground escape. We can fool them."

"Oh, uh, yeah, that would be smart." She almost sounds disappointed. Pearl wants to have a sleepover with me? What part of me screams I like having sleepovers?

I try to override the system again, but nothing works. "Guess you'll have to borrow some clothes from Headquarters or something." Pearl is still shaken up, so I need to calm her. "Please tell me you don't snore."

Her sullen face is replaced by a smile. "I don't, I swear."

"Good." I hold up a finger. "Also, I call right side of the bed. It's closer to the AC."

Pearl furrows her eyebrows. "It's not that hot."

I shrug. "I like to sleep cold. Too bad my room doesn't have dual climate control like my parents' room." I reach across the console and pat her arm. "We have tons of blankets, don't worry. You'll be fine."

She rubs her hands together. "I haven't slept over at someone's house in forever. And on a work night?"

"Look at you, living on the edge. It suits you."

"Thank you." She shimmies, fingering her pearl necklace, her worry now gone, and I breathe a sigh of relief.

CHAPTER EIGHTEEN

WHEN WE GET HOME, we talk to Dad for a bit before we "go to bed." I set my bedroom up on a timer, leaving the lights on for another hour before they go to sleep mode. I also have a fun program Lincoln created that can put shadows in the room, so it looks like people are inside. The men will sit outside watching an imaginary Harper and Pearl hang out.

I send a message to Rigg and Scarlett, letting them know we're on our way. Seconds later, Rigg is calling. I accept it and his grumpy face hovers above my watch.

"Does you coming here have anything to do with your recent antics on the streets?" Rigg asks.

"How did you know about that?" I ask.

Rigg rubs his goatee. "I had Lincoln install a special software in your car system. It alerts me when you do anything stupid."

My hand balls into a fist, and the man is lucky he's not

in front of me. "You're behind Code OHRP? What does that even mean?"

A rare smile spreads on his face, actually reaching all the way up to his eyes. He's really enjoying this, which pisses me off even more. "Override Harper's Reckless Plan."

"Can you even legally do that?" I know the answer to the question before it finishes leaving my mouth. It doesn't matter if it's legal or not. Since when has DPS cared about being on the up and up?

Rigg's eyebrow quirks, giving me the only answer I'll be getting from him.

I flick a hand over my buzz cut hair like it will wipe off the anger boiling out of me. "We're being watched, so we're taking the tunnel. See you soon."

I end the call right as a curious expression lands on Rigg's face. I'll just let him stew in that until we get there. And maybe we'll walk really slow.

Pearl and I head into the tunnel underground, and a small disc descends from the ceiling, floating above our heads and offering us light as we walk.

It's quiet for a while, giving me time to simmer down. But, of course, Pearl can't be in silence for long stretches of time. Like, anything over a minute.

She clears her throat next to me. "So, let's say, hypothetically, what if B were to ask me to Homecoming. How could I politely turn him down?"

I pause in the tunnel, waiting for her to stop and back-track to me.

"Pearl, do you like him?"

She twists her hand. "Well, I mean, he is pretty cute, and he makes me laugh and—"

"Yes or no."

She sighs. "Yes."

"Would you actually want to go to Homecoming with the guy? Like have dinner, spend the whole evening dancing and crap, and then have him be the one to walk you to the front door?"

She puts her hand on her hip. "Who says *he'd* be the one to walk *me* to the door and not the other way around?"

I roll my eyes. "Because you like that kind of crap. The guy treating you like a princess, making sure to pull out a chair for you, making your night magical, and then topping it off with a goodnight kiss at the door."

She blushes. "Okay, that's true." A cute, little snort comes out with her laugh. "Which is so the opposite of you."

"Oh, for sure. Akiro is you in our scenario. Except, he can pull out his own chair, and I'm not giving him a pansy kiss at the end of the night. It will be a decent make-out session in the car, definitely on the handsy side of things."

Now it's her turn to roll her eyes. "There are so many things wrong with you."

I take off down the tunnel. "Me? I'm perfectly fine. It's the rest of you that have your heads put on wrong. You're all stuck in a fantasy when I'm perfectly comfortable chilling in reality."

She snorts. "Keep telling yourself that, Harper."

She spends the rest of the trek to Headquarters showing me some of the animations Bellamy has sent to her, and I do everything in my power to pretend like I'm interested.

CHAPTER NINETEEN

RIGG, Scarlett, and Lincoln are waiting in a meeting room, along with The Brick. He gives me the briefest nod of acknowledgement.

To my surprise, however, Everly Stuart is here in the flesh, along with her burlesque show. Sans Wyatt, because, well, he's in jail. For now. Also, he tried to kill Everly, so there's that. He's probably not her favorite person.

Paul tips his imaginary hat when I come in, which I do in return. He's usually sporting aviators, but since we're inside, he's ditched them, so we can see his obnoxiously smoldering brown eyes. He's wearing his typical three-piece suit, his tie and little pocket handkerchief a pale pink. "Miss Harper. How are you doing?"

"Great. It's so good to see you."

Two hefty arms wrap around me, and suddenly I'm being lifted in the air and twirled around like a little girl.

"You can put me down, Dwayne," I say with a grunt.

Laughing, he sets me on the floor, all smiles. He's got on a two-piece suit, the top three buttons of the lavender silk shirt undone, showing off his smooth chest.

"Always a joy to see my little Harper." Dwayne pats me on the head, then pauses on my buzz cut before he rubs his hand back and forth on it.

I duck away from him. "Why does everyone think they can do that?"

"It tickles," Dwayne says, still smiling.

Ignoring him, I turn to my favorite burlesque show member, Alan Echols. Since his parents gave him such a lame name, I refer to him as Echols. He's rocking a white three-piece suit, no tie as usual, but he only unbuttons the top button. He pulls out a tin of mints and offers one to Pearl and me, which we both happily accept.

"How are Brutus and Sam?" I ask Echols. He has two huskies that are freaking amazing. Now that we have our own yard, I've been trying to talk Dad into letting us get one. He never wanted one because we had our hands full with Mom. Now that she's gone, maybe he'll change his mind.

My lips twitch into a frown for a second, thinking about Mom. But I'm at work. I need to focus. So, I switch my smile back on.

"Of course, you'd ask about them first," he says in his scratchy tone. "They're doing great." He winks, his blue eyes lit up in amusement. "And so am I."

The three members of the burlesque show share a look, then glance at Everly, who shakes her head.

Dwayne huffs. "I'm sorry. I just can't *not* bring it up." He wraps me up in another hug, and why is he being so freaking affectionate? "I'm so sorry about your mom." I sigh. That's why. "We all wanted to be at the funeral but wanted to give your family space." He sniffs, lets me go, and wipes at his eyes. Is he crying?

He pulls a handkerchief out from his pants pocket and blows his nose.

Paul comes to me next, hugging me tight. "She was a good woman, and I know she's proud of you."

When Paul finally releases me, Echols arches a bushy eyebrow. "Will you kill me if I hug you?"

Tears are welling in my eyes, and it's pissing me off. I don't want to cry in front of them. I try to speak, but the words get lodged with the lump in my throat.

Echols comes to me anyway, hugging me close. "I lost my mom around your age. If you ever need someone to talk to, you have my number."

Everly is next, her hug as soft as her skin. The smell of jasmine accompanies her, as always. Her tight pants and heels are royal blue, along with her eyeshadow, making her soft blue eyes pop. Her white silk blouse has the top two buttons undone, so a compromise of Echols and Dwayne's style.

She gently places a hand on my cheek, her usual snark nowhere to be found. "It sucks, doesn't it?"

A laugh finally inches around the wedge in my throat, coming out in a squeak. "Understatement."

She nods. "It's okay to be mad. Ticked. Sad. Let it all out, Harper. Don't bottle it in."

I hate that she's come to know me so well. She always says I remind her of her when she was my age. I've never known if that's a compliment or insult. I like her, but sometimes she pisses me off. We don't always see eye to eye.

But she's done so much for my family and DPS, and I can't look past that. I owe her a lot.

So I'll stop crying like a baby and turn my focus to the newest member of the burlesque show. A woman. She's a petite thing, friendly and calming. But there's a fire behind her eyes that tells me not to cross this woman.

Everly follows my gaze. "Harper, this is Mayleen. She joined my security detail a few months ago."

Mayleen comes forward, extending her small, dainty hand, her shake everything but. Man, the woman is strong. "Nice to meet you. I've heard great things."

Dwayne smiles at me. "After working with you, we realized tough things can come in small packages."

Paul rubs his shoulder. "Don't get in a ring with the woman. You'll be regretting it for days."

"Weeks," Mayleen says, smirking at Paul. "Maybe if you weren't so worried about your hair staying in place, you'd actually be able to keep up."

And, she's officially my favorite person in the world.

I turn back to Everly. "So, what are you—"

My question is cut off as the door swings wide open, and Zia slinks into the room, wearing a long black coat. Her dyed-white hair is split between three layers. Buzzed on the bottom, about an inch long in the middle, the top a good three inches and sticking up into the air in a single spike. Her straight bangs fall to the bottom of her eyebrows.

"Sorry I'm late." She undoes the buttons and lets the coat fall into a heap on the floor, revealing a bright orange dress, the same color as the cat-like glasses she's wearing. "The group of terrorists I tracked down really gave me a run for my money. I had to stop all five of them escaping, disarm the bombs—" She holds up a slender finger. "Yes, *bombs*, as in plural, release the hostages, and jet out of there before the cops showed up." She motions to her dress. "Pearl, my precious pudding, this dress you designed is brilliant. All the hidden pockets, the breathable material, not to mention the range of motion I have in this beauty is off the charts." She brushes her bangs out of her eyes. "What did I miss?"

Everyone stares at Zia in silence before I finally turn my attention back to Everly and finish my question. "Why are you here?"

Her lips twitch up into an amused smile. "Wyatt Mitchell."

CHAPTER TWENTY

EVERLY TAKES a seat at the head of the table, clearly irking Rigg who twitches his jaw, but he doesn't say anything. Instead, he takes the seat to the right of her, followed by Scarlett, Bo, Lincoln, and Zia. Aside from Echols—who takes a seat to the left of Everly—the rest of the burlesque show remains standing, spread throughout the room. They're constantly in reconnaissance mode.

"How come no one told me I have a cousin?" I ask.

Almost everyone looks at me, confused. Except Bo. He's a nice, shiny statue with three braids and a knife up his sleeve.

I fold my arms. "Wyatt has a kid."

Pearl plops down in a chair. "Whoa."

Rigg grunts in annoyance as Scarlett and Dwayne snicker.

"Did I miss something?" Mayleen asks. "I didn't know Harper and Wyatt were related."

I huff. "We're not. I call him Uncle W. It's a long story." I turn my attention to Rigg and Scarlett. "You knew about this?"

Scarlett leans back in her chair, one arm resting on the back, the other resting on her kicked-up leg while she holds a cup. "I found out not too long ago. After the gala." She does a one shoulder shrug. "Didn't think you needed to know."

Rigg narrows his eyes at me. "I didn't want you to hunt her down."

I open my mouth to protest but realize he's right. I would have, and I don't know how our first meeting would have gone down. If she's anything like her dad, it might not end well for her.

"Your priorities were right where they needed to be," Scarlett says softly.

My mom.

Echols reaches forward, grabbing a bottle of scotch and pouring a drink for himself and Everly.

Everly takes the glass in her hand and abruptly changes the subject, expecting us all to follow. "Unfortunately, I think Wyatt is telling the truth. We've been keeping a close eye on the Fukunaga family ever since the gala."

Rigg leans forward and clasps his hands on the table. "We have, too."

I sit down next to Echols. I'm not surprised DPS has been watching them, I'm just shocked they never said anything to me. Though, I knew the shipments have been continuing and never told them.

I look at Rigg. "Why keep that a secret?"

Zia kicks her feet up on the table and crosses her ankles. The heels of her orange shoes are ridiculously long. How she fights in them is beyond me. "Love makes us extraordinarily blind, you prickly pear."

I jump, my chair flying back and colliding with the wall. "I'm so not in lo ... in lo ..." I grunt. "I seriously hate that word."

Pearl tries to guide me back to my chair, but I yank my arm away from her. She smiles at me. "There's nothing wrong with *love*."

I grunt again.

Lincoln turns on the computer, probably trying to get us back on track. "The Fukunagas have still been getting steady shipments, about twice a month, ever since the gala." He pulls up photos from the transport, Mr. Fukunaga and Akiro showing up in some of the photos. "Just like the previous ones, they're all crates and people."

"The people have been transported to different cities in the western United States." Everly runs her finger along the lip of her glass. "They've given them all new identities and a chance at a new life here in America."

Scarlett spits some sunflower seeds into her reusable cup. "The majority of them have gone to the same cities, namely Seattle, Albuquerque, Salt Lake City, Boise, here in San Diego, and the capital."

"Las Vegas," I say, finally taking a seat again.

After the war left Washington D.C. practically demolished, they relocated the capital to the most thriving city at the time, Las Vegas. I've yet to go there, even though we're not too far, but, you know, the whole being poor thing kept us away.

Now we have some money, but it still goes to pay off Mom's medical bills, now the funeral on top of that. Plus, I don't really have the time for luxury travel. Or any kind of travel.

"I thought we established that them importing people wasn't that big of a deal," I say, pushing my chair back so I can kick my feet up on the table. "Well, besides the fact that we don't have a trade agreement with Japan. I mean, is having people here illegally *that* big of a deal?"

"It is when they're sporting this," Rigg says, pulling up an image on the feed.

A yellow and orange cobra slithers onto the projection, fangs bared, glancing at everyone at the table. It settles in the middle, coiling up. It's then that I notice the bottom half of the snake is a fox tail, and giddiness erupts inside me. I know exactly who this symbol belongs to.

"Have you heard of the Corbox Clan?" Everly asks.

I try to rein back the excitement in my voice. "They're only the most notorious gang in Japan. Highly skilled, as lethal as a cobra, as sly as a fox." I point to the image and glance at Pearl. "Life goals, right there."

Pearl tightens the bun on her head. "Only you would want to join a ruthless gang."

I slap her arm, making her grimace. "I don't want to join them, stupid. I want to infiltrate them and crush them from the inside out with my bare hands."

Scarlett chuckles across the table. "Well, you might get your chance."

Everything around me freezes. Normally, my brain is flying at a million miles per hour, but I'm suddenly in slow-motion, all my thoughts breaking down into savory pieces.

A chance to take down the Corbox Clan. Christmas came way early this year.

Something flicks my cheek, and I startle, turning to find Pearl's fingers flying toward my skin again.

I swat her hand away. "What are you doing?"

"Just making sure you're still with us." She points to my chin. "I think you're drooling."

I wipe at it, only to find it dry, then snarl at her before I turn my attention back to Scarlett. "What do you mean, I might get my chance?"

She lowers her leg. "Thanks to Wyatt, we've been keeping a closer eye on Hitoshi, and it's a good thing we have. A shipment came in two days ago. One Tomi didn't know about. Hitoshi oversaw the whole thing." She points at the cobra with a fox tail. "One of the people getting off the ship had this image tattooed on his arm."

Wyatt was right. Hitoshi has been working with crime

bosses in Japan. It better be because they're threatening him, because if I find out Hitoshi's doing this of his own free will, I'm going to rip him to shreds for doing this to Akiro and his family.

Lincoln pulls up a video of a scrawny guy leaving the ship, a rip on his shirt sleeve, showing part of the fox tail. There's a small glimmer on his skin when a light reflects off it. I reach forward, pausing the video.

I point to the shimmer. "What's that?"

Lincoln is beaming. I've never seen the guy so excited before. "Only the most amazing technology." He leans forward, pointing to a sliver of the man's skin. "He's using disguise technology, making him look skinnier than he really is. We've never been able to I.D. any of the people coming off the ship because of it. It can alter anyone's appearance, from skin tone, eye color, weight, height." His jaw is practically on the floor. "It's mind-blowing."

"Seems like something you could have created," I say.

Bo makes a weird noise, like he doesn't agree with me. He's never thought highly of Lincoln, mostly because of his gentle demeanor. Bo likes fighters. It's one thing Bo and I don't see eye to eye on. I think Lincoln is brilliant. Who cares if he doesn't have a get-up-in-your-face attitude? DPS already has too many of those.

Lincoln blushes. "I wish. I mean, I have a lot of things that are close, like being able to alter images on camera, but this is a sheer material that changes what the eye sees."

He scratches his smooth chin. "If I could get my hands on one of these, I could probably duplicate it."

Scarlett pushes Lincoln gently on the arm—over his shirt, avoiding skin contact—bringing him back to the topic at hand.

"Oh, right," Lincoln says, using the top of his index finger to lift the bottom of his glasses. "Once I knew what I was up against, I was able to run a program that decoded what the man with the tattoo looked like in real life and compare it to a database DPS has of known Corbox members."

A muscular man pops up in the projection, his massive frame reminding me of Rigg. Compared to the altered image of the man getting off the ship, there's no way anyone would tie them together.

"Meet Kazumi Ito," Rigg says, motioning to the burly man hovering above the table. The projected man scowls, showing off three platinum teeth. "Younger brother to—"

"Raiden Ito," I whisper. "Overlord of Corbox."

Dwayne chuckles near the door. "Overlord. A bit much in the title, no?" He stops laughing, wiping his massive finger along his pearly whites, probably thinking about getting them in platinum.

"Also, a bit much," I say, pointing at Dwayne.

He quickly lowers his hand, tucking it into his pants' pocket. "I'd look better in gold anyway."

Paul eyes the large gold ring on his middle finger, the lights in the room reflecting off the diamonds almost causing me to go blind. He lifts his upper lip, baring his teeth.

I sigh. "No gold teeth, guys." I turn back to Rigg. "Where's Kazumi now?"

"Vegas," Everly says, leaning forward, her shirt dipping low. "Which is why we're going there."

Pearl squeals next to me. "Vacay!"

Bo—who normally remains quiet during meetings—glares at her, his voice coming out low. "It's work, Pearl. No gallivanting." He's also not the biggest fan of Pearl. She's way too much of an overly happy teenage girl for him to handle. Really, his list of people he's fans of is super small. It's probably just himself on the list.

Zia hisses at Bo. Like actually hisses.

Pearl shrinks back in her chair, red climbing up her neck to her cheeks.

I hold up a palm. "How in the world can we get close to Kazumi Ito? You know his security detail will be impossible to get through, and, as much as I'd like to, we don't have time to infiltrate his organization."

"Unless we send in someone he already knows," Echols says next to me.

"Wyatt," I say, not hiding the irritation in my tone.

Everly sits back, clasping her hands and resting them on her stomach while she nods. "Wyatt."

Lincoln pulls up a blueprint of Calloway Penitentiary on the computer. "Which is why we're going to break him out."

143

BREAKING Wyatt out from his cell is impossible. The walls and door are impenetrable, even with the gadgets DPS has. So, we need to move him to the room I met him in last time. A lot easier to get through the glass wall.

Everly is standing, just like everyone in the room. We all stood the second Lincoln pulled up the blueprint. Apparently, standing around the table makes the situation more serious or something.

Everly leans her palms on the table. "I'll arrange a meeting with Wyatt at Calloway on Thursday morning."

Rigg has his arms folded, muscles twitching under his shirt. "Pearl, you'll be posing as a local high school student working on a summer project, wanting to do an interview with Wyatt."

I hold up a palm. "Wait, you're sending Pearl in?" It should be *me* going in there. I'm the full-time DPS agent.

She's just a part-time operative, who doesn't know the art of being subtle.

The anger must be apparent in my voice, because everyone is staring at me with either a frown or wide eyes. Except Bo. He almost looks impressed.

"What?" I ask, folding my arms to match Rigg. "I've worked hard to get where I am. I know the way Wyatt thinks better than anyone in this room. I have more training than she does."

Bo cracks the tiniest of smiles.

Rigg's jaw is pulled tight, though, and he's about to spew something I'm not going to like.

Thankfully, Scarlett gently sets her hand on his shoulder, stopping him. Her soft eyes turn to me. "Patience, Harper. We haven't gotten to your role yet."

Zia frowns dramatically. "Ah, but we all know patience and Harper have never gotten along. Don't see eye to eye, those two."

Heat flares from my cheeks, and I hate it. I don't get embarrassed. But why is it suddenly so hot in the room? Everyone staring at me is like being under interrogation. I do the interrogating, not the other way around.

Everly pushes away from the table, gently putting a hand on her hip. She nods her head at Paul. "Paul can be Pearl's teacher, since he's the closest build to Wyatt. Of course, they'll both be using aliases."

"Why does his build matter?" I ask.

Out of the corner of my eye, I see Pearl shyly smiling

at Paul. He's a good-looking dude, but way too old for her. If her parents won't like Bellamy, they certainly won't like a guy in his late thirties.

Scarlett smiles at me. "Patience." Zia sings the word along with her.

I snort but keep my mouth shut.

Rigg's still glaring at me, not liking my behavior, but I really don't care. I have every right to question Pearl being chosen over me. This isn't her area of expertise.

Scarlett has to elbow Rigg so he'll start talking. He runs his hand down his goatee. "Harper will be coming in from the roof."

"It's ninety floors high!" Pearl squeaks.

All the annoyance flies out of me and is replaced by a giddiness I need to keep in check. "Drop in?"

Rigg nods. "We'll fly in, you hop out, using a small parachute to guide you to the roof."

"Sweet," I say under my breath.

Echols smiles next to me, then pops a mint in his mouth.

Lincoln zooms in on the roof on the projected image. "You'll use a scrambler on the keypad to get through the roof door." He swipes his finger, showing the hall inside the building. "Then you'll take the elevator shaft down to the fiftieth floor."

This keeps getting better and better.

"We'll have to time it just right," Scarlett says. "You'll want to be there right when Pearl and Paul are coming out of the meeting room and sneak inside before the door closes."

I'm nodding, looking at the images as Lincoln adjusts them while we're talking.

Rigg tosses me a laser pen, which I catch in my hands. His anger has finally melted and he's in full-on mission mode. "You'll use that to cut a piece out of the glass, give Wyatt an outfit to change into."

"Same as what I'll be wearing," Paul says from near the door. His lips twitch in amusement. "Harper will wear the same thing Pearl's wearing."

"So, if we're caught," I say, "they'll think we're them."

We'll install a Trojan horse to remove all traces of us from the video feed, plus erase Pearl and Paul's fake names from the visitor's log, so there will be no physical evidence of our presence that day. It will just be what the guards remember of us.

Pearl claps her hands together, jumping up and down next to me. "We'll be twinners!"

And, she totally ruined the moment.

"We're not wearing pink," I say. "Or dresses. Or anything paisley."

"I'll pick something fashionable yet sensible," Pearl says.

"But—"

Pearl waggles a finger at me. "I'm in charge of wardrobes here, Harper. That's my job. You have to trust me."

It is why we hired her, but that doesn't mean I can't be worried about it.

Zia motions to her bright orange dress. "The girl does have excellent taste."

I need to change the subject before I explode again. "How are we getting out?"

"After you use the elevator shaft to get back to the roof," Bo says, his voice gruff from lack of use, "you'll zipline to an adjacent building. A helicopter will be waiting for you."

"Perfect," I say, not able to contain my grin.

"Doesn't this seem a little dangerous?" Pearl asks, wariness in her tone.

"Harper can handle her own," Rigg says, and my heart warms despite the tightness in his voice. He's clearly not happy with me right now. "We hired her because she can."

Echols pats my shoulder. "I'm more worried about Wyatt. Hopefully he can handle it. He hates heights."

"Well," Rigg says, "if he wants out of prison, he'll have to suck it up."

A thought crosses my mind. "Wait. Won't the guards on Wyatt's side come in once the interview is over?"

Lincoln grins at me. "You know how my Trojan horse can make someone disappear from cameras?"

I nod.

"Well, I figured out how to add them as well," Lincoln says. He pulls up video footage of the interview room at Calloway. Wyatt is standing there in his fuchsia jumpsuit, all shackled up, looking clearly annoyed. "We'll cause a glitch in their system, and the guards won't be able to open the door on his side. When they check the feed, they'll see this video, thinking Wyatt's still in there, so there won't be a panic."

"You'll still have to move quickly," Scarlett says. "We can only hold it for so long without detection. You'll need to be off the building before we lift it and the alarms sound."

"Will do," I say. "Will we be ready by Thursday?"

Scarlett nods. "We have to be."

No way I'm going to be able to sleep tonight, and not just because Pearl will be there. I can't wait for Thursday.

Before Pearl and I leave Headquarters, Rigg pulls me off to the side, out of hearing range from the others, although Scarlett is lurking awfully close.

He's got that fatherly scolding look in his eyes that I hate. "Are you sure you're ready for this?"

"Why wouldn't I be?" I ask.

He pinches the bridge of his nose like he's trying to calm himself. "You've been off your game. Doing reckless things."

Scarlett joins us, the concern in her eyes telling me she heard everything. "Harper, no one will blame you for needing some more time. You just lost your mom."

I want to appear calm, but my balled fists are betraying me, so I clasp them behind my back. "This is my job. You both trained me to work in every circumstance possible."

My gaze shoots to Rigg. "You're the one who said I can handle my own."

"When you're not emotional, yes," Rigg says.

Scarlett opens her mouth, probably to say something incredibly stupid that will push me to my breaking point, so I back away from them, my chin held high. "I'm fine."

With that, I turn around, go to Pearl, snatch her away from Paul—who she's disgustingly flirting with—and tug her toward the exit.

Pearl tries to yank her arm from my grasp, but I'm way stronger than her. "I can walk by myself, Harper."

"Once we're far enough away from Paul, I'll let you go," I snarl, dragging her up the stairs and out the door.

Her cheeks flare. "What's that supposed to mean?"

"You're flirting with him like a lovesick girl. It's embarrassing."

This time, when she jerks her arm away from me, she does it with so much force that she actually gets away. "You know, I think I'll sleep at my own house tonight."

"There are guys watching my house." I check my watch. "The lights have already gone off in the bedroom. They think we're sleeping."

"So, they're probably gone, then."

I spin around to face her. "Hey, if you want to risk getting abducted, be my guest."

"Fine." She takes off in the opposite direction of my house, stomping across the old football field in a graceful manner. Then she pauses, turning back toward me. "Listen, I know you're in mourning, but that doesn't give you the right to treat me like this." She spins around in a perfect pirouette, disappearing into the night.

This is exactly why I don't have friends. Way too much drama.

CHAPTER TWENTY-TWO_

Pearl and I don't speak again until Thursday morning. I thought about messaging her a few times, but everything I typed out sounded way too snarky. In the end, I figured silence was better than shoving my foot in my mouth again.

Same goes with Akiro. I've kept our interaction to a minimum. I don't trust myself to be around Hitoshi without tying him up and beating his involvement with the Corbox Clan out of him.

In the meantime, I focus my energy on training, a couple of those times with Bo. I'm sure his sudden interest in working with me is because he feels sorry for me, and my mom dying, but I push my annoyance aside and use it to my advantage. His willingness to help might not last long.

I also search for Wyatt's daughter, but I'm coming up empty. Wherever she is, she doesn't want to be found. I don't blame her. I wouldn't want anyone to know that man was my father.

Pearl and I are standing in Headquarters, waiting to leave. The brown wig is light on my head, the material breathable. It's the only redeemable quality it has, otherwise it would currently be on fire in the trashcan near me. They also made us wear contacts, changing my brown eyes and Pearl's blue eyes to hazel.

Pearl fixes the bangs on her light brown wig in front of a full-length mirror projected from her watch. She swapped out her pink paisley watch for a DPS-issued one that matches mine. "My first DPS mission," Pearl says. "Like, in the field. This is so exciting." Satisfied with her appearance, she presses a button on her watch and the mirror dissipates.

"This whole get-up is stupid," I say, folding my arms tightly across my chest. She forced me to wear a lavender drawstring jumpsuit, an old-school fashion that is making yet again another comeback. "I look like an idiot." I mean, they're impractical. What if I have to pee? I'll have to unbutton the top and pull the whole thing down. They could at least create a flap down there, like on those old pajamas you see in westerns.

Pearl tries to wipe at my chin, but I swat her hand away. She huffs. "First of all, you look gorgeous, just own it. Second, you have lipstick on your chin."

I wipe furiously at my chin, wishing I could wipe my lips as well.

It's her turn to swat my hand away. "You're rubbing your skin raw." She places her hands on her hips. "If you do your job right today, no one will see you." She removes a loose string on my shoulder, letting it fall to the ground. "Don't pass any judgment until the mission is over. I know the look is not your style, but I swear you're going to love the material."

I rub my hands together. "I can't wait to jump out of the plane."

"You're crazy. No way I could do that."

"Maybe if you grew a backbone, you could." The words come out rougher than I mean to. I'm just so on edge, and this outfit isn't helping. I don't feel like myself.

Pearl takes a step back, hurt flashing across her eyes as her lips tremble. "Not all of us are superheroes, Harper." She goes to clutch the pearls at her neck, only to remember she's not wearing any. We had to ditch anything that screams us.

Which is why I look like a walking flower. I'm just glad we can't take any photos or videos, because I don't need a reminder of this day, or any blackmail material readily available.

We stand there in silence for a good three minutes. I know, because I'm staring at my watch, like it could teleport me out of here.

She's pouting, still upset by my outburst. I hate seeing her like this, because it's annoying. She looks stupid when she's acting like a hurt little girl.

"Any recent animations from Bellamy?" I ask.

"B!" she hisses.

"Fine. Any recent animations from *B*?"

She narrows her eyes at me, trying to detect my sincerity. She did tell me I have to get used to playing a character for the day, so I feign the best interest I can.

"I'm still convinced he broke into my house to use Casper in that last one you showed me," I say. "That cat was the spitting image of him."

A smile breaks out on her face. "They were twins. So crazy." She pulls up one of a fox scattering rose petals all over the place. The fox reminds me of the Corbox symbol.

"Think he knows we're looking into Corbox?" I whisper.

Pearl gasps. "What? No!"

I put a hand on her arm. "I'm kidding."

She lets out a breath of relief. "Right."

Scarlett, Rigg, and Paul join us in the lobby. Pearl smiles at Paul, a little twinkle in her eyes. He returns the smile in a friendly way, like 'I'm your uncle and you're just an adorable little thing,' clearly not noticing she's smitten. Then, her gaze goes to me and she shrinks away, embarrassed. As she should be.

Scarlett bumps my arm. "You ladies ready?"

I rub my hands together, eager to get on with the mission and end this conversation and gag fest with Pearl. "Yes."

Paul tips his imaginary hat. "Good luck, Harper." He

moves toward the exit, expecting Pearl to follow. They're taking a helicopter most of the way, then switching to the rails to get to the prison.

Rigg, Scarlett, and I will be going on the plane.

Pearl suddenly throws her arms around me. "Don't die, Harper."

I pat her back. "Hey, if I do, you can just throw me in my mom's casket. Save some money."

When I pull back, they're all staring at me in horror.

I awkwardly laugh, going to rub the back of my neck, only to remember I'm wearing a stupid wig. "It was a joke."

"A horrible one," Pearl says.

Scarlett regains her composure. "Alright, let's stay focused. We have a mission to do."

"Consider it done," I say.

With one last fleeting glance at me, Pearl hurries out of Headquarters, and I swear I see tears welling in her eyes. I hate the weird feeling of betrayal worming through my veins.

We're about to move toward the exit ourselves when Lincoln comes running out, Zia skipping behind him.

"I found his daughter," Lincoln spits out, pulling up an image on his datapad. "I found Wyatt's daughter."

The projection hovers above the screen, a girl around fifteen, strawberry-blonde hair, light spattering of freckles, and an innocent smile that looks nothing like her dad's. She must take after her mom.

"Meet Viana Vale," Zia says, pointing to the image. "Fifteen years old, lives in Arizona, a Sagittarius, is deathly allergic to peanuts, and is a talented young artist." She leans toward me. "Water coloring is her medium of choice, but if you ask me, she's much better with charcoal."

Scarlett blows out a breath of relief as she checks her watch. "Zia, how soon can you get to Arizona?"

Zia backs away, her yellow dress swishing side to side. "I'm already on my way, my exquisite ruby. I won't come back without her." She wriggles her fingers in a wave. "Ta-ta for now." She smiles at me. "Good luck, prickly pear."

She saunters out, humming the whole way.

"Do you really think it's wise to send her on this mission?" Rigg asks with a guttural growl that comes from deep within. "Can we trust her with Wyatt's daughter?"

Scarlett places a hand on his arm. "I wouldn't have sent her if I thought otherwise. Rigg, Zia's good at her job. Eccentric, yes, but she knows what she's doing and will keep it professional."

I feel like I'm missing something, but I know they won't tell me if I ask. This isn't the time or the place.

Rigg storms toward the exit. "Everyone, on the jet. Now."

Scarlett and I share a smile before we follow him out.

CHAPTER TWENTY-THREE

THE WHOLE FLIGHT to the prison, Rigg keeps drilling me about the mission, making me repeat every single step I have to take. He's never pushed it so far, and it's starting to piss me off.

I hold up the piece of glass I just cut out from a mini replica of the glass wall at the prison. "This is the tenth one, Rigg. I know how to use the laser."

He tosses me the grappling hook gun so hard, it whams against my chest, making me stumble back and stinging a little. "Show me how you use that."

I point it at the replica target, making sure the coordinates on the projected screen are exact. "Also, for the tenth time, I line up the trajectory and pull the trigger." I wriggle the gun in my hand. "I secure the handle on the roof, then use the wrist grips to zipline across."

"And your body?" Rigg asks.

I have to hold in my sigh. "Parallel to the cord."

Rigg resets the diagram hovering above the table. "Let's start from the beginning."

"Rigg," Scarlett says as gently as she can. "She's got it."

I, on the other hand, am not so gentle. "What's your problem, Rigg? I know what I'm doing. I'm not new to this."

"I need you focused!" he roars.

I stumble back, his words slamming into me. "When am I not?"

Rigg rubs furiously at his goatee. "Maybe this is a bad idea." He turns to Scarlett. "Let's have you go in."

"I'm not as young as Harper," Scarlett says. "As much as I'd love to, I can't pass as a teenager anymore." She motions to me. "This is why we hired her."

"Why are you questioning this so much?" I ask.

"Because you just lost your mom, Chandler!" He slams a fist down on the table. "We need your head on straight."

He's switched to usage of the last name, which is never good. I mean, didn't we just go over this the other night? Why does he keep pushing this?

I put my hands on my head. "I'm fine! I can handle this. I won't lose focus, and I won't make any emotionally rash decisions."

He points a thick finger at me. "You can't promise that. Emotions aren't always rational. They pop up at inconvenient times."

I point my finger at him, just inches away from his

chest. "You're the one who taught me how to rein in the emotions during a mission."

Scarlett steps between us, putting her hands on our chests and pushing us away from each other. "That's enough." She growls at Rigg. "From both of you." She waits for both of us to stop heaving and take a step back before she lowers her hands. "Everything is already in motion. We can't change or stop any of it. We're going to have to trust that everyone will do their job."

Lincoln's voice comes over the intercom. "Almost to the drop-off point."

Rigg stomps over to the wall, snatches a parachute, comes back, and shoves the bag into my chest. "Strap this on." He turns around, heading for the cockpit. Seriously, the man is acting like a child.

I move like I want to strangle him, but Scarlett waggles her finger at me. "Give him time. He'll cool down."

I zip on the chute with more force than necessary. "I don't know why he's so mad at me. I've been doing my job."

She calmly walks over to me, gently placing her finger under my chin to get me to look up. "Baby girl, it's okay to admit you're in a bad place. You just lost your mom. I know you're trying to keep yourself busy, but you still need to mourn. It's part of the process."

I slap her hand away and back up. "I said I'm *fine*. Why won't anyone believe me?"

Lowering her hand, she sighs. She checks her watch. "One minute before the jump."

I follow her to the door, checking all my straps to make sure they're secure. I have the bag with Wyatt's change of clothes strapped to me as well.

I may have gotten on Pearl's case about the jumpsuit, but the material is comfortable, and more importantly, breathable. Squatting, I test the flexibility. Also awesome. I might have to actually thank her for it later. Maybe.

Scarlett sets her hand on my shoulder. "You need to remember, you and Rigg are a lot alike. He wants to be there for you but doesn't know how. Anger is his go-to emotion." She peels back some of the wig's hair stuck to my eyelashes. "Stay focused. You got this."

I nod.

She presses the button to open the door and smiles softly. I don't know what comes over me, but I throw my arms around her, squeezing tight. Her lips press against the top of my head as she rocks me back and forth. I don't know what I would do without her.

Everyone around me is trying to help, trying to console me, and while I know their hearts are in a good place, it's annoying the crap out of me.

With Scarlett, though, everything she says is wanted and appreciated. Her opinion means more to me than anyone else's. While people try to understand me—Akiro especially—none of them quite gets me like she does.

Her watch beeps, letting me know it's time to jump.

Without looking at her, I run and jump out of the plane, the heavy wind welcoming me into the sky.

CHAPTER TWENTY-FOUR

This feeling of absolute freedom, complete abandonment of everything that matters, this is why I love my job.

The air slapping against my cheeks as I plummet to the earth gives me a thrill I can't really explain to the average person. In this moment, there's no one around to bother me. No one to get inside my head with meaningless notions.

I wish I could soar forever, just me, the wind, and the sky, an endless amount of refuge. Unfortunately, that's not reality.

It's a short jump. The chute opens at the correct time, having calculated my falling speed and distance to the landing coordinates, yanking me back up and slowing my descent.

It would be so nice if everything in life worked that

way. All calculated out to the exact measurements, no interference, no second-guessing. Just logic and precision.

My feet land quietly on the roof of Calloway Penitentiary. The Trojan horse has already been installed, so the cameras won't pick me up. I quickly undo the chute, the material disintegrating before my eyes. One less thing to carry around.

There are no security guards on the roof. I mean, it's ninety stories high, and they have high-tech equipment that alerts them if anything lands on the roof, or if there's even pressure on the ground I'm walking on.

DPS is the only one that can crack their code, and since the prison doesn't know we exist, well, they aren't looking for us.

There has always been a concern about what would happen if the DPS software were to land in the wrong hands. If terrorists could do what we could, they'd win every time. If the government had what we had, I worry about the power trip it would give politicians and what they'd do to other countries or those who don't agree with them.

My wrist warms, my watch letting me know it's time to begin my descent into the prison. Paul and Pearl should already be in place, doing their "interview" with Wyatt.

All of us are without communication devices. We can't risk anyone intercepting our feed. The likelihood of that happening is so small, but even DPS isn't foolproof.

Keeping my feet light, I go over to the door and place

the scrambler over the keypad to get in. Since Calloway has a difficult system to crack, it's going to take at least thirty seconds to unscramble the code, which we counted on.

Twenty-eight seconds later, the light on the keypad turns green, and I slowly open the door as I tuck the scrambler back in my bag.

My training instincts have me wanting to have my tranquilizer gun out, ready to shoot, but I'm trying to minimize the threat I pose. If anyone sees me, I have to claim the innocent schoolgirl who got lost in this massive prison.

There's no one in the stairwell, relieving me. I'm not that good of an actress when it comes to pretending to be innocent.

I hurry down one flight of stairs, my boots not making a sound on the concrete floor. When I get to the door, I quietly open it and use a telescoping rod with a camera attached to make sure no one is in the hall before I slip through.

Staying close to the wall, I creep down the hall until I'm standing below a vent. I pull a stick-em out of my bag. It's a handle that will stick to the roof while I try to open the hatch. After a quick sweep to make sure the hall is still empty, I run at the wall, push off, and leap into the air, pressing the stick-em to the ceiling. Thank goodness for all the curls I do at the DPS gym.

I have one hand wrapped around the stick-em, holding me in the air, the other working to open the hatch. It takes a few light punches before it lifts into the ducts, and I can push it off to the side.

Hefting myself inside the ducts, I press the release valve on the stick-em, then replace the lid. My watch automatically turns on a light, just bright enough for me to see down the ducts, but not too bright to alert my presence. A compass projects from above my watch, calculating the coordinates and which way I need to head. I crawl to the east, going toward the elevator.

It's a tight squeeze as I work my way through, doing an army crawl as quickly as I can. I don't have much time to waste until Pearl and Paul will be done with their interview, and I'll need to be at the door.

Ugh. Paul and Pearl. P-squared. Their names go together like an annoyingly lovey-dovey couple that have stupid nicknames for each other and use baby voices when talking. I really hope Pearl doesn't do anything stupid. Paul's a class act, so I'm not worried about him being attracted to a teenager. I am worried about Pearl letting her crush go too far and not paying attention to the guy her age that actually likes her.

My fist tightens, hating that I'm even thinking about this crap. I need to be focused on the mission, not my friend's love life.

It does make the time go by faster as I crawl through the narrow vent. I arrive at the opening to the elevator shaft, slipping down and out of the hole with ease. Using a retractable cord, I repel down, keeping close to the wall.

I'm halfway down when I hear the whoosh of the elevator zooming toward me. Pressing my body against the wall, I try to make myself as flat as possible, not wanting to get crushed by the elevator. What a horrible way to die. Not to mention completely messy and would definitely give away how we got in the building.

The elevator rushes by so fast, I'm afraid my wig is going to rip off with the gust. Thank the stars it stays in place and I continue my decent, not wasting any time as I hurry out and down the hall.

I'm slinking around the corner right as the interview room opens and P-squared waltzes out.

Pearl immediately starts talking to the guard outside, her back to me. Paul makes sure to step right behind her and to the side, blocking me from their view.

As I pass Paul, I lightly tap his back to let him know I'm here, then I slip into the room, the door closing softly behind me.

Wyatt's about to knock on the door on his side, probably wondering why they haven't opened the door yet.

"I have a cousin?" It comes out of my mouth before I can stop it.

Wyatt whips around, his wide eyes narrowing when he sees me, then a smirk breaks out on his face. "I think this is the first time in my life I'm happy to see you."

I snort. "Feeling is so not mutual."

His smirk fades. "Leave Viana out of this."

"You brought her into it in the first place. Is she your plus one?"

He answers with silence, his tired eyes lit up in anger. He somehow looks worse than he did a few days ago.

As much as I want to grill him about his daughter, we don't have time. I start the countdown on my watch, so I know how much time we have to get to the roof. "Let's get this over with."

CHAPTER TWENTY-FIVE_

I RUSH TO THE GLASS, taking a pen out of the bag wrapped around me. Flipping on the laser, I begin to cut a line through the glass, needing an opening for Wyatt to fit through. The laser cuts with precision, the line perfectly straight, just like I practiced with Rigg.

"Why are you wearing a jumpsuit?" Wyatt asks. "Are we trading places? If so, you got the wrong color."

I keep my focus on the glass. "Fuchsia doesn't go as well with my complexion as yours does. Besides, my outfit is way more fashionable than your prison garb." Ugh. I hate that those words came out of my mouth. I sound like Pearl.

I make a square cut, wide enough for Wyatt to slide through. I gently lower the piece of glass to the ground, then help Wyatt through the hole, ignoring his protests for me to slow down.

"We don't have time to waste," I say.

Using the laser again, I slice open the shackles on Wyatt's wrists and ankles. Lincoln already disabled the tracker on his ankle, so the prison will be none the wiser until we're long gone.

I throw down the shackles. "Take off your jumpsuit."

As he unbuttons his ugly jumpsuit, I pull Paul's replica outfit out of the bag. Wyatt puts the shirt and pants on, jumping around on the ground like an idiot, trying to not put too much pressure on his left leg. There's a small scar on his thigh from the bullet wound. Then I look at the long, jagged scar on his arm from when I stabbed him. Guess it makes sense why he hates me. I have a habit of giving him scars. But, if we're being honest here, he deserved them.

Right when he yanks his head up after zipping the pants, I use the opportunity to shove contacts into his eyes.

With a shriek, he bounces away from me, rubbing his eyes. "What are you doing?"

"Disguising you," I say.

He glares at me with all the hatred in the world, and it's almost touching. I've never been hated so much by a person. I feel like I've reached some milestone in my life.

"I could have done it myself," he says as his eyes water.

"I know. But that was more fun." I twirl the wig around on my finger. "Do you want me to put this on you as well?"

He snatches it from my hands, tugging it on as he glares at me. The second he finishes, I toss him a pair of socks and shoes, which he barely catches against his chest. The guy is a little sluggish, probably from being locked up in this horrible place.

"Hurry." I glance at the countdown hovering above my watch. "We have six minutes to get to the roof."

The clothes are a tad too big for him since he's lost some weight, but they'll work. As I watch him struggle with the laces—his weak hands shaking—I can't help but wonder if we're making the biggest mistake ever. I mean, we're breaking Wyatt freaking Mitchell out of prison. Felony if we get caught aside, he doesn't deserve to be free.

The image of Ned being blown into pieces at the gala flashes in my mind, and I press the back of my hand to my mouth. The whole scene was horrid. Ned didn't need to die, yet Wyatt obliterated the poor dude. Ned was no saint, but no one deserves that kind of death.

Wyatt is suddenly in front of me, snapping his fingers together. "Harper! We don't have time for you to daydream!"

Resisting the urge to head-butt him, I hurry over to the door, using the scrambler to unlock it.

Wyatt keeps looking over his shoulder at the door across the room. "Why haven't my guards come?"

"That door *malfunctioned*," I say, drawing out the last word. "Right now, they're watching video footage of only you in the room, glass still intact, you shackled on the other side." I smile up at him. "Don't worry, you look pissed in the video, scowling away at the camera."

His eyebrows lift in surprise, and he actually looks impressed.

I open the door just a crack and use my telescoping rod to check the hallway. Empty. I glance back at Wyatt. "Stay close at my side. If anyone sees us, I'm a student, you're a teacher, here to interview Wyatt Mitchell."

"So, myself."

I shake my head. "You're not Wyatt Mitchell right now. You're Jack Wheeler, a high school criminology teacher."

He grunts. "I think I'd prefer prison."

"You're welcome to stay here," I say.

His gaze lands on the countdown hovering above my watch. "We're wasting time."

I bite my tongue, holding back all the snarky remarks I want to make. We slip into the hall, walking lightly and staying close to the wall. For every turn we make, I use my telescoping rod to make sure no one is heading down the hall. Thank goodness that since the prison is so big, there aren't tons of people walking all the halls.

Once we get to the elevator, I use a trusty Scarlett creation to open the doors. Placing it against the pad, I use it to send a digital message to the doors, making them open, even though the elevator isn't on this floor. We don't want to go inside, just use the shaft.

Wyatt peers inside, looking up and then down into the blackness below. "Please tell me we're not scaling this."

I pat his arm, then pause, squeezing his bicep. "Man, I

remember when there used to be muscle here." I snatch my hand away when he bares his canine like he's going to consume me. Pulling the scaling gun from my bag, I show it to him. "The magnet on the end of this baby is strong enough to hold our weight, so you won't have to do a thing."

Again, he looks impressed. I quickly wrap the support straps around us, putting me way too close to Wyatt for my liking. His grunt tells me he feels the same way. But we don't have time to argue.

Then we hear the whiz of the elevator. It's on the way up, so we only have a few seconds to act.

As I aim the gun at the top of the shaft, it calculates the distance, and the magnet launches, soaring up the shaft. I switch the ascending speed to the fastest it can go. As soon as the magnet latches to the roof, we're yanked into the shaft, flying up at an alarming rate. So fast, I can't even look down to see how close the elevator is to smashing us.

I say a quick prayer that the elevator isn't going to the ninetieth floor. Ugh. Praying. Akiro is rubbing off on me. But I have to admit it has calmed me at times or helped me through a tough situation.

The speed of the scaling gun slows as we reach the top, jerking us to a stop inches from the roof.

"I think I'm going to be sick," Wyatt says.

Reaching back, I palm his head and turn it away from me. He hacks up everything inside him, raining down in the void. I can't hear the splatter when it hits the roof of the elevator, so the elevator must not have gone past the eightieth floor.

Oh, the stench. I dry heave, pressing my fist against my mouth. That smell is of the devil.

The elevator starts up again. I shine the light from my watch down and see it ascending. With all the energy inside me, I grab Wyatt by the shirt and heft him into the opening of the vent, knowing he can't do it himself since he's weaker than my mom.

Sorrow twists inside me like a thousand daggers clawing at me. She's gone. She's really, actually gone.

"Harper!" Wyatt yells loud, but it's almost a whisper compared to the whiz of the elevator.

Pushing my sorrow aside, I fling myself into the opening seconds before the elevator comes to a stop next to us.

As we both lie there in the vent, gasping for breath, all I can think is that, for a tiny moment there, I wanted to join my mom on the other side.

CHAPTER TWENTY-SIX

We need to get out of here and onto the roof. Only two minutes remain until we need to be clear of the building.

We only have to wait a few seconds before the elevator goes back down, giving us a chance to switch positions so I can be in front. We army crawl like a baby on meth, not caring about making noise or being cautious.

The coordinates on my watch take me back to where I originally entered the ducts. Using the telescoping rod, I do a quick scan of the hall to make sure it's empty before we jump out of the duct. I land lightly on my feet, glancing all around to make sure no one is heading toward us.

Wyatt lands with a thump next to me. I look down to see him curled on the concrete floor, groaning in pain.

Rolling my eyes, I grab him by the shirt and yank him to his feet. "I don't like this new version of you."

"I wouldn't be in this shape if it weren't for you," he snarls.

I slap his cheek, making him yank back from me. "Keep telling yourself that, darlin'. But you brought this on yourself."

Wyatt flinches when I say, *darlin'*. He's probably thinking of Paul, because he loves to use that word.

"Also your fault," I say, heading down the hall at a trot. "If you hadn't turned on everyone, you'd still be friends with the guy."

We hurry into the stairwell, taking the steps two at a time. I'm surprised Wyatt keeps up with me, but it's like he's got a newfound strength.

"I didn't turn on anyone," he says, panting behind me. "I was making things right."

I stop at the door leading to the roof, my hand wrapped around the handle. "Telling yourself lies won't turn them into truths." I stroke my chin. "I should embroider that onto a pillow or something. Mom would totally—" Do that for me. If she were still alive.

Wyatt leans toward me. "Mommy dearest is dead, *darlin'*. She can't do anything for you."

I punch him right in his nose, smiling at the crunch it makes. "I'd watch your words, Wyatt. You're making it awfully tempting to pitch you off the roof of this building." I shake out my hand, loving the blood pouring out of his nose. "Except, that would be too easy a death for you. You'd have a heart attack before you even hit the bottom."

He's holding his hand over his nose, and I don't need to see his mouth to know that canine of his is hungry to have me.

Right as I open the door to the roof, the countdown on my wrist goes off, the beeping in sync with the sirens now blaring overhead. We're out of time.

Wyatt and I move at the same time, heading for the edge of the roof. I'm pulling out the grappling gun as we run, getting it ready.

"How are we getting off this roof?" Wyatt asks.

I wave the gun as we come to a stop at the edge of the roof. "Ziplining. Heard it's your favorite hobby."

If he hadn't already thrown up everything inside him, more would be dumping out on the roof right now. I love seeing him squirm. Especially when he's covered in blood, courtesy of me. Not sure if this day could get any better.

I send a quick message to Rigg and Scarlett, letting them know we're on our way.

"Hey!" A deep voice comes from behind us.

We whip around to see a security guard standing about ten yards away near the air conditioning unit. A repairman is next to him, staring at us with wide eyes.

"What are you doing up here?" The guard asks, moving toward us. He has his hand wrapped around a communicator, probably about to call it in.

"School project!" I say. I elbow Wyatt in the stomach. "Too bad my teacher is a total wimp."

The guard pauses, confused by my words.

With a grin, I spin back around, aim the grappling gun at an adjacent building, pull the trigger, and watch the hook and cord soar in the sky.

"No way, Harper," Wyatt says.

I point at the guard that's now running toward us. "It's me or him. You choose." I shove a set of hand and feet grips into his chest, then anchor the gun into the roof, and jump onto the cord, making my body parallel to it. My hand and feet grips secure me in place as I soar downward, heading for the other roof.

I'm moving too fast to know if Wyatt got on behind me. I didn't show him how to use the grips, but hopefully he's smart enough to figure it out. I mean, all he has to do is put them on and take hold of the cord. The magnets will do the rest.

I'm too frustrated to enjoy the ride. I hate that I'm helping Wyatt escape. I hate that my mom's dead and Wyatt knows it's a weakness of mine. I hate that I even have a weakness. I hate that he slowed me down during our escape. We should have been off the roof before the sirens blared.

My feet connect with the roof of the other building before I can get all my frustrations out. I turn around, only to see a blur of Wyatt before he crashes into me. We fall to the ground, rolling across the roof. I use the momentum to roll into a standing position and rush to the grappling hook, pressing the release valve. The cord shoots back toward the gun on the other building, and I know the second it's coiled back inside, the gun will self-destruct. Such a waste of an awesome tool, but we don't want any of our technology falling into someone else's hands.

Wyatt's still curled up on the ground, so I reluctantly help him to his feet.

"I'm so flattered you chose me over the guard," I say.

He brushes off his hand that touched mine like he might catch some sort of disease. "Just be glad you're not him."

I glance back at the roof of the prison, but it's too far away to see anything. I glare at Wyatt. "What did you do?"

He smiles, all teeth. "I used your brilliant idea and pitched him off the roof."

I don't even think. I punch him in the gut, then in the nose again. This is why I didn't want the man free. He kills without even batting an eye.

I'm about to pick him up and drag him to the edge of the roof so I can toss him off, but, aside from the fact that I'd be turning into him, a cord unfurls right next to me. I glance up to see our airplane, barely visible, thanks to its reflective mirrors.

I want to hop on and let Wyatt fend for himself, but I need to complete my mission, which was to break Wyatt out and deliver him to DPS.

Flexing my hands a few times, I finally reach out and help him to his feet—again—and secure him to the cord hanging from the plane. As it lifts him up, another cord comes down for me.

I look over my shoulder at the edge of the roof, thinking of the guard. "Sorry, dude. You didn't deserve to die. Trust me, I'll get revenge however I can." With a quick salute, I give him five seconds of silence since that's all I can afford. Then I secure myself to the cord, and once again, I'm soaring into the air.

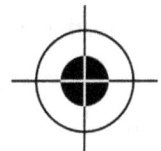

CHAPTER TWENTY-SEVEN

THERE's something mighty pleasing about seeing Scarlett smirk at the sight of Wyatt's appearance.

Rigg pats my shoulder. "You sure cut it close." He nods at Wyatt, who's getting cleaned up by a reluctant Pearl. "Guess he gave you a hard time?"

I ball my hands into fists. "Well, I gave him one back."

Rigg chuckles. "You did good, kid."

Relief washes through me. I'm glad he's not mad at me anymore. Maybe Scarlett talked to him about what a jerk he was being.

Pearl squeals as she quickly backs away from a frustrated Wyatt, dropping the bloody gauze in her hands. Whatever Wyatt is saying to her has her cowering. Paul comes up, gently placing a hand on Pearl's shoulder, and she melts like butter in a frying pan, the spark in her eyes sizzling.

"I've got this, darlin'," Paul says in his charming accent.

I swear I hear Pearl swoon, but maybe I just imagine it.

I rip off my wig, happy to feel the air on my buzzed hair once again.

Pearl's gaze swings between Wyatt and me. "You two are—"

"If you finish that sentence, Pearl," I snarl, "you'll end up like Wyatt."

Knowing her, she was about to say twinners. I don't care if we have the same haircut. We are *not* twinning in any way.

I pull Rigg and Scarlett out of hearing range of Wyatt and the others. We sit down on some couches in the back corner of the jet. Curling my legs underneath me, I let out a breath of relief, grateful to have that part of the mission over.

"He pitched a security guard off the roof," I say.

Rigg pulls his jaw tight. "Why didn't you stop it?"

"I went first."

Rigg rubs his eyes with his thick thumb and index finger. "You were supposed to let him go first."

"The security guard was coming toward us, Wyatt was whining about the height, and I didn't want to get caught. I told him to choose between me or Calloway." I shrug. "He chose me."

"He chose freedom," Scarlett says, looking over at him.

Paul finishes bandaging Wyatt, guides him to the rear of the jet, shoves him into a seat, and shackles him to a table. He stays close, keeping an eye on him.

I reach up, touching my empty earlobes. I couldn't wear my mom's angel wing earrings on the mission.

As if on cue, Pearl sits down on the couch next to me, handing me the earrings. I quickly put them on, sighing in relief. Then I look over and see that we're still wearing the same outfit—minus the wig—and almost dry heave.

She's grinning ear to ear, and against my wishes, my lips betray me and break into a smile of their own.

"That was so awesome." Pearl does her famous shimmy, my smile growing. "First time in the field a success." She motions to Wyatt. "What happened on your end?"

I don't want to mention what he did to the security guard, because I know how hard Pearl will take it.

"He took a jab at my dead mom," I say.

Horror crosses Pearl's face, and suddenly she's on her feet, storming toward Wyatt, her hands in fists, and practically leaving a trail of ashes from the swear words blazing from her mouth. Scarlett has to rush to stop her from pummeling the man. Water wells in my eyes, betraying me just like my lips. I love seeing this side of Pearl.

Rigg, who had been looking over his shoulder, watching the event unfold, turns back to me, shaking his head. "I'm sorry you're in this situation, Harper." He leans forward, an intensity in his eyes that warms my heart. Why is everyone making me all sappy all a sudden? "I swear to you he won't walk free. We'll stop the terrorist attack, and then that animal will be shackled behind bars once again."

I hold up a finger, trying to blink back my tears and take the gooiness out of the conversation. "Technically, he'll be behind a concrete wall, not bars."

Rigg leans back, a small smile slipping onto his face. "Either way, I'm not letting him escape."

I want to say thanks, but a lump jams into my throat, and I really hate emotions. This is why I didn't have friends or let anyone in. Emotions get in the way.

Clearing my throat—and sending that stupid lump straight to its grave—I lift my legs and set my boots on the table in front of me. "What's the plan now?"

Rigg rubs the back of his neck. "I think you should take a crack at Wyatt."

"Me?" I may have reached full DPS operative status, but actual mission-assigned interrogation isn't something I've done before. Rigg has said on many occasions that he worries I'll get out of hand if I have a chance to question a suspected terrorist. Says I'm too "unpredictable." Whatever.

He releases a defeated sigh. "For some reason, the guy only responds to you. I think you have a better chance of getting intel out of him than anyone else."

That lump I sent to its grave is starting to resurface,

184

clawing its way up my throat. I can't cry. I will not cry. Not in front of Rigg, and definitely not in front of Wyatt.

Before I break down into a mushy mess, I interlock my fingers and stretch out my arms, giving my knuckles a good crack. "Let's do this."

CHAPTER TWENTY-EIGHT

Shaking out my nerves, I go to Wyatt, sit on the table near him, and cross my feet at my ankles.

"How do we decode the papers from Alcatraz?"

We don't have the papers from the island anymore, but I want to see his reaction when I talk about them.

Out of the corner of my eye, I see Rigg and Scarlett come closer but still stay out of the conversation. They know Wyatt is more likely to talk to me alone.

Wyatt pulls back in surprise, his raised eyebrows telling me he's impressed. "You found them."

"Why do you always sound so shocked when I'm able to do my job? This is why DPS hired me, idiot."

He snarls, flashing his canine, his tongue running across the bottom of it. "I'd be careful how you talk to me if you want information."

I lean toward him, sporting my own snarl. "I can talk to you however I want. We can still send you back to

Calloway, and honestly, I'm *begging* for you to give us a reason to."

He moves closer, but his shackles stop him just inches from my face. Still too close for my liking, but I'm not cowering in front of this puny bulldog.

"Then thousands of people will die," he growls, low and throaty.

In my peripheral vision, I see Scarlett move toward me, but Rigg holds her back. With his shackles, there's nothing Wyatt can do to me. Although, maybe Scarlett is more worried about me killing Wyatt than the other way around. But I don't kill. Seriously injure, though? The smug look on his face is making it awfully tempting.

All I have to do is place my hand on his head and slam it into the table. It would crush his already broken nose.

But Rigg has been waiting for me to step out of line. Give him a reason to suspend me, so I can have time to mourn. I worry what will happen if I'm left with just my thoughts, Casper's sorrow, Dad's despair, and Mom's empty spot on the couch. I could crumble into a million pieces.

"How do we decode the papers, Wyatt?" I ask.

He slowly pulls his head back, not breaking eye contact with me. His face and body language aren't giving any indication that he's surprised we still have them. He might not know about the self-destruct function. "You need the key."

The muscles in my hands tighten, like they want to

fold into a fist, but I keep my composure. "Why don't you just tell me what's on the papers and save us all the hassle?"

Sitting tall in his chair, he finally tears his gaze away. "I'm hungry."

"Tell me what's on the papers, and I'll get you something to eat." I'm sure I can find a stick of celery in the fridge on the jet, and then throw it at his face.

"Food." He whistles a tune similar to an annoying electro-folk song he listened to all the time. When we make eye contact, he winks at me.

All the composure in me evaporates, and my anger takes over, all the hatred I have for this man fueling me.

In a swift movement, I leap off the table, palm the side of his head, slam the other side into the table, holding it there while I bend down to look him in the eye. "What's on the papers?"

Wyatt squirms, trying to get away, but it's useless. Aside from being shackled, the guy is incredibly weak.

A twisted grin breaks out on his face. "I like this side of you, Harper. We have more in common than I thought."

Like he's seared me, I let go and leap back, wiping off my hands on my pants. "We are nothing alike."

Still smiling, he moves his jaw side to side like he's trying to alleviate the pain. Amusement dances in his eyes. "You'll need the encryption key if you want to decode them."

I kick Wyatt's chair. "And where's that?"

He sighs. "Corbox Headquarters. Good luck getting in."

Discomfort wrangles my insides. No way he'd give that information up after a couple of minutes of questioning. Which means he's lying, or he wants us to go there for some reason.

"Do you know where that's located?" Rigg asks from behind me. I turn around to see him holding a large knife in one hand, and a tranquilizer gun in the other.

"In Vegas," Wyatt says in a deadpan voice.

I turn back to him, rolling my eyes. "Obviously. We need an address."

Wyatt shifts uncomfortably where he sits, his gaze on the table.

I groan. "You have no idea, do you? Seriously, we should have left you in Calloway."

"We can always take him back," Rigg says, slipping his tranq gun into the holster at his side.

Scarlett steps into view, nodding. "I like that idea."

Wyatt wriggles his jaw a little bit, like it still hurts. "I can get you the address *and* the key from the Ito brothers. You just gotta get me in the same room as them."

Rigg and I lock eyes, and I can see the torment in his, probably mirroring mine. The thought of letting Wyatt loose, giving him the opportunity to be alone with the Ito brothers is a disaster waiting to happen. But it's why we got him out of Calloway.

"I hate this," Scarlett whispers, turning away and heading toward the front of the jet.

I know exactly how she feels. I pretty much hate everything right now. Especially Wyatt.

"Tell me about Viana," I say.

Wyatt's nostrils flare. "I don't want to talk about her."

"I hear she's an amazing artist," I say, leaning against the table.

The little color he has drains from his face.

"We know everything about her, Wyatt."

A look lands in his eyes I've never seen him sport before. His usual anger is boiling over, but there's a small patch of fear added to the mix. His tone comes out low and strained, like he's fighting back tears. "Don't you dare touch her."

"Too late for that," I say. "Zia's on her way to Arizona."

Recognition flashes in his eyes. Zia worked with Everly the same time Wyatt did. Something else settles in his eyes. A fury laced with venom, making me giddy. Guess we sent the right person to fetch his daughter. He hates Zia more than Rigg does.

"You really thought we'd let you out of prison without leverage?" I pat his shaved head. "Sweet, naïve Wyatt. You can never outsmart DPS."

With that, I step away, creating a large distance between us, because the urge to beat him up is taking over.

CHAPTER TWENTY-NINE

As soon as we land, I head home, wanting to spend some time with Uncle Forest before he has to leave. Also, I need more time away from Wyatt.

Casper is curled up on my lap as I sit on the couch in the front room. He's been very needy since Mom passed. It probably has something to do with the fact that I have her fleece blanket on my lap as well. It has her smell, and I hope I never have to wash it.

He's purring loudly, kneading my leg. I pet his head, and he leans into my hand, wanting a deeper pet. Who knew you could attach to an animal so much?

Uncle Forest's suitcase sits near the front door, waiting for his departure.

"How was school?" Uncle Forest asks. He's sitting next to me on the couch, a bottle of Diet Coke in his hands. He's been sober for almost two years.

Since Uncle Forest doesn't know about my job, and we

want to keep it that way, he thinks I'm taking some summer school classes to get ahead with credits.

I shrug. "Aside from Criminology, boring." It's of course my favorite class—when school is actually in session—and the only one I easily ace.

Dad's in his recliner, also drinking a Diet Coke. "Criminology. They sure didn't need that class when I was a kid."

"This world has gone to pot." Forest takes a long drink from his bottle.

Dad glances at me briefly, knowing what I do for a living. DPS is trying its hardest to stop all the terrorist attacks in the area, but we're a small operation and can only do so much. The west coast has been doing so much better than the east, and I like to believe it's thanks to us. Most people won't travel past Texas. Not if they want to live.

The doorbell rings, and the image of the person standing on the other side pops up above Dad's and my watches.

My heart skips for a second before I jump from my seat and rush to the door, swinging it wide open. "Ike!"

I haven't seen the night manager at my old apartment building in months. He stopped being a school janitor a few months back as well. Aside from Pearl and Akiro, he was the only other person at my school I could tolerate.

Ike grins from ear to ear, making his massive form not so intimidating. "Hey ya, Harper." He's still got that smoker's growl, but by the lack of smell, I wonder if he finally quit. He must have had enough of his wife and me nagging him.

I'm not one for hugging, but I can't stop myself from throwing my arms around his waist and squeezing tight. He'd also been a victim of Wyatt, back when he guarded our apartment. Wyatt and his men attacked him when they broke into my apartment and attacked my mom. Thank goodness they didn't do much damage to him. Just a tiny scar above his eye remains.

Ike hugs me back. "I'm so sorry I wasn't at the funeral." When I pull back, he has tears in his eyes. "I was out of the state. But the Mrs. and I really wanted to make it. Your mom was an extraordinary woman." He pats my shoulder. "Just like you."

I snort, wiping the tears that escaped down my cheeks. "I'm nowhere near her awesomeness, but thanks."

It's then that I finally notice he's wearing a fancy suit. Whenever I saw him, he was in his janitor coveralls, or outdated clothes.

"You're looking sharp," I say.

Dad appears at my side and holds out a hand. "Ike. It's good to see you."

Ike ignores Dad's hand and pulls him in for a hug. I watch the two guys awkwardly pat each other's backs before settling into a real hug.

When they end their embrace, tears shine in both their

eyes. As Dad wipes his cheeks, he motions for Ike to come in.

I'm surprised yet again. No limp. He'd been injured in the war, making it difficult for him to walk. Maybe he had some type of surgery.

Uncle Forest grabs his suitcase from the entryway. "I gotta head out so I don't miss my flight back to Salt Lake."

I hug him, and so does Dad. Forest nods at Ike before he leaves, closing the door behind him.

"Have a seat," Dad says, motioning to the front room.

I head back to the seat I had vacated, noticing that Casper has curled up on the blanket that fell to the floor during my jump. Which meant he fell as well. Which explains why he's glaring at me.

"Sorry, boy," I say, bending down to pet him. He swats my hand away with a small growl. "I deserve that." With one last glare, Casper finally closes his eyes and settles into the blanket, falling fast asleep.

Dad has reclaimed his recliner, and Ike has taken the spot Forest vacated. It's weird seeing Ike in my fancy new house, wearing a fancy suit, and smelling like a rugged mountain man.

I sniff. "New cologne?"

Ike smiles. "You can say that."

"What's with the suit?" Dad asks, eying it. He adjusts his old cardigan, playing with a loose button.

Ike clears his throat, and it turns into a cough. He pulls a white handkerchief out of his breast pocket and dabs at his mouth before tucking it back in. "I'm here on business."

Dad puts up a hand. "If you're here to sell us some type of insurance or stock investment, I'll stop you right there and tell you you're wasting your time."

Ike chuckles. "That's not why I'm here, I promise." His smile fades, replaced by a sadness in his eyes. "I really hate to do this so soon after you lost Diane, but the situation is getting urgent."

I arch an eyebrow. "What situation?"

Ike settles back on the couch, resting his arm along the back. "There's no easy way to say this, so I'm just going to cut to the chase. I work for the CTB."

The Counter-Terrorism Bureau? Ike?

Well.

This changes everything.

CHAPTER THIRTY_

I STARE at Ike in shock, trying to see if he's telling the truth. I look in his eyes, check his posture, all his body language, and, son of a terrorist, it's all true.

"They're hiring old people now?" It's the first thing out of my mouth and though I want to take it back, I can't.

"Harper," Dad says in a warning tone.

Ike laughs again. "First, I'm not *that* old."

"You're seventy," I say.

"Again, not *that* old," he says. When I don't argue the point, he continues. "I've actually worked for them for over forty years."

The shock just keeps on coming. "I'm sorry, what?"

Honestly, the more I think about it, the more it makes sense. I always thought Ike was way too smart to be an apartment manager and a school janitor. He has this air of greatness about him. A sophistication that comes with real-life experience.

Ike scratches his smooth chin. "I was sent out a couple of years ago to keep tabs on your family."

All the color drains from Dad's face, and I know exactly what, no, *who* he's thinking about. President Boggs.

Ike nods, like he knows what Dad's thinking as well. "I think it's safe to say that everyone in this room is hiding who they are. I'm just the first to admit it."

Now the color drains from *my* face. Does he know what DPS actually does? Like, how we don't just provide personal security but are essentially our own slightly-illegal-with-questionable-tactics counter-terrorism unit?

"The CTB is working to get Gladys Boggs back in the President's office. We *need* her back. The United States needs her."

I nod. "That I agree with."

She had to go into hiding after the War of 2098 and the U.S. went crazy. She had so many death threats, even though the war wasn't her fault. People were just wanting someone to blame. And who better than the president?

Dad still hasn't commented. I have no idea what he's thinking.

There's a moment of silence, and I think Ike's waiting for Dad to say *something*. Anything.

Finally, Ike just continues talking. "We've been trying to get all the pieces in place so she can have a safe return. Now we just need to find her." He points at Dad. "Which is where you come in."

Dad finds his voice. "I have no idea where she is."

Total lie, but I'm not calling Dad out in front of the CTB.

"I'm not trying to be rude or anything, Ike," I say, "but do you have any proof that you are who you say you are?"

Ike pulls his badge from his breast pocket and hands it to me. Everything about it looks official, but it's easy to make knockoffs. Question is, would the Ike I know be capable of doing such a thing? It doesn't fit his character. But he's obviously been lying to us for years, so maybe the Ike I know doesn't exist.

The thought makes my stomach churn. I really like that version of Ike. He's cool and easy to talk to. The limp had a cool swagger to it.

"I'm sure you have some type of equipment that can verify my credentials," Ike says, narrowing his eyes at me.

I swallow, hating this whole situation. Why has everything been sucking so bad lately?

My wrist vibrates, and Akiro's image pops up above my watch, doing a sweet ninja kick. He's calling. I hit decline.

"I'll be right back." I'm already off the couch, hopping over a sleeping Casper and sprinting to my bedroom.

"Call Scarlett," I say to my watch as I fish though my DPS supplies in the closet. I find a scanner and use it to validate Ike's badge. It scans the front and back before doing an X-ray of the inside. The light blinks green.

Real.

There's no name listed on the card, just an ID number, so, it could belong to anyone. I send an image of the badge to Lincoln.

"How's my favorite girl?" Scarlett asks, her smiling face hovering above my watch.

I just cut to the chase. "Ike Daniels—if that's his *real* name—is in my house, claiming to belong to the CTB."

The smile on her face comes crashing down. "What?"

Lincoln's suddenly in the projection behind her, his eyes wide. "Did I hear that right?" He glances at his watch, probably receiving my message.

I nod and wave the badge so they can see it. "His badge is real."

Lincoln disappears from sight, I'm assuming to go do a search on his computer.

"What does he want?" Scarlett asks, concern in her voice.

"His focus seems to be mostly on my dad," I say, keeping my voice low. "He's claiming the CTB wants to pull Gladys Boggs from hiding and reinstate her as the president."

She frowns. "Can they legally do that?"

I shrug. "I don't know. I mean, honestly, the current president is a total idiot, and one major reason why this country is still in a downward spiral."

Scarlett nods. "I agree with that. We could use her right now."

It makes me wonder if she were still president, would

the terrorist attack Wyatt knows about have even been in play? President Boggs was good at sniffing that stuff out. Granted, she couldn't stop the EMP attack, but who could?

Certainly not President Poulson. The guy's completely incompetent. I hate bad-mouthing a president, but the man doesn't know how to handle threats. He cowers from them like Lincoln when someone tries to touch him.

Lincoln comes back in the projection. "The badge belongs to an Isaiah Danielson. He works for CTB." He pulls up a photo from the DPS database for me to see.

"That's definitely Ike." I scoff. "Not too creative on the undercover name. They're practically the same."

"Sometimes those are the best disguises," Scarlett says. "I mean, we never put it together."

We could have, but we weren't aware we needed to look. The man never showed up on the DPS database.

Akiro's calling again, so I hit the decline option.

I peer into the hall to make sure I'm still alone. "So, what do I do? I think he knows more about DPS than the average person. He knew I'd have the equipment to see if his badge was real or not."

Scarlett rubs her forehead. "Let me talk to Rigg and get back to you. For now, don't say anything about DPS. Even if he knows everything, keep your mouth closed."

"Got it." I end the call and the projection dissipates.

When I get back into the front room, Ike is standing like he's ready to leave. I hand him back his badge.

"It was good to see you, Harper," Ike says, tucking the badge back in his pocket. "If you could let Rigg and Scarlett know I'd like to speak with them sometime soon, that would be great." He hands me a business card. "Either way, I'll be in touch."

There are so many questions bouncing around in my head, it's hard to pin them all down. But I let them bounce and keep my mouth shut like I was ordered to. I don't want to be the downfall of DPS.

He sets a hand on my shoulder. "I will add that you have nothing to worry about. I think DPS and the CTB are on the same page about most things."

I know he meant to calm me, but holy freaking crap that means he knows a lot. If the government knows what we do, we could all be arrested. I could end up in Calloway with Wyatt.

Ugh. That means a fuchsia jumpsuit. No, thank you.

CHAPTER THIRTY-ONE

AFTER IKE LEAVES, Dad grabs another Diet Coke from the fridge, downing it in one chug. He tosses the empty bottle in the recycle bin and snatches two more from the fridge before he goes and sits down on the couch.

"It's times like this, I wish I drank something stronger." Dad reclines the chair, kicking his feet up.

"Then you'd end up like Uncle Forest, and we can't have that happen."

I grab a Dr Pepper from the fridge and join Dad in the family room. Casper's still passed out on Mom's blanket on the floor.

"Was it real?" Dad asks.

I nod. "Yep. DPS confirmed it, too."

Sighing, he takes a long swig of his drink.

"Are you going to help him?" I ask.

Dad twirls the glass bottle around in his hand. "I don't know where she—"

"Please, for the love of every locked-up terrorist, stop lying to me, Dad. I know you know where she is."

He sighs again, longer and louder. "You know, I'm proud of your career choice, but it sure makes my life difficult."

I tuck my feet underneath me and turn my body to face him. "I would never tell DPS if that's what you're worried about. The only thing they care about are terrorists, and we both know President Boggs isn't one of those."

He stares at the glass bottle in his hand. "Tomi and I have worked so hard to keep her location a secret."

"Have you asked her what she wants?" I ask.

Dad looks taken aback.

Now it's my turn to sigh. "Seriously, Dad? It's *her* life. You and Tomi can't decide what's good for her or not. Give her the option and let her choose."

"When did you become so logical?"

"I've always been this way."

Dad lets out a small laugh. "True. You've been observant since the day you were born." He wets his lips. "I guess I'll get in touch with Gladys and see what she wants to do."

I lean back against the couch, resting my hand on my cheek. "Do you really think the CTB wants to help her become the president again?"

My wrist vibrates. Akiro. Why does he keep calling? Usually when someone doesn't answer, it means they're busy and they'll get back to you when they can. Or, they don't want to talk to you.

"I do. I can read people well, just like you. He was telling the truth." He points his bottle at me. "He wants a meeting with me, Tomi, Gladys, you, and DPS."

"I really don't like the sound of that."

"Me, either," he says, scratching the scruff on his chin. "There's just so much at risk here."

I think about the tens of thousands of lives supposedly at stake. If having Boggs back in office could help lower the number of these situations, shouldn't we try?

"Guess you have to ask yourself if a safer future for the country is work that risk."

Dad's face is a mix of annoyance and pride. "You're too smart for your own good."

"That's my job." I twist my watch around on my wrist. "Dad, if Wyatt is being honest about the terrorist threat right now, so many lives are in danger. I mean, I love having job security and all, but if lowering the number of attacks means putting me out of a job, I'd do anything and everything in my power to make it happen."

Dad rubs his bum knee, grimacing a little in pain. "I think Gladys will agree with you."

I lean back. "I'd so love to go with you to talk to her, but I'm heading to Vegas tomorrow."

He arches an eyebrow. "You're going to Vegas tomorrow, and you're just *now* telling me?"

I throw out my arms. "Surprise!"

"Not a good surprise, Harper." He takes another sip of his drink. "Should I be worried?"

"Always," I say. "But I have to go."

He nods, accepting my answer. I'm so lucky to have this man for a father. I think it helps that we're so much alike. He understands how I think and that he can't talk me out of anything, even if he wanted to.

"I'm not going to see her, anyway," he says. "Just reach out."

I lean forward, placing my hand on his arm. "I think this requires a face-to-face talk. You and Mr. Fukunaga should both go." Because if Mr. Fukunaga is preoccupied with all this Boggs stuff, it will distract him from anything going on with his brother.

"I'll call Tomi tonight," Dad finally says.

"Speaking of Mr. Fukunaga," I say, "did you ever talk to him about Hitoshi?"

Dad slowly nods. "I poked around a bit. There's definitely something off about him, but I can't pinpoint anything. And Tomi doesn't seem to think he's a threat in any way."

Of course he doesn't. Who would want to think that about their own brother?

"Just make sure Tomi doesn't mention anything about President Boggs to Hitoshi," I say. "We can't have information falling into the wrong hands right now."

The doorbell rings and Akiro's face flashes above mine and Dad's watches.

"I'll let you get that." Dad's eyes narrow in on the projection. "Wait. He looks mad. Maybe I should get it?"

I sigh. "I'll handle it."

The second I open the front door, Akiro is yelling.

"Why don't you answer your phone?"

"I've been a little busy," I say, trying to rein in my annoyance.

He looks past me, seeing Dad just chilling in his recliner. "I can see that."

I step out onto the porch, shutting the door behind me. "I don't need to explain myself, but first we were saying goodbye to my uncle who I haven't seen in years." I hold in the smile when he flinches. "And second, Ike was just here. We were catching up."

He flinches again, realizing what a jerk he's being. "How's Ike doing?"

Well, he works for the CTB and might know what DPS really does and wants to get Gladys Boggs out of hiding. Nothing too important. "He's doing good." I glance down, noticing he's wearing his sad panda T-shirt. "Uh-oh. What's going on?"

Akiro sighs, rubbing the back of his head. "I think my Uncle Hitoshi might be in some kind of trouble."

CHAPTER THIRTY-TWO

Taking his hand, I lead him to the porch swing, trying not to think about the fact the last time I sat on it was with my mom.

We settle in, finding a calm rhythm. I intertwine our fingers, and his body relaxes against mine. He only did one spike with his hair today, standing tall and sure, which clashes with his slouching body.

"What kind of trouble?" I ask.

"He has this friend, Nozomu."

I'm not sure if I should mention I've met him or not, so I just keep it to myself for now. Gotta see how this plays out.

"He ... arrived recently," Akiro says, drawn out. Read: Nozomu was on one of the ships Mr. Fukunaga illegally imported.

"Ever since then," Akiro continues, "Uncle Hitoshi has been acting funny."

"Funny, how?"

He rubs circles on my hand with his thumb. "Usually, Hitoshi is all smiles and jokes. Since Nozomu showed up at our door, he's been gloomy and has absolutely no sense of humor." Read: He's now acting like Wyatt on a daily basis. Sans canine tooth.

I don't really want to bring up the fact that we suspect his uncle to be a terrorist. I mean, we already went through this with his dad. He's going to start thinking we're just targeting the Fukunaga family.

So, I tread lightly. "Maybe he's just missing home and didn't realize it until his friend showed up."

Akiro shakes his head. "It's more than that. They're always talking in whispered voices. Sneaking in and out at odd hours of the night."

I bump my arm with his. "Sounds like you've been spying on him."

He squeezes my hand. "I learned it from watching you." He grimaces. "I mean, watching what you do for a living, not that I've been spying on you."

I hold back a laugh. "I got it."

He goes quiet, and the silence stretches on. I'm not sure if I should say anything or not. His mind seems to be whirling.

I'm not really good at navigating this whole relationship thing. The making out? Awesome. I could do it all day long. The listening, comforting, keeping tabs with someone else, it kind of sucks. Okay, it really sucks. It's why I didn't want a relationship. I like Akiro. A lot. But sometimes it can be draining, so I choose to keep my mouth shut instead of saying something I'll regret. Because I know whatever I do say, I'll definitely regret, because it won't be nice or tactful.

He finally lets out a long sigh, releasing my hand and leaning forward, resting his head in his hands. "I don't like accusing anyone of something bad, especially someone I'm related to, but I think they're planning something."

When he doesn't continue, I lean forward, putting my head close to his. "Like what?"

Akiro yanks at the spike on his head, practically tugging off his hair. I reach up and stop him, keeping his hands in mine.

"Akiro, look at me."

He stares at the ground.

"Whatever is bothering you, just tell me. You'll feel better if you do."

He finally looks at me. "Will I?"

I shrug. "Okay, I don't know, but it's obviously eating you up."

"The thing is, it might sound crazy if I explain it to you."

"I live crazy."

He cracks the smallest smile. "Which is why I thought I'd come to you. But I don't know if what I've pieced together is real or not, or if I'm just wanting to crack some super code and be all cool as you."

I push his arm. "You'll never be as cool as me."

He stands, yanking at his spike again. "I don't even know where to begin. I've uncovered all this stuff. I didn't want to come to you until I had anything substantial, but I think I do."

I stand, folding my arms. "Lay it on me."

He stuffs his hands in his pockets, pushing far down like he's forcing himself to keep his hands there and not have them yanking off his hair. "Is there somewhere *private* we can go?"

"Don't want my dad to overhear?"

"I don't want *anyone* to overhear."

"We can go to my room."

"Actually," Rigg says, suddenly stepping onto the porch.

"Ah!" Akiro jumps in the air, clutching at his chest like his heart is going to burst through.

"I think the tunnel under Harper's house will work just fine," Rigg finishes, not even flinching from Akiro's outburst.

I look behind him to see Scarlett and Bo standing there, all business. Lincoln stands off to the side, looking completely out of his element.

"Uh, what's going on?" I ask.

"Whatever research Akiro has been doing on his uncle

has triggered our system," Scarlett says as gently as she can.

Read: Akiro is now on the DPS watch list, marking him a potential terrorist.

CHAPTER THIRTY-THREE

DAD DOESN'T SAY anything when we all step into the house and head for the door that will lead us underground. He just watches with a ton of curiosity while knowing we wouldn't tell him anything if he asked.

The tunnels under the house will block out anyone from overhearing our conversation. I turn on the noise-canceling filter on my phone as added protection, but it means we have to keep in a tight circle since the radius isn't that big.

Akiro shifts nervously where he stands as Scarlett, Rigg, Bo, Lincoln, and I stare at him, waiting for him to speak. He swallows, opens his mouth, then snaps it shut.

Rigg folds his arms. "Akiro, we need you to tell us everything you discovered about your uncle and Nozomu."

Akiro looks at the ground. "I don't want to get them in trouble."

"If they didn't do anything wrong," I say, "then you have nothing to worry about."

"And if they did do something worthy of DPS' attention," Scarlett says, using her gentle tone, "then we need to know so we can stop it."

When Akiro doesn't speak, Rigg does. "Listen, Akiro, there's a lot going on at DPS you don't know about. We've received some intel that we have to act upon. We still have some holes, though, and we think you can fill them."

Akiro licks his lips, nodding likes he's taking in all the information.

"And unless you want us to treat you like a suspected terrorist," Rigg says, "you need to explain all the things you were searching online."

Lincoln pulls up the information on his datapad, all of Akiro's searches filling the projected screen. Including a search of bulldogs.

Hitoshi and Nozomu were talking about a bulldog named Duke, but as far as I know, Hitoshi doesn't have a dog.

Akiro takes in all the searches, his shoulders sagging in defeat. He rubs the back of his neck. "Do you want the long or short version?"

Scarlett buttons up her red leather jacket, the coolness of the tunnel probably getting to her. "Let's go with condensed. We're running on a short timeline right now."

Akiro straightens out his shirt like it might make him look more professional. It doesn't. "Basically, Hitoshi has been acting weird ever since Nozomu arrived. Hitoshi claims they went to high school together in Japan, but after a search ..."

"Not only did they not graduate the same year," Lincoln cuts in, "but they didn't even go to the same high school."

"Correct," Akiro says, pulling up the documents on the datapad to prove it. "There was a weird vibe going on between the two of them, and I couldn't quite pin it down." He pulls up photos of Hitoshi and Nozomu meeting in secluded locations, both acting all shady. "I've been following them, trying to collect my own intel." He folds his arms. "It all comes down to this. Hitoshi and Nozomu have been planning a party for a bulldog named Duke."

Scarlett arches a red eyebrow. "A dog?"

"Hey, people love their pets," Akiro says.

I nod. "It's true. Pearl's family throw their dog, Daisy, a birthday party every year. Presents, cake, and everything."

Bo grunts as Rigg rolls his eyes.

"Anyway," Akiro says, standing tall, trying to appear serious, but I can see the uncertainty behind his eyes. "They've been inviting friends from all over, selecting a venue, caterers, everything like that."

Bo's grizzly voice booms through the tunnel. "Just get to the point."

Akiro stares wide-eyed at him, and for a second, I

worry he might wet himself. He clears his throat. "Right. So, this is my theory, and I'm like only eighty-four ... eh, eighty-seven percent certain I'm right. There's a lot of variables in play—"

"The point, Akiro," Scarlett says with her firm tone that tells you not to question her and do as told.

Akiro takes a huge gulp of air. "They're having a party Sunday night at the Promenade, eight p.m. sharp, where they will hold a ceremony to honor Duke, the dog. Which is actually all code for, they're planning to invade a charity event at The Wilshire Events Center in Vegas and assassinate Duke, aka, President Poulson."

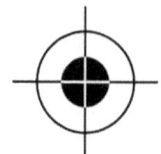

CHAPTER THIRTY-FOUR

THE ONLY NOISE in the tunnel is everyone's breathing. I'm not sure what everyone else is thinking, but I know what's racing through my brain.

If all of this is true, how did DPS not pick up on any of it? I mean, aside from flagging the Fukunaga family last year. I know DPS' system can't pick up on every threat, but this is against the president, the highest threat possible, even if the guy is a complete moron.

Also, how does Wyatt fit into all of this? Does he know about the assassination attempt? I've heard him make off-colored jokes about the president before, but really, who hasn't? Does Wyatt really want to help us, or does he want to help see the threat through?

How did Akiro's uncle get wrapped up in all of this? Are the Ito brothers behind it all, like we suspect?

Man, I can't stop the questions from coming, thanks to my hyperactive brain.

Like, if DPS couldn't pick up on it, how on earth did Akiro piece it together? I stare at him in a whole new light. I mean, yeah, he's a ninja. Yeah, he's hot and an excellent kisser. But he's able to decode an overlord's operation in just a matter of days?

I kind of want to make-out with him right now.

Rigg's sudden voice startles me as he points at Lincoln. "I want all the information Akiro found up here *now*."

Lincoln nods, quickly pulling up file after file, expanding the perimeter of the screen hovering above his datapad and filling it with documents, photos, videos, everything Akiro found. We all scoot back to give the 3D projection room.

Scarlett, Bo, Lincoln, and Rigg are sorting through all of it, circling the screen as they do. They're passing documents and photos around to each other, separating them at lightning speed and putting them into corresponding folders.

"This is my favorite part of the job," I say under my breath.

Akiro is watching in awe. "Is this how they always work?"

"Yep," I say.

Then I remember I'm a full-time agent now. I know the way they work together and their patterns. I quickly fall in sync, finding any and all references to the guest lists. Scarlett sends a few messages my way, and I sort them into the file. Rigg sweeps out a hand, an image flying my way.

"Can I record this?" Akiro asks.

"No," Rigg and Bo growl at the same time.

"Yeah, okay." Akiro's voice cracks.

Ten minutes later, it's all sorted through. Everything Akiro has pieced together makes sense, but there's probably more our system can find.

Lincoln adds everything we learned during the first Fukunaga investigation to the mix, along with everything we have on the Ito brothers, Nozomu, Hitoshi, and Wyatt. The information Akiro provided expands our search, connecting all the dots in a glorious way.

We watch the computer work, the system using our previous sorting to add to the feed, creating so many layers to the screen, I can't see Scarlett and the others on the opposite side.

"I want one of these at home," Akiro says.

I smile at him. "Me, too."

"Good work, Akiro," Rigg says from the other side of the screen, though we can't see him from all the images flooding the air.

Akiro beams and does a little fist pump, and it's probably a good thing Rigg can't see his reaction, because he'll find it as lame as I do. I mean, it's a kind of cute lame, but still lame.

"This plot is much more complicated than I originally thought," Scarlett says. "We have a lot of work to do."

And we only have a few days to do it.

As much as we want to figure out how DPS didn't pick

up on a plot this big, we have a more important question at hand: How do we stop the assassination of the most protected man in the United States?

The screen shuts off, and Lincoln tucks the datapad under his arm, the light filling the tunnel dimming.

"Change of plans," Rigg says, moving down the tunnel toward the stairs that will lead back to my house. "We're leaving tonight. I'll call Everly and let her know."

Akiro raises his hand next to me as we hurry to keep up with Rigg and the others, all moving at lightning speed. "Uh, am I included in this 'we'?"

"No," Rigg says as he pounds up the stairs.

Akiro worms his way up, pushing everyone out of the way until he's at Rigg's side. "With all due respect, sir, I'm the one who pieced this together."

Out of the corner of my eye, I see Scarlett squirming. It's killing her as much as it is me that DPS didn't catch this.

Rigg stops at the top of the stairs, rounding on Akiro. "And we appreciate it. But we'll take it from here."

Rigg's sharp tone would have me shutting my mouth and taking a step back.

But Akiro's eyes are determined. "I earned my right to go."

Rigg's jaw twitches as his gaze flits over to me for a second. He wants to tear Akiro a new one but doesn't at the same time, because he's my boyfriend. And a regular civilian.

Bo steps close to Akiro. "DPS operatives only."

Again, I would have shrunk back at his steely tone, but Akiro doesn't even flinch. "Hire me."

Bo stares at him for a few seconds before he lets out a deep rumble of a laugh. He slaps Akiro's arm. "I like this kid." He disappears out the door and back into my house.

"Does that mean you'll hire me?" Akiro calls after him.

Rigg grunts. "No." When Akiro's face falls, Rigg sets a hand on his shoulder. "Listen, kid, I get it. You put in a lot of work and discovered some important intel. But you aren't trained for missions." He nods to me. "It was a year before we let Harper go on a mission of this magnitude. She had to work her way there." He scoffs. "Sometimes I question if we let her go too early."

"Hey!" I say.

Scarlett puts a hand out to stop me. I didn't realize I was moving forward, my hand in a fist, until she did that. I relax at her touch.

Rigg checks his watch. "We don't have time for this. Harper, grab anything you need here, then meet us outside."

He takes off with the others, leaving me on the stairs with Akiro.

Akiro's shoulders sag in complete defeat. "I thought this would impress them."

"It did," I say. "But they can't just hire you on the spot. It doesn't work like that." I reach up on my tiptoes, softly kissing his lips, something I rarely do.

Akiro's lips linger on mine, like staying connected to me will help heal his sorrow. I want to be here for him, but I need to leave. We have something bigger on our hands than Akiro's sadness.

I end our kiss and place my hands on his cheeks. "I have to go."

He pulls back, away from my touch. "Yeah, I know." He takes off, his footsteps fading until I hear the front door slam shut.

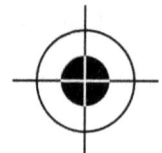

CHAPTER THIRTY-FIVE

Rigg messages Pearl, telling her to meet us at Headquarters. She's sitting in a chair in the lobby when we get there, a mix of confusion and intrigue on her face.

Rigg immediately springs into action, barking orders at everyone. "Bo and Scarlett, get all the equipment we'll need on the jet."

With a nod, they jog off down the hall.

"Lincoln," Rigg continues, "gather all the tech you think we'll need for the job."

Lincoln heads toward the hall, his face in such deep concentration that I know his mind is whirling, making a list of equipment we'll need.

"Pearl," Rigg says, his voice firm and commanding, making her sit tall in her chair, "our trip to Vegas has been pushed up, and we're on limited time. You'll stay here, working on our disguises for a charity event. I'll send you everything you need to know about it. Gather all the

222

clothes, make-up, shoes, whatever we need. We need to blend in with the crowd, so research the attire people will be wearing. All of us need something elegant, but light and breathable. Bullet-proof. Fire-proof. Use whatever you need."

Pearl stands. "When do you need the disguises by?"

"With same day shipment, just make sure they're on their way to Vegas by Sunday morning."

"Yes, sir." She turns and leaves the room, her eyes lighting up in excitement like she's already had an idea of what she wants to do. I love how fast she thinks. Which is good, because it's Friday night. She doesn't have much time.

Rigg turns to me, unease in his eyes.

"Something's wrong," I say.

He nods. "I know."

DPS didn't pick up on *any* of it. Nothing. Our system isn't foolproof, but it's also not this shoddy. Which means the Corbox Clan worked so secretively that we couldn't sniff them out, or it's something way worse.

My stomach clenches. "Do you think someone hacked the DPS database?"

He rubs his forehead. "Either that, or it's an inside job."

I'm not sure which one is worse. We want to believe our system is hack-proof. Any of it falling into the wrong hands could be catastrophic. But an inside job?

"How well did you vet Zia?" I ask.

Rigg closes his eyes, his deep breaths coming out ragged, like he's trying to keep calm. "Not as much as I did everyone else. Everly vouched for her, saying she had already done a thorough check before she hired her."

I snort. "Yeah, and she hired Wyatt. Her record isn't all that clean."

His jaw pulls tight. "I know. It has to be Zia. Who else could it be?"

Scarlett would never turn on us. Ever. Neither would Lincoln or Bo. They're as loyal as they come. The other operatives are out in the field, but if they were a part of this, they wouldn't have gone to the other side of the country.

Unless the attack is monumental, and they want to be as far away as possible when it happens. Wyatt did say tens of thousands of lives were at risk.

Rigg sighs. "I'll have Lincoln check on everyone in the field, plus Zia."

"Where is Zia anyway?" I ask. I haven't seen her since we left for Calloway.

Rigg's words are tight. "She's in hiding with Viana."

I remember Wyatt's face when he heard Zia was the one snatching up his daughter. "Do Wyatt and Zia have a history?"

He nods. "They used to be an item. Not sure what happened, but I know it was an ugly separation. So ugly, Everly sent Zia away to work somewhere else for a while."

No wonder Rigg questioned Scarlett about sending

Zia on the mission to get Viana. But Scarlett didn't seem at all worried about it.

I place a hand against my stomach, wishing I could quell the unease. "What if they got back together? What if they planned this whole thing?"

Yeah, Wyatt looked royally pissed when I mentioned Zia's name, but it could have been an act, trying to throw me off his scent. If I think they hate each other, then I'd think they wouldn't work together.

"It's a possibility we can't rule out." Rigg sets a hand on my shoulder. "Let's keep this to ourselves for now. I'll keep tabs on Zia. And you, kid, I need you on alert. Your gut has always been right, so follow it."

I nod. "Consider it done."

CHAPTER THIRTY-SIX_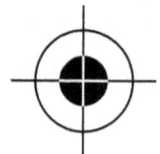

BEFORE THE WAR, Las Vegas was known as Sin City. Gambling, heavy drinking, no clothes, were pretty much the theme they had going.

Once the EMP struck, Vegas took the biggest hit. They had to rebuild from the ground up. For some unknown reason, the Vegas community came together better than anyone else. They made something magical, and quick. They focused on commerce and technology, wanting to make it stronger than it had been before the EMP.

The eastern U.S. was practically demolished during the war, including Washington, D.C. It was wiped from the face of the earth.

During that time, the western states banded together, creating a barrier around Las Vegas. It was the perfect hub for a new capital and they had the resources to make it into one. The new Vegas was sleek and advanced.

I've seen tons of pictures and videos of Vegas, but nothing could prepare me for what I saw when I stepped off the jet.

The curvy, sleek high rises pierce the night sky, all the soft lights illuminating the area for miles. Floating oval billboards roam the city, advertising the newest tech and current job opportunities.

There are no cars in Vegas. Only commuter rails run in the area, covering every major street. It means a little more walking for some people, but Vegas has been crowned the fittest city in the country. There's hardly a drop of alcohol or any drugs in the city.

If it weren't for the history books, no way you'd think this was once Sin City.

The second Wyatt walks off the jet, I almost cry out. He's not shackled.

Before I can shout, Lincoln is at my side, pulling me away from everyone else. "They're invisible."

"What?" I ask.

Lincoln uses the top of his finger to lift the bottom of his glasses. "The shackles. He's bonded, you just can't tell."

"But he's walking like his hands and arms are free," I say.

"We can't see it, but he can feel them. If he gets farther than five feet from any of us, he'll be electrocuted."

I grin. "So, if I shove him really hard and he falls out of the perimeter, oops!"

Lincoln shakes his head, but he's smiling. "I would advise against that, but I know there's no stopping you once your mind is set." He leans down, keeping his voice low. "Just save it for the right moment."

I look up at him. "I think that's the wisest advice you've ever given me."

He pulls a small box from his pocket and removes the lid, showing me what's inside. There are five black dots, each the size of a flea.

"What are those?" I ask.

Lincoln can't contain his smile. "Locators." Using his index finger, he presses down on one in the box, and it comes out with his finger, resting on his skin. With his watch, he scans the locator, and its stats suddenly hover above the watch. He moves his hand toward Wyatt, the coordinates on the screen changing as he does. When he's lined up with Wyatt, the screen turns green. With another smile at me, Lincoln turns his attention back to the locator, blows it off his finger, and it floats in the air toward Wyatt.

Seconds later, Wyatt glances down at his arm, his face scrunched together.

"He felt a small pinch," Lincoln whispers. "That was the locator inserting itself into his skin. He probably thinks it was a bug bite." He motions to the coordinates above his watch. They change as Wyatt moves on, unable to see anything on his arm. "We can keep track of him at all times now."

I can't hide the awe in my tone. "How long do they last?"

"Until I give the order for it to self-destruct."

My eyes go wide. "Please tell me it's going to explode in his arm, setting it on fire."

With a small laugh, Lincoln shakes his head. "It will just disintegrate. He won't even know."

My shoulders sag. "That's disappointing."

Lincoln flicks the bottom of his glasses with the top of his index finger. "The whole point is so that the person doesn't know they're being tracked."

I stare at all the others in the box. "Can I have one?"

"Sure." He pulls a small container out of his pocket and hands it to me. "I figured you'd ask for them. There are five in there. Software is already installed on your watch. Just scan it, line it up with your target, and blow."

"This is pure genius, Linc." I hold out a fisted gloved hand for him to tap the side with his fist.

Even in the night, I can see his blush. "Scarlett and I built it together. I can't get all the credit."

Feeling someone staring at me, I glance over at Wyatt and my good mood slips away. That man knows how to ruin everything.

CHAPTER THIRTY-SEVEN

AFTER WE GET CHECKED into the hotel, I meet Rigg, Scarlett, and Bo in the lobby. Lincoln will be running tech from his room. Dwayne and Mayleen are babysitting Wyatt while Everly and Echols do whatever they are doing. I didn't care enough to ask.

Rigg zips up his DPS jacket. "Bo and I are going to scope out the president's hotel. Scarlett and Harper, scope out The Wilshire."

Bo just nods at us before he and Rigg leave the hotel.

The Wilshire—the venue for the charity event—is a massive oval dome structure right across the street from where we're staying. Lincoln has all the blueprints for the building, but we're going to do a complete scan of the building, making sure nothing has been moved or added since the last update.

Scarlett and I split up, with me taking the north and

west sides of the building and Scarlett taking the east and south.

I slip on my owl mask Scarlett created, the gel fusing coolly to my skin. Any camera that picks up my face will just see a reflection. Anyone who sees me in person will just see a sweet owl mask. The mask moves perfectly with every movement my face makes, the material so light I can barely feel it.

On top of The Wilshire, in the center of the dome, the roof is a flat area of space for guests to mill about. Using a grappling gun, I aim it at the north side and let it fly. It connects seconds later, and I begin my scan, going left to right, ascending floor by floor, using my watch to take X-rays of the entire side of the building, plus the domed side of the roof.

By the time I reach the top, my thighs are tender from all the scaling. I unhook the grappling hook and head to the west side of the building, right as Scarlett hops onto the roof on the south side. Her mask is a fox, matching with her stealthy and cunning personality.

I grin, walking backward on the smooth concrete toward the edge of the roof. "Getting slow in your old age."

Scarlett narrows her eyes at me, the mask moving perfectly with her skin. "Or maybe I do a more thorough job."

I point a gun finger at her. "Keep telling yourself that, Scar."

I'm about to set the grappling hook into the center of the roof on the west side when the door to the roof exit opens.

Both Scarlett and I roll into a dive, finding cover behind air ducts, hers a few yards away from mine.

Three sets of boots squeak across the concrete, heading straight toward me.

The first few words I hear are Japanese. I quickly turn on the translator on my watch, pushing in my earpiece to make sure it's securely in my ear. My Japanese is getting better, but not enough to listen to three natives speak at their normal rate, using slang. I don't want to miss a word.

"Don't get views like this in Japan," one guy says, my watch translating the Japanese to English. Nozomu.

"We'll get them soon," another man says. I don't recognize the voice.

The three come to a stop near the edge of the roof, just a couple yards away from me. I'm hidden behind the duct, and I need to be careful not to make a sound. My watch is on silent, so I'll have no interference from incoming messages or anything.

"His landing time has been pushed back a couple of hours," the third voice says, and I tense. Hitoshi.

"Will it be a problem?" the second guy asks. I need to see who it is. Voice recognition might be able to pick it up later, but it would be nice to have a visual.

"My contact says it's just a scheduling error," Hitoshi says. "They aren't on to us."

They're talking about the president's arrival, which adds the possibility of Hitoshi having a contact in our government. That could also explain why nothing has pinged DPS. They could be clearing out anything that would cause an alert. Which would put Zia in the clear. But how would Hitoshi get a contact in our government?

"Good," the second man says.

Using a reflective pane in my bag, I lean toward the edge of the duct, angling the mirror so I can see behind me.

The three men are standing in a line, looking over the city. The closest one to me is Nozomu. I can't see the faces of the other two guys. I need a better angle.

My mind whirls as I scan the area. There's nothing in front of me to hide behind. If I create a distraction to my right, it would expose Scarlett. A distraction behind me would require going behind or over the guys, which would be risky. If I toss something over there, they could see it flying in the air. Though it's the middle of the night, Vegas is lit well, thanks to all the lights and floating billboards.

Floating billboards. They're all wired with cameras, doubling as surveillance for the city. Lincoln had prepared for that, installing a Trojan horse in all of them so they wouldn't catch any DPS agents on their mission.

But Hitoshi and the others would surely show up. Using my watch, I scan the network for the billboards and hack them, flipping through their feeds until I find the one closest to the building I'm on.

I change its trajectory so it'll pass by the west side.

Suddenly Hitoshi breaks out in swears, dropping them like they're burning his tongue and he needs to spit them out.

"What's wrong?" Nozomu asks.

"Akiro," Hitoshi says, breaking my concentration on the billboard for a moment. "He's here in Vegas."

I freeze. Akiro is *here*? Rigg is going to be ticked something fierce, and I don't want to be the one who tells him. I'll let Scarlett handle that.

"What?" the second man asks. "I thought he'd be taken care of."

Taken care of? As in kill?

"His locator just pinged him here," Hitoshi says. "He must have left before our men got to him."

Locator? Looks like DPS isn't the only ones tracking people. And Hitoshi sent someone to kill his nephew? Man, I want to hurt him so bad right now. But I have a job to do.

Stifling my shock, I turn my attention back to the billboard as it floats closer to where the men stand. I can see their outlines in the camera feed but can't make out the faces quite yet.

"Find him," the second man says with a growl. "And let me know when you eliminate the problem."

My stomach clenches as it realizes two things simultaneously. First, if I don't find Akiro before they do, he's

234

dead. Second, the billboard hovers just close enough to the guys that I see the second man clearly, capturing the image and saving it to my watch.

Raiden Ito. Overlord of Corbox.

CHAPTER THIRTY-EIGHT

My MIND CAN'T STOP SPINNING. So many things have just been verified. Raiden Ito is in the U.S. The Corbox Clan is planning an attack. Hitoshi Fukunaga is in on it.

While this information is mind-blowing, it's not sitting well in my stomach. There's this nagging sensation that something's not right. As weird as it may sound, I hate when things fall into place so easily. Granted, we still don't know their exact plan. We don't know where or when the assassination attempt will happen. And we still don't know *why*. What would Japan or the Corbox Clan gain from our president being dead?

I also hate coincidences. Like, these three guys happen to come out on the roof at the same time Scarlett and I are on the roof. Why this roof? Why right now? Maybe I'm overthinking things, but that's my job—inspect every angle, repeatedly. Maybe this is where the attempt is going down, and they just happened to be here, doing their own reconnaissance.

But if it's not a coincidence, why would they want us to catch them? If they did, that means they know we're here and want us to know.

I want to bite my fingernails, but my gloves are on, and I can't risk leaving any of my DNA behind.

Part of me wants to rush out there and pummel all of them repeatedly until they tell me what's going on. Another part wants to go over and push them all off the roof. I mean, Raiden Ito is only a couple of yards away from me. He's the leader of the Corbox Clan, the most ruthless criminal organization in Japan and the cause of thousands of deaths. I could just end everything right here and now.

But I'm not a killer. That's not how DPS operates. Our job is to stop lives from being taken, not take them ourselves, even if it's the bad guy we're talking about.

A smile creeps its way onto my face as I rememberi the trackers Lincoln gave me. Being as quiet as I can, I reach into my pocket, pull out the container, and retrieve one of the bugs. Using my phone, I scan it, then peer around the air duct, lining the trajectory up with Raiden. I softly blow, and the bug leaves my hand, floating toward him.

Raiden suddenly slaps the back of his neck, grimacing. "I hate this place."

The tracker is in. *Locator 7* hovers above my watch for

237

a second before it fades out. That must be the number assigned to it.

After a few more minutes of idle chitchat, the three men retreat, heading back into the building. We wait a full five minutes to come out from our hiding places. I killed the time by calling Akiro a million freaking times. No answer.

"Did you get it all?" Scarlett asks as we meet in the middle of the roof.

I nod. "You?"

She nods. "Did you know Akiro was coming?"

"I had no idea. I swear I'm going to beat him senseless when I find him." What on earth was he thinking, coming here?

"Rigg might beat you to it," Scarlett says. "We need to find Akiro before the Corbox Clan does." She sighs. "Do you feel uneasy?"

"Yep."

"I couldn't see who the third person was," Scarlett says. "I sent the recording to Lincoln. He can probably run it through voice—"

"It was Raiden Ito," I say, cutting in.

The fox eyebrows of her mask shoot up. "Raiden Ito? You saw him?"

I pull up the image on my watch and show her.

Scarlett narrows her eyes at the picture, then looks over at where the men were standing. "How did you get that angle?"

"Billboard," I say. It's already floated away, moving on to another location. "Hacked it."

Scarlett smiles, her nose scrunching, which looks awesome with her fox mask on. "That's my girl." She folds her arms, looking at the picture.

"I also planted a locater on Raiden," I say, pulling up the feed on my watch. A small dot shows him outside of the Wilshire Center, about a block down. They sure took their sweet precious time leaving. "Maybe we can track them to their headquarters."

"Good." She looks at me, her fox eyes soft. "What's your gut telling you?"

I close the image hovering above my watch. "That something's going to happen in this building, whether it's an assassination attempt or something else. The Corbox Clan is dangerous. Whatever they're planning is big. I can't see them smuggling themselves in from Japan, taking one of the longest and horrid ways—on a ship—just to assassinate our president. And Wyatt did say that people I love could be in the crosshairs."

Scarlett nods. "Which could mean something else outside of Vegas. There's more to this that we need to uncover, and quick." She adjusts her gloves. "Hitoshi's contact is going to make it difficult. They'll keep Corbox a step ahead."

"We need to find a way around them." I sigh. "I hate the thought that there are Americans helping the Corbox Clan." I tug at the strap of my messenger bag. "Well, if you consider Wyatt an American. That man's far from being a true patriot."

Scarlett smiles. "True. Sounds like someone in the government could be helping."

"I was thinking that, too. Plus, there's always Zia."

"Rigg told me about your assumptions," Scarlett says. "I hate to admit it, but I think you guys might be right on an inside job. It means anything that alerts DPS can be deleted before we see it." She pauses. "Someone could be framing us."

"True. We've made a lot of enemies over the years."

We're quiet for a moment, thinking everything through.

"Hey, Scar?"

"Yeah?"

"Do you think they knew we were out here?"

She sighs, looking out over the rooftop. "I'm not sure. If they didn't, Ito is very daring to just walk out into the open like this and say everything they did."

"The man thinks himself invincible."

"True. If they did know, they wanted us to know the Corbox Clan is here and means business. It also means they think we can't stop them."

Either way is not good. We're dealing with heavy hitters, probably the toughest we've been up against. DPS has never lost a battle. It's come close a few times, but we've always stopped them.

I hate this feeling that's telling me DPS is going to lose this time around.

CHAPTER THIRTY-NINE_

After trying to call Akiro—no answer—I do a quick scan of the west side of the building, and then meet back up with Scarlett. I try calling Akiro again, but it goes straight to voicemail.

So, I try messaging him.

Why aren't you answering me?!

No answer.

Maybe I'll try a video message. I pull up the screen and hit record. "Akiro, the Corbox Clan knows you're here. They put out a hit on you. Stop being an idiot and answer your phone!"

After I hit send, I wait a minute. Nothing.

Another video message. "For the love of every locked-up terrorist, you better be alive and just unable to answer your phone right now. If you're ignoring me, I'll never forgive you. If you're dead? I'm so not going to your funeral. CALL ME BACK!"

I really hope he's just being a stupid boy and not answering me, because the other option is that the Corbox Clan already has him, which means he's dead, and I can't even stomach that thought right now. Or ever.

I call Lincoln and his face is above my watch seconds later. "Linc, can you track down Akiro? He's here in Vegas, and if we don't find him before the Corbox Clan does, they're going to kill him."

If they haven't already. No, I can't think like that. I need to stay positive, which is something I'm not very good at.

"On it," Lincoln says. "I'll send you his coordinates when I do. Just give me a couple of minutes." His face disappears.

"What if they already have him, Scar?" I whisper.

She puts an arm around me. "They couldn't have found him that quickly. We'll find him before they do. I promise."

Her words are meant to be encouraging, but they're not. That's a promise no one can make.

"I'll send a message to Rigg," Scarlett says, working on her watch. "I'll update him on the Akiro situation, along with Raiden. They're probably still at the hotel. There's a lot of ground to cover."

So I don't explode with rage, I think about why we're here. Planning an assassination attempt at the hotel is pretty bold, seeing as it's the most protected place in Vegas right now, but we can't rule it out.

Lincoln was able to find the details of the president's stay. He'll be flown to the roof, his suite on the hundredth floor, so he doesn't have far to go. If he has to leave by the streets, there's an elevator that takes him straight from his suite all the way down to the lot in the basement where an armored tank awaits him, the only vehicle allowed in the city. The tank can resist a bomb, so killing him in there is out of the question.

Any time the president enters or leaves a building, he not only wears a bulletproof robe that covers his bullet-proof suit, he's surrounded by a few circles of guards. He usually just holds all meetings and correspondence from his suite to make everyone's lives easier. Oh, and his suite has bulletproof windows.

Your only opportunity to get him is when he speaks at a public event, which is rare. He wears a bulletproof suit and gloves, leaving only his head as a target. When he's giving a speech, bulletproof glass surrounds his head, so you'd have to be close enough to shoot between the box and his body, angled to make contact with his head.

Even the most skilled assassins couldn't pull off a stunt like that.

I'm pacing the street, rage pulsing everywhere in my body. Akiro can't be dead. He just can't.

"What was he thinking?" I spew the words out in anger.

"Who?" Scarlett asks. She's watching me pace, keeping cool and calm.

"Akiro!" I throw up my hands. "Coming to Vegas? That's just insane. What does he think he's going to do? Stop the attack himself?"

My phone vibrates with an incoming message. Lincoln sent the coordinates of Akiro's location. I route it into my GPS, and Scarlett and I take off, sprinting toward the location. Getting on the rails would make no sense. There are too many stopping points, and by looking at the map, he's only about a mile away. Scarlett and I can run a five-minute mile.

Thank goodness the streets are practically empty. Not many people are out walking around this time of night. I only have to push a few people out of my way, and to make matters worse, they actually shout apologies to *me* for being in *my* way. What's wrong with these people? Don't they know being nice gets you nowhere?

As we draw near to Akiro's spot, we slow to a jog. We're suddenly in the swanky part of Vegas, pop-jazz music playing from floating speakers. They follow you as you walk, really immersing you into the experience. I look at the one above us, tempted to shoot it out of the air, really immersing it in a Harper experience.

The outfits get more colorful as we near a club on the corner, the music getting louder.

"I hate this place," I growl.

Everyone around us is so ... happy or something.

They're all smiling and laughing, holding glasses of their fruity-vegetable juices, giving them fuel they really don't need.

Scarlett bumps my arm. "There's nothing wrong with being happy, Harper."

The only thing that really made me happy were my parents. Now one of them is gone and the other is broken from the loss. I'll probably never know happy again.

A map pops up above my watch, and a red circle blinks where the club is. *Locator 7* is written above the dot.

"Raiden Ito is in that club," I say to Scarlett.

We come to a stop just around the corner, staying in a quiet spot without much light.

"You don't think Akiro is in there with them, do you?" I ask, unable to hide the unease in my voice.

Scarlett looks at the coordinates of Akiro's location. "It almost looks like it's off to the side, like maybe he's outside the club."

I scan the area, taking in everything I see. A couple in bright pink outfits, arm in arm as they enter the club. A line of people, waiting to get in the club, all bouncing with excitement. Two bouncers flanking the doors to the club.

There's a dumpster behind me, a dark point sticking up on the other side of it. No, not a point. A spike. Of hair.

Clenching my jaw, I hurry over and round the corner, grabbing Akiro by the front of his shirt and yanking him up. "What are you doing here?"

Before he can answer, I press my lips to his, grateful

he's alive and not lying in a pool of blood in the club. Then I shove him away, pushing back down to the ground and spin around, glancing at Scarlett, who's watching the whole exchange.

"I can't look at him right now," I spit. "I'll meet you back at the hotel."

Without waiting for a response, I take off, sprinting toward our hotel and thinking about the fact that I almost lost Akiro on top of everything.

Mom really, truly gone.

Akiro almost gone thanks to his stupidity.

Although, if I wasn't in a relationship with him, I could get rid of all these feelings and shove them into a dark pit so they can never see the light of day again.

Relationships ruin everything. My control. My reasoning. My ability to think clearly.

I'd be better off on my own.

CHAPTER FORTY

I SLAM open the door to the room Wyatt is being held in. I'm huffing from my run, but, boy, did it feel good to let off some steam. Maybe now I can face Akiro without wanting to pummel him.

I take in Wyatt and my mood lifts. He's tied up to a chair in the corner of the room, the shackles binding his wrists and ankles making me smile. Add in the fact that he's now stick thin and has a broken nose, and it's one of the most beautiful sights I've seen in a long time.

Noise-canceling earphones cover his ears. They'll only be removed when needed.

Everly is lounging on the couch, a glass of scotch in one hand, her feet kicked up on Echols' lap. Echols has unbuttoned his cuffs and rolled his sleeves up to his elbows. He also has a glass of scotch in one hand, the other resting on Everly's leg.

It's the most affection I've seen them show in public.

I've always sensed their relationship is purely professional, and even with the way they're sitting right now, it still feels that way. They're just always around each other and have reached that level of comfort, I guess.

Dwayne and Mayleen—both with guns in their arm holsters—flank Wyatt, hands clasped in front of them, all business, like they're expecting Wyatt to try a disappearing act. I wouldn't put it past him.

Paul has his back leaned against the wall near the couch, his feet crossed at his ankles, his smolder cranked up for some reason.

My wrist vibrates, and I look down at my watch to see *Locater 7 disabled.* What? I quickly open the app and check on Raiden's locator. It's gone. Not in the system at all. It's been wiped.

Clenching my hands into fists, I let out a yell that feels good.

"What's got you all worked up?" Paul asks in his southern drawl when I'm done.

I close my eyes and count to ten before I speak. A little bit of rage still burns behind my heart. "Akiro is in Vegas. Raiden Ito is here, but we no longer have a tracker on him. The Vegas citizens are so freaking happy that it's beyond annoying. Wyatt isn't in prison. Something's not right about this whole entire thing. We're missing something big. Something important."

Slipping the knife Bo gave me from my sleeve, I rush to Wyatt, rip off his headphones, and push the tip of the knife into his neck. "What's the Corbox Clan planning? And don't give me any crap that you don't know, because you do."

He's breathing deep, his head stretched back as far as it can go, trying to clear my blade. "Prove to me my daughter is okay, and I might cooperate."

"Shouldn't we be stopping her?" Mayleen asks from my right.

Dwayne chuckles on my left. "Nah. Let Harper do her thing."

Mayleen stays tense next to me, so I know she'll put a stop to me seriously injuring—or killing—Wyatt, which is probably a good thing. I don't need his death on my conscience on top of everything.

"Give me something, Wyatt," I growl.

He leans close to me, my knife pricking his skin. "Let me talk to my daughter."

With a roar, I push back, walk away, stop, turn on my heels, and hurl the knife at Wyatt. It drives into the chair between his legs, just below his crotch.

"Are you out of your mind?" Wyatt yells.

I shake my head. "No, *you* are out of your mind to think we'd *ever* let you go free."

"Harper," Everly snaps.

Wyatt glances between Everly and me. "Is that true? You're not going through with your end of the deal?"

"Not if I can help it," I say.

"Then you'll get *nothing* from me," Wyatt says in a low, harsh tone.

We stay glaring at each other, both fuming so bad, I'm surprised our skin isn't smoking.

Out of the corner of my eye, I see Echols take a sip of his scotch. He clears his throat. "Did I hear you right? Akiro is here?"

"Yes," I say, my gaze not leaving Wyatt's.

Wyatt's lips twitch into a small smile. "The Corbox Clan will kill him."

"We already found him," I say.

Behind me, the door to the room opens, and multiple people step into the room. I can peg the footsteps of each one. The thick, commanding ones belong to Bo. The calculating and firm ones belong to Rigg. The stealthy, light ones are Scarlett's. And the scared, shaking ones belong to Akiro.

"Is everything okay in here?" Rigg asks, coming to my side. His gaze goes to Wyatt, then the knife stuck between his legs. He sighs. "Harper, maybe you should take a breather."

Going over to Wyatt, I grab my knife, tuck it back up my sleeve, spit on his face, and then leave the room, not making eye contact with anyone.

CHAPTER FORTY-ONE_

EVERY CELL in my body ticks. It pulses with a rage I'm not sure I can control much longer. Why on this terrorist-infested-earth did we let Wyatt out of prison? What could he possibly do that we can't?

I pace my hotel room, all the thoughts swirling through my brain in a haphazard way, nothing quite linking together or making sense.

Why would Akiro come to Vegas? What could he possibly do to stop this attack?

What exactly is the attack? Just an assassination attempt? I don't buy it. Those other cities have to tie into it, unless sending Corbox Clan members to other major cities was a red herring. There's so much more that we're missing.

Someone hacked the DPS system, or someone is betraying us. If I find out it's the latter, I may break. How could anyone turn on DPS? After everything we've done for this country. After all the attacks we've stopped, the lives we've saved, even the crappy lives like Wyatt's, who we just should have killed at the gala last year.

I squeeze my eyes shut. No. I can't let those thoughts into my head. DPS doesn't kill. *I* don't kill. I'm *not* Wyatt. I'm *not* the Corbox Clan. I'm *not* a terrorist.

I'm a problem solver. I stop the bad guys, which is what I'm going to do. I'm going to figure out what the Corbox Clan is up to, and I'm going to stop it.

But I need to calm down, and an overly happy Pearl can usually do it.

Knowing she'll be awake, working on the gear for the charity event, I call Pearl, accepting projected images.

When she answers, she's in the materials and armor room at Headquarters, her eyes red, bright, and wide like she's probably downed a million energy drinks to stay awake.

"Hey, Harper," she says, focus on the outfit in front of her.

"I need to apologize," I say, wanting to get it over with.

She looks at me, shocked. "I'm sorry, what?"

I sigh. "I was a total jerk earlier." I rub at my eyes. "Losing my mom has been harder than I thought. I'm not really sure what to do with my emotions."

She grins. "I do. Beat the crap out of some terrorists. That always makes you feel better."

I chuckle. "It really does." I close my eyes, fighting back tears. "I took my anger out on you, and I shouldn't have. You've been the greatest friend through all of this, and I'm lucky to have you."

When she doesn't say anything, I open my eyes to see her crying, tears falling down her face and probably onto whoever outfit she's working on. Hopefully not mine.

She starts talking, but it's coming out in a blubbery mess, and I can't understand a word of it. I try to interrupt, but she keeps on going, speaking through her sobs, and wiping furiously at her nose with some extra fabric she found next to her. At least, I hope it's spare fabric.

She finally shudders, her tirade coming to a stop as she looks at me expectantly.

"Uh," I say, scratching at an itch on my neck, "I honestly didn't understand a word of that."

She laughs, which lights up her eyes. "Basically, I'll always be here for you, and you don't need to hide your feelings from me. I love you so much. It's been fun having you for a friend."

Love. A word I rarely use, because it holds so much weight.

But what does love mean? Caring for someone so much that you'd do anything for them? Throw down your life for them? Put up with their insanity and wild ideas because, well, you love them?

"I love you, too, Pearl," I say.

She squeals, and I almost take it back. But I do still love her even with her incessant squealing that makes my hairs stand on end.

"I'm never saying that again, you know," I say.

She wipes her cheeks. "Doesn't matter. I'm recording this whole conversation, so I can watch it back whenever I want."

I roll my eyes, making her laugh.

"Are you working on my outfit?" I ask.

She nods. "You're going to love it. It'll be there in time, promise."

The door to my hotel room opens, and Scarlett calmly comes in, giving me a soft smile. I say a quick goodbye to Pearl and end the call.

"How are you doing, baby girl?" Scarlett asks, her tone grittier than usual.

"Fine."

She bumps my arm with hers. "You almost cut off Wyatt's manhood."

I snort. "Pretty sure that would have been a favor to the world."

She turns her body to face me. "You don't have to lie to me, Harper. It's okay to miss your mom. She was one of your best friends."

I love and hate how well Scarlett knows me.

A tear trickles down my cheek, so I swipe it away. "I just hate that I'll never talk to her again. Yeah, I have recordings of her, so I'll be able to see her face and hear her voice, but it's not the same as being in person. I won't watch her get old. She won't see me graduate high school, college, or get my first gun. She's going to miss everything."

"I know this isn't easy. The only thing you can do is work hard, doing everything in your power to make her proud."

I pull my arms close to my chest. "Do you believe in an afterlife?"

"I do. Which is why I think you'll see her again, and how I know she's watching over you. She hasn't left you, Harper. She never will."

I want to believe her and Akiro. He believes in all that crap, too. All I know is if I don't believe, the hole in my heart will expand until there's nothing left but a hollow cavity. Believing gives me courage. Offers me hope. Gives me the strength to carry on during the days I just want to give up. What's the point of life if there's nothing after this? What are we working toward? I need to believe I can see Mom again.

More tears have escaped my eyes, so I shut down the topic. I can't cry on a mission.

But I can make my mom proud.

Scarlett pulls me into a hug, and I sink into her, breathing in her musky scent.

"It's going to be okay, Harper," she whispers. "I promise. We'll get through this together."

Together. Am I really better off on my own? Or is putting trust in others worth it?

Scarlett pulls back, resting her hands on the sides of my arms. "Akiro wants to talk to you."

I shake my head. "I'm not ready to see his face right now."

She offers a small smile. "I thought you'd say that." She lowers her arms and backs toward the doors. "Get some sleep, Harper. We have a big night ahead of us."

I check my watch. We're already well into Saturday morning. Not much longer and the sun will be peaking through the windows.

Scarlett rubs the back of her neck, her face telling me she doesn't want to say whatever she's about to say. "Wyatt and Bo are going to the club tonight to talk with the Corbox Clan and hopefully get us some answers."

She hurries out the door before I can protest.

How did they get Wyatt to help us? Especially after what I said. Unless he's helping for ulterior motives.

My gut twists as I wonder if we're about to make the biggest mistake of our lives.

CHAPTER FORTY-TWO_

WATCHING Wyatt walk out of the hotel, unchained and unguarded, is one of the worst moments in my life.

He's back in his three-piece suit, his blue tie matching his pocket-handkerchief. He's got an e-cig in hand, the clouds of smoke hovering around him bringing back all the bad things Wyatt did, like beat my mom.

The thing that I really hate is that I had to hand over the gold and diamond tie clip. Wyatt's greedy eyes gleamed when I set it in his stupid hand, his tongue running along his sharp canine tooth. I kind of want him to try to eat it, only to end up choking on it and dying. What an amusing twist of fate that would be.

The only thing that makes me sorta happy is that he's so gaunt, he doesn't look as tough as he used to. But we're still letting Wyatt loose into the world. Yeah, he's still got that tracker in him that he doesn't know about, but the smug look on his face, like he's outsmarted us, is really pissing me off.

Even with the tracker in him, he can still do a lot of damage before we can find and stop him. And what if his tracker gets wiped like Raiden's did?

"He's the only way to get inside the Corbox Clan," Scarlett whispers, putting her hand on my shoulder.

My tense muscles loosen under her touch. "I hate it."

"We all do," Rigg says, coming up beside me. "But, remember, we're sending Bo in with him. He'll keep an eye on Wyatt."

Bo comes out of the elevator, jogging to catch up with Wyatt. He's in a fancy suit, his usual three braids undone, his long, curly hair hanging well past his shoulders. Wyatt and Bo exchange a few heated words, then they disappear.

"At least you're sending the scariest-looking person of our group," I say. Add in the fact that the guy hardly talks, and he's really the perfect candidate. The Ito brothers won't suspect a thing.

Paul and Echols join us on the outing. The others stay back at the hotel, sorting through what intel we have, trying to uncover something. Anything.

I guess Akiro made a fuss about wanting to come with us, bringing up the fact that he's a ninja, but Rigg shut him down. I don't know exactly what happened, because I still can't look at Akiro. If I talk to him now, I know I'll say something I regret, because that's what I do when I'm all charged up.

We follow Bo and Wyatt to the club, keeping a safe distance behind them so we won't be spotted.

The second we step into the swanky part of town, my mood plummets. I'll be happy when I can go home, back to my family. To my dad. Away from all this happiness.

We have to sit back and watch as Wyatt and Bo enter the club, the bouncers letting them in after only a brief interaction.

The background chatter of the club drifts through our earpieces as Wyatt and Bo work their way through the club, each of them only grumbling a few things now and then to inquire where the VIP lounge is located.

Bo's voice cuts clearly through the earpiece. "We're about to be let into the VIP lounge. Hold steady."

Seconds later, static clatters through our earpieces. I tap mine, hoping it's some random interference.

"I lost audio," Lincoln says through the other earpiece.

"Can you get it back online?" Rigg asks.

"I'm trying," Lincoln says. "But it's like we've been locked out."

Scarlett leans against the wall nearest us. "They could have something surrounding the VIP lounge that blocks outside communication."

"But wouldn't our equipment override that?" I ask.

Rigg looks down at me. "Not if someone learned how to hack our system."

"We're losing valuable time here," Scarlett says. "We need to hear inside that lounge."

A thought zips through my mind. "Lincoln, find me a secret way inside the club. Air ducts or something."

Echols arches an eyebrow at me. "You want to climb your way through?"

"You have a better idea?" I ask.

He shakes his head. "None of us can walk into the club. Our only option is an alternate route."

"I can't find another way in," Lincoln says, his voice bouncing like he's moving feverishly on his side. "It's guarded too well."

Which is one of the reasons why we sent Bo and Wyatt in alone in the first place. We had no other option.

I clasp my hands and place them on top of my head. "What if something happens to Bo?"

"Bo can take care of himself," Rigg says, but there's a tiny hitch in his voice, ratting out his unease.

I glare at him. "Against the Corbox Clan? Really, Rigg? I don't care how tough that man is, he doesn't stand a chance against that many enemies."

What were we thinking? Sending Bo in alone with Wyatt. We've basically handed him over on a gold tie-clip-platter.

Someone across the street catches my eye. The guy from Alcatraz.

"I'm following him," I say, moving away from the group, grateful for a distraction. "If anyone wants to come with me."

Scarlett and Rigg hiss in low tones behind me, their voices fading the farther I get. Paul just chuckles.

"I'll go with her," Echols says, jogging after me. He's quickly at my side. "Is that the guy from Alcatraz?"

"Yep," I say. He may lead us to nothing, but I can't just stand outside a club for hours, wondering if one of our own will make it out alive, and if Wyatt will be free forever.

Echols and I keep a good distance from the man, not wanting to give our position away.

"I lost my mom when I was fourteen," Echols said as he keeps pace next to me. "Car accident. Worst moment of my life."

"Were you close?"

"Very. Not to mention, she was the thing standing between me and my dad." He lets a long, deep breath. "That man had a temper. Mom always took the brunt of it, saving me and my little brother from his rampages."

"What happened when she died?"

The man from Alcatraz is leading us to the quaint side of Vegas, full of soft colors and a peace in the air that takes me by surprise. It's quiet on the streets, with only a light breeze and the floating billboards making noise.

I sniff. Lavender. It's everywhere.

"Dad switched his preferred target to me," Echols says. "So, I took my brother and ran. We tracked down my mom's dad in Oregon and lived with him for a while." He takes his tin of mints out of his pocket and offers me one, which I happily accept. "Grandpa carried this tin with him everywhere he went. He wasn't a man of many words, but he did his best to take care of me and my brother. He ended up dying five years later."

I clench my hand into a fist, tightening it around the strap of my messenger bag. "Did you ever have this rage burning inside of you, while wondering why she had to be taken so young?"

The man enters a building, so Echols and I stop outside, using our watches to scan the perimeter.

"It's still there," he whispers.

I turn to him, surprised.

"Harper," he says, "you'll never get over the loss of your mother. The anger does fade, yes, but it's never fully gone. The best thing you can do is use it to drive your life. Let it make you stronger. Let it fuel you." He looks at me, his blue eyes full of sorrow and determination. "Loss can either break you or build you. Same goes with love. The way I see it, if you lose someone you love, let it build something inside of you that's impenetrable. A force that even your biggest enemy can't break down, because, no matter what, the worst has already happened."

I let the words stew inside me, allowing them to really settle in.

I always knew Echols was my favorite burlesque show member.

"Oh, is there already a line forming?" a guy says from behind us.

I whip around to see a group of men and women, all dressed up as dogs. Ears, collars, make-up, and everything.

Then I look up and see the sign outside of the building.

Scrawled in neon blue letters are the words: *Pup Mates*.

Echols chuckles next to me. "Well, this night just got infinitely better."

CHAPTER FORTY-THREE

ECHOLS OPENS the door for the people waiting behind us and they all scamper in, their fakes tails wagging.

When I don't move, Echols motions for me to go inside.

I shake my head. "Nah, I think I'm good."

Echols arches a bushy eyebrow. "Don't tell me you're not at least a little bit interested."

Well, yeah, I am. Not only did I witness grownups dressed as dogs go inside a building, but that big, beefy Polynesian guy from Alcatraz is in there.

"Maybe it's a cover for something?" I stare at the door, trying to build up some courage to go inside.

Echols puts a hand on my shoulder and pushes me inside, not giving me much of a choice.

I come to a stop just beyond the doors, confused by what I'm seeing. Tons of couples fill the room—each couple being one dog and one human. Some are playing cards, some having dinner, some doing jigsaw puzzles.

"Please tell me this is just a cover for something really shady," I whisper.

A petite lady bounds up to us, her skin painted white with black spots and a blue collar around her neck. "Welcome to Pup Mates! First time?"

"Yes," Echols says in a casual manner like this isn't the weirdest thing he's ever seen.

The lady barks twice. Like, an actual bark. All of a sudden, everyone else in the room lets out a bark, some turning and howling at us.

"We love first timers," she says. She hands us a menu. "We have a variety of puppies and different activities for you to choose from." She points a thumb behind her. "We even have frisbee golf in the adjacent rooms. Always the biggest hit of the night."

I glance around, spotting Alcatraz man in a booth off to the side. He's perusing a menu as a collie sits across from him, looking at its own menu. A waiter comes up, dressed as what I'm assuming to be a beagle, thanks to the floppy ears and brown tail with a white tip sticking straight up. He takes their orders and then leaves them alone. Alcatraz man easily slides into a conversation with the collie, the dog nodding like he understands what he's saying.

"What is happening?" I whisper, clutching the strap of

my messenger bag like it can protect me from whatever is going on here.

"Excuse me?" the Dalmatian host says to me.

"Just give us a second to look over the menu," Echols says before he pulls me off to the side.

We watch as the beagle waiter brings Alcatraz man a pitcher of beer, along with a bowl of water for the collie.

"I think this is exactly what it looks like," Echols says, glancing around the room with an amused smile. "A place to hang out with a dog for the evening."

"But why?"

"Dogs do make the best of friends."

I snort. "Then buy one and have it live with you like a normal person."

Echols pops a mint into his mouth. "Some people live in places where pets aren't allowed, or maybe they have a partner that's allergic."

"It doesn't make it right." I look up at Echols. "Please tell me you don't do this with your huskies."

He laughs, low and gruff. "No. Sam and Brutus would never go for it." He rubs his chin. "They might be up for the frisbee golf, though. Might have to try that when we get back home."

"Just don't dress up as a dog, and it will be fine."

The beagle waiter comes back out with a steak for Alcatraz man and a bowl of dog food for the collie. They both dive into their meals, Alcatraz man sporting the biggest smile.

"Can we go now?" I ask, already moving toward the exit.

"Yes, please," Echols says.

"Did you make a decision?" the Dalmatian host asks.

Echols hands her the menu. "Thanks, but we're going to take off."

"I'm more of a cat person," I say, putting my hand on the door handle. "Dogs are way too needy and have no idea of personal space."

I hurry out the door, leaving the Dalmatian host with her jaw dropped.

Echols meets me outside, a smirk on his face. "Vegas sure has its share of eccentric people."

His words make me think of Zia. "Hey, Echols, how well do you know Zia?"

He stuffs his hands in his pockets as we head down the street. "Fairly well. She's worked for Everly for a long time."

"Do you trust her?"

He glances over at me. "Yes. Why?"

I'm not sure how much to reveal to him. I have a feeling he tells Everly *everything*. But he also seems like he can keep his mouth shut when asked.

"What I'm about to say, can it stay between us?" I ask, looking up at him.

He stares at me a second before he nods. "Of course."

I search his eyes and know he's telling the truth. He's a trustworthy guy.

"I think someone has been messing with our intel," I say carefully. "Getting into DPS' database and deleting anything that will give us information on this mission."

The words sit in the air for a minute as we walk, Echols deep in thought.

"You think it's Zia," he says as a statement.

"She's a strong contender," I say. "Rigg told me that she and Wyatt used to be a couple."

"They were," he says. "A long time ago." He pauses, still thinking deeply. "I'm not sure what you've come across, but I can tell you this: Zia would *never* help Wyatt. Not in a million years."

"You're positive?"

He nods. "Everly and Scarlett wanted to send Zia to get Viana so she couldn't come to Vegas."

"Why?"

His voice is strong and sure. "If Zia ever gets into the same room as Wyatt, she'll kill him."

CHAPTER FORTY-FOUR

I WILL GIVE Pup Mates some credit. They distracted me for a limited time. Enough to release some of the pent-up energy inside of me.

Echols' revelation also gives me something to think about. Maybe Zia isn't working *with* Wyatt. Not in the way he thinks. Maybe she's trying to get him in a situation where she can carry out her plan and kill him. Having his daughter with her would be the perfect way to get him to do what she wants.

But why would she delete everything so we can't find out what's happening? Does she think the second we piece everything together, we'll deliver Wyatt back to Calloway and she won't have an opening to kill him? Maybe she's stalling, trying to buy time for her to get here and end his life.

Wyatt. Man, I hate him. He really should be in

Calloway and not in that stupid club with the Ito brothers, planning out an attack on the U.S.

And he has Bo with him.

I dial Scarlett as we walk down the street. As soon as she answers, I speak. "Any news on Bo or Wyatt?"

She shakes her head, a frown on her lips. "Nothing. Lincoln's been trying to get the feed back up, but it's useless." She glances off to the side and then turns her attention back to me. "Did the guy take you anywhere interesting?"

"You could say that," I say, not able to hide the amusement in my tone. "But nothing vital to the mission."

Her eyes light up in intrigue, but she doesn't push it. "You two should just head back to the hotel. Help sort through all the intel."

"What are you guys going to do?" I ask.

She sighs. "Wait for Bo and Wyatt to come back out. Hopefully alone and alive."

"And if they don't?"

She rubs her forehead, her eyes closed tight. "We'll regroup. We can't really storm the place with no intel. They could very easily outnumber us. Plus, that will give away our presence in Vegas. We don't need that information falling into the wrong hands." She licks her lips. "I'll let you know when we're on our way back to the hotel." With a weak smile, she ends the call.

I'm not sure if I've ever seen Scarlett so defeated. This

whole mission is weighing on all of us. There's just so much as stake, and so many unknowns.

Maybe a night at Pup Mates will cheer everyone up. Or, at least weird them out enough to ease some of the stress.

Echols and I hurry back to the hotel, joining Lincoln, Mayleen, Everly, and Dwayne around the computer. The large screen hovers in the air, information filling every inch. They're all concentrated on different parts, sorting through what we have.

I glance around the room. "Where's Akiro?" I expected him to be here, trying to involve himself as much as he can.

"He went to bed about an hour ago," Lincoln says as his fingers move swiftly across the screen. "He's in the next room over if you want to talk to him."

Not yet. If I see him, I know I'll melt into a puddle, ruining my focus. I don't have time for that kind of distraction. It will have to wait until this is over.

"Any luck?" Echols asks, taking a spot next to Everly.

She shakes her head. "Any time we stumble on something we think might tell us what's going on, it ends up being nothing, or it disappears from the feed."

Someone is definitely messing with our system.

I turn to Lincoln. "Send me the contact info for Zia. I need to talk to her."

"About what?" Everly asks, the intrigue in her eyes blazing.

I chance a glance at Echols. He's watching me, waiting to see what I say. I'm not sure if I should say anything to Everly. Zia is one of her employees. Well, every DPS operative is technically Everly's employee, but she vouched for Zia. They have a long history.

I take off my messenger bag, tossing it on an empty chair in the corner of the room. "Just want to talk to her about Viana."

"Is that really important right now?" Everly asks, sauntering over to me.

She's ditched her high heels, her bare feet a stark contrast to the dark gray concrete beneath them. Her purple toenails match her pants and jewelry.

I shrug. "Maybe she has information about her dad that can help us."

Everly's eyes narrow as if she's trying to see if I'm telling the truth. No matter how hard she glares, she won't find her answer.

"How tech savvy is Zia?" I casually ask.

Everly blinks rapidly, confused by my question. "She knows how to use her phone to make calls, if that's what you're asking."

I shake my head. "I'm talking the stuff Lincoln does. Knowing the inner workings of a computer system."

"Why does that matter?" Everly asks.

Echols is a few feet behind her, his inquisitive eyes on me. Even Dwayne and Mayleen have paused their searching, waiting for my response.

My gaze goes to Lincoln, and he gives the tiniest shake of his head, telling me to keep my mouth closed. If I tell Everly I think Zia is working with Wyatt, she might explode, taking the concentration off the mission at hand. We don't need that right now.

I turn to Everly. "Viana has to have some electronics with her. If not a datapad, then her watch. Maybe there's something on there Zia can find, like communication between Wyatt and Viana. Something that tells us what he's up to."

Dwayne nods. "That's not a bad idea."

Echols stays quiet.

Everly motions to Lincoln. "Can't he hack that from here?"

I roll my eyes. "Of course he can. But, as you can see, he's a little busy. I'm just trying to come at this from a different angle."

"We really don't have time to waste right now," Mayleen says, her quiet, yet firm tone commanding the room. Man, I really like this woman. "We should get back to searching and let Harper do what she does best."

The number for Zia pops up on my watch. I head toward the balcony and step into the night, shutting the door behind me.

We're high up, which lets me get a good look at Vegas. It's lit up in a calm, sophisticated way, not flashy and bombastic like the old Vegas. There's a smoothness to the curves of the buildings, all sleek and shiny. As much as I hate it, there's still a part of me that's impressed by the way the city has held up. The government has taken great care, leaving it one of the true beauties in our country.

Crossing my arms, I lean them on the railing and then dial Zia.

Her bright face pops up, a knowing smile on her lips. What she knows, I have no idea. "Well, hello, prickly pear. Whatever do I owe the pleasure?"

"I want to talk to Viana."

Zia frowns. "No small talk?"

"When have I ever done small talk?"

She twists her lips in amusement. "Come now. I'm stuck in this awful safe house with a brooding fifteen-year-old. I'm dying of boredom. I haven't heard from anyone, and no one answers my calls."

"We're a little busy right now with a possible terrorist attack about to happen." But her mention of a safe house intrigues me. "Where are you anyway?"

She waggles a manicured finger at me. "Tsk, tsk, prickly pear. We can't have someone intercepting that information."

I try to take in her surroundings, but the projection isn't that wide. It does look like there's floral wallpaper behind her, telling me she could really be in a house.

She glances over her shoulder at the wall. "It's hideous, isn't it? Of course, out of all the houses Rigg could pick as a safe house, he chooses one that hasn't seen an update in over fifty years. I should have just found my own place to hide out." She leans close. "Please tell me you're close to ending this. I'm not sure how much longer I can take being cooped up, especially with *his* daughter."

She says *his* with so much venom, confirming that she really does hate Wyatt.

But I still need to confirm that she's working with DPS, not against us.

"Viana, please. And can you give us a moment alone? I think she might open up more without you hovering around."

With a long, exaggerated sigh, Zia gets up, sweeps into what appears to be a kitchen and hands the datapad over to Viana.

"I'm going to use the bathroom," Zia says in the background. "Don't try any funny business and try to leave. Trust me when I say you'll regret it."

"Whatever," Viana says, sounding an awful lot like her dad.

The screen shakes and the next thing I know, I'm face to face with Viana Vale, daughter to the man I hate most in this world.

CHAPTER FORTY-FIVE

VIANA's soft features take me by surprise.

"You look nothing like your dad," I say in awe.

She smiles. "I'm glad to hear that." She pauses, looking to the right before turning her attention back to me. "Can you tell me what's going on? This lady is really weird and creeping me out."

"She's an acquired taste," I say. "Did she leave the room?"

Viana nods, then grips the top of her sweater. "Does this have something to do with my dad?"

I search her eyes, trying to see the deceitful Mitchell traits, knowing she could be just as cunning as her dad, but all I see is a scared fifteen-year-old girl.

"How well do you know him?" I ask.

"I don't." She sniffs, then wipes her nose with the sleeve of her arm. "Mom never talks about him. She gets mad if I ask. It's like she wants to forget he exists."

I stifle a laugh. "I know the feeling."

She frowns. "So, you know him?"

"Unfortunately. Listen, Viana, we don't have a lot of time. I need you to tell me everything you know about your dad."

She shakes her head. "Like I said, I don't know anything. I've never even seen a picture of him."

"Has he ever reached out to you?"

"No. Is he in trouble or something?"

"It's complicated." I try to soften my face, something Pearl has been teaching me to do. She says it would make people open up to me. If she's wrong, though, and I'm looking like an idiot for no reason, I'm releasing the truth about her Barbie doll obsession to the entire school.

"Viana, I need to know where you are. Can you explain your surroundings?"

She glances around. "We're in a really old house. It smells funny, like it hasn't been used in ages. She keeps calling it a 'safe house' but I don't feel very safe here." Her voice turns to a whisper. "Or with this lady."

I furrow my eyebrows in concern. "Has she hurt you in any way?"

"No. It's just, she keeps mumbling about 'killing Wyatt' if she ever sees him again." She bites her bottom lip, adding another layer to her innocence. "Is that my dad's name? Wyatt?"

This girl really knows nothing. What was Wyatt planning on doing? Abducting her and taking her out of the country? That would be a horrible way to start off their relationship. She'd never trust the man.

"Yes," I say. "Can you tell me what's outside of the house? Are you in a forest, the desert?"

She wipes her nose again. "I hear the waves of the ocean. I can smell it, too. I think we're in California."

So, Zia took her back to San Diego. Which means she's definitely not here in Vegas, trying to murder Wyatt. She could still be working with him, but the possibility of that is really dropping.

Viana tenses, her eyes going wide as she looks to the side.

"Prickly pear," Zia's voice rings out in the background. "Can you pass a message along to the others? Tell them to hurry up. My patience is wearing thin, and I didn't bring a change of clothes." I hear the padding of feet, telling me she's moved back out of the room. The way Viana eases, all the tension fluttering away, confirms it.

"Viana, just hold on for a little while longer. This will be explained to you soon. Just know you aren't in any danger. Not with us."

"Who's *us*?"

"We're the ones with your best interest at heart." I turn my face back to a steely determination, the soft Harper gone, and the real me shining through. "I'll make sure you're reunited with your mom. I swear on my mom's grave."

"What's your name?" she asks.

"Harper."

"Thanks, Harper." Viana smiles softly. "Good luck with whatever you're doing. I hope you win."

I return her smile. "We always do."

I end the call and look out at Vegas. How can we win when we don't know what we're up against? We need answers, and we need them soon.

If Zia isn't working against us, who is?

CHAPTER FORTY-SIX

I GO BACK inside the hotel room, taking everyone in. Lincoln has the best access to our system, giving him ample opportunity to destroy evidence. But why would he do that? Lincoln isn't the vindictive type. He may be timid at times, but he's loyal to DPS. There's no way it's him.

I turn to Everly.

Everly. I went about assuming it was someone working *inside* DPS, but she owns the company. She has just as much access to everything as we do.

My gaze slides to Dwayne, Echols, and then Mayleen. The burlesque show would too.

But are any of them capable of working with the Corbox Clan? One of the most notorious gangs in Japan?

I immediately rule out Echols and Paul. I know them well enough to know they aren't capable of hurting the U.S. I saw the hurt and betrayal in Paul's eyes when everything went down at the gala with Wyatt.

I know how strong and fierce Echols is. He said himself that losing a loved one makes you break or build something inside yourself. He's a builder and as tough and loyal as they come.

I can't imagine Dwayne turning on DPS or the country. Granted, he didn't seem as angry as the others at Wyatt's betrayal, but the man doesn't get that angry often. I don't think he has enough hate in his body to do something this catastrophic. Someone planning this magnitude of an attack will have a hatred in their core, fueling their every move.

Mayleen. I don't really know her. Yeah, her words and actions have made me like her, but that doesn't mean much. And Everly doesn't have the greatest track record of hiring the most dependable employees.

Which goes back to Everly. She does have a history of violent behavior. She was practically a heathen in high school. She says she's changed, but has she really? She's one who takes matters into her own hands. If something isn't going the way she likes, she'll do everything in her power to fix it.

Maybe getting the president out of power is her way of fixing things. I wouldn't put it past her.

The door to the hotel room suddenly opens and Scarlett walks in, followed by Paul, Wyatt, Rigg, and just a beat behind him, Bo.

I blow out a breath of relief before I hurry over to them.

"What happened?" I ask.

Paul escorts Wyatt over to a chair where he chains him back up.

"We were right about it being something worse," Bo says in a low voice. "I found out some crucial intel." He looks at Rigg. "You really didn't hear a thing?"

"The feed shut off the second you went into the back room," Rigg says.

Bo folds his massive arms. "That does explain why it was radio silence on your end." He smirks at me. "I was expecting at least some snarky comments by Harper."

"Oh, those would have been a plenty," I say.

Bo looks over, making sure the noise-canceling headphones are on Wyatt. Then he rounds up everyone around the table.

"I can confirm that both Raiden and Kazumi Ito are here," Bo says, "and they're planning an attack. But it's not an assassination on the president. Not quite." He takes a deep breath. "They're planning on killing everyone in attendance at the charity event. A mass shooting."

"What's their motivation?" Scarlett asks.

Bo shrugs. "They were pretty tight-lipped. I could tell they were wary of me, even though Wyatt vouched for me. Honestly, I was surprised they revealed that much." He ties back his massive amount of curly hair. "From what I can sense, they hate the president and this country. They want to kill him and his entire staff in one fell swoop. Basically, crush our government from the inside."

"Are they planning a takeover?" Everly asks.

"That's what I'm thinking," Bo says. "Kill everyone in attendance, then infiltrate the Capitol Building."

"Do we contact the local government?" I ask. "If they know what's going on, they can cancel the event."

"I have a contact in the FBI," Everly says. "I can reach out to them and let them know what's going on."

A contact in the FBI? A contact that could get close to the president and kill him? A contact that could wipe out any data that would raise a red flag?

"We can't cancel the event," Scarlett says. We all turn to her. "Not completely. We need to make sure the day continues as if the event is going down. Guests can show up, but then we can escort them to the bunker underground."

"So, we can still catch the Corbox Clan," I say, nodding. "I like it."

Rigg nods at Everly. "Reach out to your contact. We'll draw up a plan."

After he barks orders at everyone, he takes Scarlett and me to my hotel room so we can talk alone.

"I had Lincoln look into all the DPS operatives," Rigg says, his arms folded and feet shoulder-width apart. "It's not any of them that has turned on us."

"I talked with Viana," I say. When Rigg and Scarlett look at me shocked, I tell them of my encounter with her and Zia. "I think we can rule out Zia." I pause before I deliver my next theory. "What about Everly?"

Rigg scoffs, then glares at me when he realizes I'm serious. "Everly would never turn on DPS. She runs it."

I hold up a hand. "Hear me out. What if it's not her turning on DPS, per se? What if it's her way of getting what she wants, which is President Poulson out of the picture?"

"But it's not just him being assassinated," Scarlett says. "It's everyone in attendance."

"Which would clear out the government she hates," I say, "and give her an opening to build it the way *she* wants."

Rigg shakes his head. "She'd never work with the Corbox Clan. Ever."

That's one thing that makes me pause. Working with her last year told me she's not very fond of Japan right now, so it would be odd for her to work with them.

I snap my fingers. "Unless it's her way of getting them here, and she's planning to take them out as well."

"Why not bring us in on it?" Scarlett asks. "It just doesn't make sense."

"I'm just going to stop both of you right here," Rigg says, the muscles in his jaw pulled tight. "It's not Everly, and I never want to hear her name thrown into this again."

I open my mouth, but the fire in Rigg's eyes cuts me off.

Scarlett clears her throat. "So, someone hacked our system. In an undetectable way, which is terrifying."

"Can't Lincoln put up some walls to stop it or something?" I ask.

"He's already done everything he can," Rigg says. "He swore up and down that our system is impenetrable, but that's obviously not the case."

The thought of someone having access to our entire system is beyond unsettling. They could do so much damage with our intel.

"What are we going to do?" I ask.

Rigg takes a deep breath. "We're going to finish this mission, head back to Headquarters, and get this figured out, even if it means switching our entire database to a new server."

"Or multiple ones," Scarlett says. "Spread out the intel so it's not all in one place."

Rigg rubs his eyes with his thumbs. "We should have done that forever ago. We were just so certain of Lincoln's system."

Lincoln is a genius, despite what Bo says about him. There's a weird, itchy feeling inside me that's saying we're still missing something, and I hate it.

CHAPTER FORTY-SEVEN

NONE of us go to bed. We stay up, figuring out how we're going to shuffle everyone out of The Wilshire without causing a mass panic, or raising any red flags.

Guests still need to come in the entrance, unaware of what's about to happen so we can keep the illusion that we haven't sniffed out the Corbox Clan's plan.

Once we empty the events center, we'll spread out, covering every inch of the place, and wait for the Corbox Clan to show up. If everything goes according to plan, we'll arrest the lot of them without any casualties.

After going back to my room to take a quick shower, I head out into the hall, going toward Lincoln's room, trying to get into the right mindset.

"Harper."

I turn around and see Akiro standing in the hallway, hesitation in his eyes.

A lump forms in my throat as I charge at him, jumping

and wrapping my arms around his neck and my legs around his waist.

He holds me close for a while, neither of us moving or saying anything.

When he finally lowers me to the ground, he moves in to kiss me, but I punch him in the stomach.

"What were you thinking?" I yell. "Coming to Vegas. You almost got yourself killed!"

He's doubled over, holding his hands against his stomach. "I wanted to help out. I'm not useless, you know."

"I know that." I take multiple deeps breaths, trying to keep myself from hitting him again. Or kissing him. "I just lost my mom. I can't lose you, too."

He slowly straightens, his face so apologetic it makes me squirm. "I'm sorry, Harper. It's just, my uncle is involved in this. I don't want to believe he's capable of this."

The anger in me starts to fade. Akiro looks up to Hitoshi. They've created a deep bond since he got here from Japan. Now Akiro realizes it was all a farce, and the man he admired is actually a terrorist.

"I get it," I say. "But coming here by yourself was still stupid." I take his hand in mine. "I'm just glad we found you before the Corbox Clan did." I point to his tall spike of hair. "I guess getting it so tall worked out in your favor. Made it easy to find you."

He pats the top of it. "I knew letting it grow out was a good idea."

The elevator pings, and I turn around in time to see the doors open. Everly wanders out, her blonde hair pulled back in a messy bun. Dwayne and Mayleen are behind her, each holding a large, silver case.

"Outfits are here," Everly says. "We should start getting ready."

I turn back to Akiro.

"Are we good?" he asks.

"We're good." I get up in his face. "But if you ever do something this stupid again, I'll kill you before anyone else can." I plant a firm kiss on his lips before I head into Lincoln's room.

Everly already has the cases open, pulling out very colorful tuxes and dresses.

Scarlett scrunches her face in excitement when she sees her bright red form-fitting dress.

Everly retrieves a note from one of the cases. "Pearl left us a message. *'Each outfit is bullet-proof, fire-proof, completely breathable, and flexible so you can do whatever you want in them. I know some of you will balk at the colors—I'm looking at you, Rigg and Harper—but it's Vegas fashion, so deal with it. Have fun!'*"

I find a gorgeous green silk dress in the case in front of me, noticing Everly's name pinned to it. "Hey, Evs, I got yours."

I toss it to her, which she greedily takes, holding it up against her. "Pearl sure knows her stuff."

"Look at this!" Dwayne holds up a bright pink suit. "It's perfect."

I choke back a laugh. Of course he'd like a bright pink suit.

"Here's yours," Scarlett says, handing me a bundle.

I take in the pale blue jumpsuit with skinny straps up front, and a bunch of straps crisscrossing in the back. It's cinched in the middle, the legs skinny as can be, telling me they're form-fitting.

"That's adorable," Everly says, coming to my side. "Go put it on."

I hurry into the bathroom, surprisingly eager to wear it. The material is soft against my skin, hugging every inch perfectly. There's a small pocket in the front that I slide my hands into, only to feel something metal. I pull out a slim knife, flipping it over in my hand. "Sweet."

I do a few squats, then a handstand, before doing a backward flip. Then, I run out into the main room. "This baby is awesome. I can do all sorts of things in it." Leaping into the air, I do a roundhouse kick, landing softly back on my feet. "I could kiss Pearl."

"Hey, now," Akiro says. His eyes go wide when he takes in my outfit, and he lets out a low whistle. "You look hot." He rubs the back of his neck, unease in his voice. "I'm, uh, going to assume there's no suit for me."

"Nope," I say. "Pearl didn't know you would be here."

"And we wouldn't let you join us anyway," Scarlett says. "This is too big of a mission."

Akiro sulks his way to the couch and plops down. He looks over at Wyatt, who's currently chained to a chair. "So this is what it feels like to be in the dog house, huh? It sucks."

Everly scrolls through a message hovering above her datapad. "Looks like my contact is good to go. They're arranging extra security as we speak."

"We should head over soon and get everyone into position," Echols says. "We need to hit the ground running."

Scarlett nods. "I agree." She turns on a commanding voice. "Everyone, suit up. We're leaving in five."

Rigg comes out of the bathroom in a sharp-looking navy-blue tuxedo. It fits him well, showing off his muscles.

Bo has a similar suit, but with no bowtie. He's got the top two buttons of his shirt undone. His curly hair is sans braids, thank goodness.

I glance over at Wyatt and Akiro. "Uh, what are we doing with them?"

"They'll stay here with Lincoln," Rigg says, adjusting the cuffs of his shirt.

Lincoln, who had been preoccupied with the computer, glances over at us, his face going pale. "You're leaving the two of them with me?" He glances around the room. "No one else is staying?"

"We probably should leave someone else here," Scarlett says, looking over at Everly.

Everly turns to her burlesque show members. "Echols is coming with me. Mayleen, too. You're our best sharpshooter." She motions between Dwayne and Paul. "I'll let you two decide who's staying back."

After a quick game of rock, papers, scissors, Dwayne is the unlucky one staying back.

He motions to his pink suit. "Man, I'm looking this good, and no one will get to appreciate it."

As everyone leaves, I glance over my shoulder at Akiro, giving him a smile. He offers me a weak one in return. I feel bad making him stay here, but he's not trained for anything of this magnitude.

I hurry back to him, cupping my hands on his face and keeping my voice low so only he can hear. "Akiro, I'm trusting you to keep an eye on Wyatt. We can't have him escaping or anyone breaking in to save him."

He nods firmly, determination setting in his eyes. "Consider it done."

I kiss him before I run out of the room.

CHAPTER FORTY-EIGHT

As WE GATHER in the lobby, we all form a tight circle.

Rigg opens his mouth to speak, but Everly cuts him off. "I told my contact that my entire security team will be there, so that includes Scarlett, Rigg, Bo, and Harper. I didn't want to tell her about DPS."

That's a good thing, because we can't have our operation blown open like that.

"You'll follow my lead," Everly continues.

Rigg shifts uncomfortably next to me. He's used to being the one in charge of a mission.

Everly smirks, amused by his unease. "We can't have her getting suspicious that you're anything other than my personal security."

I glance around the circle, noticing someone missing. "Where's Bo?"

Rigg pulls back, looking over at the elevator.

Bo strolls out, pausing when he sees all of us staring at him.

"Where were you?" Rigg asks.

Bo's jaw twitches, and we sit there in uncomfortable silence, no one moving or saying anything.

He finally huffs. "I had to use the bathroom, okay? I wasn't aware I had to report every time I go pee."

Paul snickers next to me.

Everly lets out a long sigh. "Let's get going. We're already behind schedule."

As everyone moves toward the exit, I reach up to touch my ears, realizing I'm not wearing my mom's angel wing earrings. I took them off to clean them and forgot to put them back in.

Rigg pauses at the doors, looking back at me. "You coming, Harper?"

"I forgot my earrings," I say.

I wait for him to make a snarky remark, saying we can't waste time over jewelry, but he nods slightly. "Just hurry it up, okay?"

"Yes, sir," I say, backpedaling toward the elevator doors. "Thanks, Rigg."

"Of course, kid." He smiles before he jogs outside to catch up with everyone else.

I bounce in the elevator, wishing it could go faster. It's probably dumb, but I don't want to do this mission without my mom's earrings. They've always felt like protection, like her watching over me.

As soon as the elevator doors open, I sprint to the hotel room and straight into the bathroom, putting the earrings on in record time.

I'm so focused that I'm not watching where I'm going. My feet kick into something solid on the ground. I glance down to see Dwayne on the floor, unconscious. I bend down, feeling his pulse. He's still alive.

I quickly scan the room, noticing Akiro and Lincoln are passed out too.

Then I see Wyatt. He's hunched over in his chair, making mild groaning noises.

I rush to him, only to see blood pouring down the back of his chair. He's been stabbed in the back.

Standing, I assess everything in a matter of seconds. Wyatt's bleeding bad and his wound will definitely need stitches, stat. Everyone else looks unconscious, like they've been given a sedative of some sort. I can see their chests moving, telling me they're breathing.

To treat Wyatt, I'll need to untie him.

"Are you just going to stand there?" Wyatt manages to squeak out.

"It's tempting," I say.

But I can't watch a man die and do nothing to save him, even if it is Wyatt.

With a reluctant growl, I retrieve the keys and undo his shackles. He immediately falls into a heap on the floor, letting out a loud groan.

"Call Scarlett," I say to my watch as I bend down to straighten Wyatt out, making sure he's face down.

My watch beeps, unable to contact Scarlett.

"Call Rigg," I say, rushing over to the medical kit we always keep on hand.

I've never stitched someone up, but it can't be that hard, can it? It's like sewing, and I watched my mom crochet all the time, and they're practically the same thing, right?

Again, my watch beeps. Rigg's not answering, either.

I try Bo, Everly, Echols, Paul, and then Mayleen with no answer.

"Why is everyone ignoring me?" I shout to no one in particular.

I fall to my knees next to Wyatt, pulling out my earpiece and popping it in. Every channel I try is dead. Which means I have no way to contact anyone.

"Bo," Wyatt whispers.

"What about him?" I ask.

Wyatt tries to say something else, but he wheezes instead.

Pushing back the desire to let him bleed out, I rip open the back of his shirt, exposing his wound. I apply pressure with a rag as I rummage through the bag, pulling out everything I'll need.

Needle. Thread. Disinfectant.

I can do this. I know I can. I have to do this on my own. There's no one here to help me.

Funny how I thought being all alone would be ideal, but at the moment, it's anything but.

My ears warm, reminding me of Mom. I close my eyes for a second, picturing her beautiful face and soft smile. She may not be with me physically, but she'll always be in my heart.

I quickly wipe away the tears that escaped, probably smearing blood across my face.

Wyatt's wound looks deep. It was a sharp knife, that's for sure. I stare at the cut a while longer, and a nauseating feeling settles in my stomach.

"It can't be," I whisper.

I pull the knife Bo gave me out of my pant leg and hold it up to the wound. They match.

Son of a terrorist.

Bo betrayed us.

CHAPTER FORTY-NINE_

As I CLUMSILY STITCH WYATT UP, MY mind reels, piecing everything together. Bo would have access to delete any potential threats that popped up on the DPS database. He'd be able to contact Wyatt, feeding him information without any detection.

He's the one that turned off Raiden's tracker and shut off the feed at the club. He deleted all the images I took at Alcatraz. He didn't have to go to the bathroom. He stayed back to knock the guys unconscious and kill Wyatt. He hadn't been expecting me to come back and find them.

But why? Why would Bo do this? It doesn't make sense. He's always seemed so loyal to DPS and our cause. And why turn on Wyatt? What's Bo getting out of this?

I shove the needle through Wyatt's skin, closing the wound. The *why* doesn't matter right now. It's what he's going to do next that matters.

I tie the ends of the thread together, then clean off all the blood on Wyatt's back. Can't do anything about the blood all over my outfit now. Pearl's going to be furious when she sees it.

After placing a bandage over Wyatt's stitches, I turn him onto his back and slap his cheek.

"You still with me, Wyatt?"

He groans softly.

I slap him harder. "I need you awake. You need to tell me what's going on. I know Bo's been working with you."

Wyatt's eyes flutter open, then close like he can't keep them open.

I need everyone awake, now. I go back over to where all the medical supplies are stacked. I know we have a drug that can wake people up from an unconscious state. It'll leave them a little nauseous, but it gets the job done.

After filling a sanitized needle with the juice, I rush over to Lincoln and inject him. Seconds later, he takes a big gulp of air as he sits straight up.

"What happened?" Lincoln asks.

"Bo," I snarl.

Lincoln fixes his glasses that are askew on his face. "Bo?" He furrows his eyebrows, thinking. Then understanding passes over his eyes. "I thought I saw him out of the corner of my eye, but I was so focused on the computer."

I clean the needle again, fill it up, and rush over to

Akiro. Then I do the same to Dwayne and Wyatt, until everyone is awake.

"You wouldn't happen to have anything for the pain, would you?" Wyatt asks from the floor. He hasn't moved from his spot, but his eyes are wide open now.

"Pain?" Akiro asks. He rubs his eyes. "What's going on? All I remember is sitting on the couch one minute, and the next thing I know, Harper is over me with a needle jammed in my arm."

"We don't have a lot of time right now," I say, getting an injection of pain medication for Wyatt. He howls as I drive it into him. "Short story. Bo is the one who turned on us. He knocked the three of you unconscious and stabbed Wyatt." I slap Wyatt's shoulder. "He's all stitched up now, so we're good."

Wyatt glares at me. "We're far from good."

Ignoring him, I look at Lincoln. "I can't get in contact with anyone on the team. Can you try?"

Nodding, he gets to his feet and stumbles over to the computer.

Akiro and Dwayne plop down on the couch, both a little woozy.

"Give it a minute," I say to them. "It will settle, and you'll feel fine." I hover over Wyatt. "Why did Bo stab you?"

"Loose end, I guess," he says, grinding his teeth in pain. The medication hasn't taken effect yet. "I know too much."

"What do you know, Wyatt?" I ask.

He closes his eyes, pressing his lips together.

I grip his jaw tight, making him open his eyes again. "I can't get ahold of anyone. What's Bo planning?"

Wyatt tries to speak, but I'm squeezing too tight. I loosen my hold.

"There is no assassination attempt or mass shooting going down," he says. "It was all a ruse."

"Why?" I ask.

He jerks his head away from my hand. "I told you, Harper, *tens* of thousands of Americans will die. Starting here, then spreading like wildfire."

"How?"

He wets his lips. "It's too late. Everything's set in motion. Better say your goodbyes, because we're all about to die."

"Enough with the games!" Dwayne roars, his voice bouncing around the room. I look at him, surprised. I've never seen the man mad before. He bends down. "What is happening, Wyatt?"

Wyatt smirks, though it looks strained. "Well, if I had my guess, Rigg and the others are in police custody, and Bo and the Ito brothers are on a jet, getting as far away from Vegas as possible, heading to the next location." He grimaces in pain. "I was supposed to be on the plane with them."

"Custody?" I ask. "What are you talking about?"

Wyatt takes a deep breath. "Bo was setting you all up

to get captured by the FBI at the event, ending DPS and throwing the lot of you in jail." He takes another breath. "Not that it really matters. We'll all be dead soon anyway. He probably just wanted all of you to feel some panic before you die."

Taking my knife, I press it into Wyatt's throat. "Tell me what's going on, or I'll finish what Bo started."

"Uh, Harper," Akiro says. "Maybe you should calm down before you do something you regret."

I shoot Akiro a look that makes him shrink back in the couch before I turn my attention back to Wyatt.

Wyatt grins. "Accept your fate. It's over. You'll soon be with mommy dearest."

I punch him in the face. "Tell me now, Wyatt."

He sighs. "Corbox headquarters will have everything you need, but I highly doubt you'll get there in time."

"Where's headquarters located?" Dwayne asks.

Wyatt squirms on the ground. He truly doesn't know. The man's useless.

I stand and straighten out my bloodstained jumper. "How are we going to find headquarters?"

Akiro raises his hand, like we're in class or something. "I know where it is."

"Why didn't you say anything?" I ask.

He shrugs. "No one asked."

"Send me and Lincoln the address." I turn to Lincoln. "Any luck contacting the others?"

Lincoln shakes his head, a frown on his lips. "Nothing."

That's probably thanks to Bo.

"You're running out of time," Wyatt wheezes.

I grin. "Then I better go get ready."

CHAPTER FIFTY

AKIRO FOLLOWS RIGHT behind me as I go to my room to gather my supplies.

"You can't possibly be thinking about listening to Wyatt," Akiro says, watching me shove things into my messenger bag.

"What other option do we have?"

"You can't trust the guy!"

"You think I don't know that already?" I throw the bag around my neck. "You're coming with me. I need your help." I glance down at my ruined outfit, but I don't have time to change.

He walks beside me as I enter the elevator, gabbing madly to the point that I just tune him out.

We have to get to Corbox Headquarters as quickly as we can and search for the truth. Finally find out what I'm missing. It's going to be tricky, but I know we can do it. I pull up the blueprints on my watch, memorizing it.

When we step into the lobby, I stop him. "Akiro, I need you to be a ninja."

"I am a ninja," he says.

I place my hands on his cheeks. "I know, but we're talking stealth mode. I *need* to get inside the Corbox Clan Headquarters."

Akiro's shaking his head, my hands still firmly in place on his cheeks. "We should stay here, especially since we can't get ahold of the others."

"We can't just sit around and do nothing!"

He places his hands on mine and pulls them away from his face. "But *why* are we going to Corbox Headquarters? It's suicide."

"It's not. Most of their members will be gone, like Wyatt said. I can handle a few guys just fine."

"And if there's more than a few?"

I pat his chest. "That's why I'm bringing you."

"That still doesn't change the fact that we're chasing nothing."

I shove him so hard, he stumbles back. "Why can't you just trust me?"

"I *do* trust you!"

"No, you don't! You keep undermining my decisions."

He throws out his arms. "You haven't been thinking rationally. You've been all over the place ever since your mom died."

My hands ball into fists. "Will you please stop

bringing my mom into this? I know she's dead. I don't need the hourly reminder."

He taps my forehead. "Then get your head back in the game. Open your eyes and see what's right in front of you. Wyatt is lying to you. It's what he does."

With a growl, I push past him and storm out of the lobby and onto the streets.

Akiro jogs after me. "Harper, let's talk about this."

"We have," I say, moving at a brisk pace. "I'm going, whether you back me up or not."

Akiro yanks at his spiked hair. "You're crazy, you know that?"

I'm not exactly sure what overcomes me, but him calling me crazy is the final straw. I stop walking and round on him, punching him right in the eye.

Akiro screams out, putting his hand over his eye and bending over. "Seriously, Harper? What's wrong with you?"

Taking him by the top of his shirt, I throw him against the building we're in front of, ignoring the comments of people passing us.

"I'm not crazy. I'm not wrong. I have a gut feeling, and I'm following it."

His eyes are watering, both from pain and sadness.

"If there's a chance a bigger attack is about to happen, I need to find out what it is."

Tears slide down his cheeks, landing on my hands that are still wrapped around his shirt. "You're letting Wyatt get in your head. You can't trust him. What if this is a set-up? Just like with Bo setting up the others."

I slowly loosen my hold on him. "So what if it is? If there's a chance I can save thousands of lives, I'm going to take it, even if it costs me my own."

Akiro grabs my hands, holding them tight. A bruise is already forming around his eye. "You're not Jesus, Harper. You can't save everyone."

"He proved my point! He sacrificed himself for all the morons in this stupid world, because if trading one life for everyone else's worked, he knew it was worth the price."

He scoffs. "Next you'll be telling me you'll be resurrected."

I roll my eyes. "I know I'm not Jesus. No one is. And I'm not trying to compare myself to him, no matter how crazy you claim I am. But I'm going to Corbox whether you like it or not. This is my life. My choice and you're not going to stop me." I back away from him. "You either help me, or just go."

"What about *my* life," Akiro asks.

I stop. "What do you mean?"

He pounds his fist into his chest. "If I help you, I'm risking my life as well. Maybe I'm not willing to die over a hunch."

"I get that, but there's only a few people in the building. I can take them." I draw a deep breath. "Just know that if you walk away, this relationship is over. I can't be with someone who doesn't trust me."

Trust means more to me than anything. Akiro has always said he trusts me, but he hasn't shown it recently.

Hurt flashes in his eyes. "You know I trust you."

"Then prove it." I spin around on my heels, storming off. I don't turn around to see if he follows, but I don't hear any footsteps behind me.

CHAPTER FIFTY-ONE_

CORBOX HEADQUARTERS IS on the twentieth floor of a swanky building not far from the club. I'm going to scale the side of the building, avoiding anyone on the floor. I install the Trojan horse, so I'll be taken off all the camera feeds.

Slipping on my mask, I let the cool gel form to my skin, calming me. This is when I feel most myself. At school, I don't fit in. The social part is the absolute worst. Even being a girlfriend can be draining. Living the nine to five life will never be for me. Being behind the scenes, doing everything I can to protect everyone around me, that's where I thrive. Because as much as I hate people, I believe in the human race. I don't care how annoying they are, no one deserves to die by the hands of a terrorist.

I don't feel normal or calm until I'm in these moments, breaking all the rules to do the right thing.

I change out the grappling hook for the magnet before

I aim the gun and pull the trigger, watching the cord sail and land against the twentieth floor window. Pressing my feet against the side of the building, I run up it.

When I get to the twentieth floor, I use my laser pen to cut a small hole, holding a suction cup in my other hand so the glass won't fall when it's cut through. I gently lower the glass inside the room, landing quietly on top of it before I release the magnet on the grappling gun.

Doing a quick scan of the room, I put together that I'm in someone's office. Actually, no one's office. It's covered in dust, meaning the Corbox members didn't even bother turning on the air filters on the floor, probably knowing they wouldn't be here long.

They probably just utilized one or two rooms on the entire floor.

Using my telescoping rod, I scan the hall outside the room, making sure it's empty before I slink out. Each room I pass proves empty, covered in dust and not used. It totally contrasts with the ritzy feel of the outside. I wonder how long the Corbox Clan has owned this floor? By the looks of it, a while, and they didn't let anyone step inside, even to clean the place.

Empty takeout containers line the table and counter, like these guys have no idea how to clean up after themselves. Or, they just don't want to. Lazy terrorists.

I'm almost to the end of a hall when I hear a couple of voices around the corner. As quietly as I can, I pull out my mirror and peer around the corner.

Two men are casually standing there, having what seems to be a boring conversation about pillows they like to use. Both are armed in multiple places, adding a layer of difficulty. If one of them gets a gun or knife out, everything will go downhill fast.

I could use my tranq gun, but I only have a couple of darts. Something inside me tells me to save them for later, just in case. Besides, I love hand-to-hand combat. I can figure out a way without the gun.

Using my mirror, I calculate the distance both men are from me, from each other, and from the wall. I need to get them disoriented at the same time.

Slipping my mirror back in my bag, I roll out my neck and crack my knuckles before I move, my mind turning on cheetah mode.

I take three long quiet steps out into the hall, run two wide steps up the wall, and spin, leaping into the air. Both my arms are out, my hands landing on the back of their heads and I shove them, their foreheads slamming together.

As they stumble away from each other, I land softly next to one guy, snatch the knife from his sock, and hurl it toward the other guy, who's reaching for the gun at his right hip. The knife sticks into his right shoulder, stopping his movement and making him cry out and distracting him for the time being.

I'm already moving on the guy closest to me, climbing up his back and putting him in a strangle hold.

A gunshot goes off, and I look over to see the other guy trying to shoot with his left hand. His second shot hits his comrade in the stomach, sending us to the ground. I dive into a roll as another shot goes off, echoing loudly off the concrete walls in the hall.

As I unroll, I throw out my legs, connecting with the gunman's. He goes flying onto his back, his gun going off again, shooting the ceiling.

Grabbing his hand holding the gun, I twist and yank back, his bones cracking under my hand. He screams again —man, this guy has a high-pitched scream—and the gun falls from his hand. I quickly kick it away from the guy, then land a kick to his face, knocking him unconscious.

I snatch some zip ties from my bag and bind his hands and legs. I'm about to get up when another guy rounds the corner, his gun pointed at me. Dropping on top of the guy below me, I grab the gun on his left hip, aim, and shoot, connecting with the third guy's right leg, sending him to the ground.

After I zip tie the guy who got shot in the stomach— he's still breathing, but I don't know for how much longer —I head to the third guy and bind him before I strip him of all his weapons.

I hurry to stand, holding a gun in my hand as I scan all around me. I wait for another person to come out of the shadows, but no one comes.

I hope that means that's the last of these guys.

There's a chance the third guy contacted another

Corbox member on the outside when he heard the gunshots, so I have to assume my time in this building is limited.

I move as quickly as I can, running from room to room. In the third room I go to, I find it full of supplies. It only takes me three seconds to piece together it's all stuff to make a bomb. I continue my search until I land in the meeting room.

It's empty, aside from a small box sitting in the center of the room. I cautiously approach, scanning it with my watch to make sure it's not an explosive of any kind. The scan comes back clean. Japanese words line the box, so I use my watch to translate it. It's a computer, but one I haven't seen before.

I'm dialing Lincoln's number on my watch in seconds, and he answers a couple of seconds after that. His face hovers above my watch. "Hey, Harper."

I show him the computer. "How do I work this?"

Lincoln squints his eyes, taking in the computer.

"There's no button that I can see," I say.

A throat clears behind Lincoln. Wyatt.

"Let me talk to Wyatt," I say.

Lincoln purses his lips. "I don't think that's—"

"I don't have a lot of time before this place is stormed," I quickly say. "So, unless you know how to work this, let me talk to Wyatt."

With a reluctant sigh, he goes over to Wyatt so I can see him.

"How do I turn this on?" I ask.

Wyatt's lip curls up into a twisted smile. "Look at you. Making it there all on your own."

"As much as I love it, I don't have time for our normal repartee. Tell me what to do."

He sighs. "I told you there's no time."

"Maybe you should man-up and do something important with your life for once."

He's running his tongue back and forth across his canine, his forehead creased in thought.

"Wyatt, this is your chance to make your pathetic life worth something."

He snarls. "You're not really good with the pep talks."

"I'm being honest, which I thought you would appreciate."

He grunts. "I do."

"You're the one who told me to come here in the first place," I say. "You also said we were running out of time. Do you really want to die?" I soften my face. "Do you never want to see Viana again?"

He gets this fatherly look in his eyes that makes me super uncomfortable. I can't picture him as a doting dad, but I can tell you one thing: this man loves his daughter.

I'm not a pleader, but my options are out. "Wyatt, please, help me. All I want to do is turn on this box. That's it."

He waits a few more ticks of the clock before he speaks. "It can only be turned on by a fingerprint."

"Whose?"

He shrugs. "I have no idea who they allowed access, but I know it's how those work."

I take off out of the room, ending the call. I have three options, and hopefully one works. Without overthinking what I'm about to do, I go from guy to guy, hacking off their index fingers, trying not to flinch at the screams of the ones who are conscious.

Fingers in hand, I sprint back to the meeting room, pressing one against the box. Nothing happens. I toss the finger behind me and try the next one.

The box hums, a blue light glowing on top. Seconds later, the room is filled with the projection.

Turning on the scanning function on my watch, I circle the room, capturing every inch. As I do, my eyes also scan the information, getting wider with everything I see.

3D images of ten different buildings throughout Las Vegas circle the room. Each one is marked in three different spots: the bottom, the middle, and the top.

I step back, putting my hands on my head, everything coming together.

They're planning on blowing up Las Vegas.

Then the image shifts, bringing up another city. Salt Lake. Then another. Boise. It keeps switching. Portland. Seattle. Cheyenne. Denver. Albuquerque. Phoenix.

And ending in San Diego.

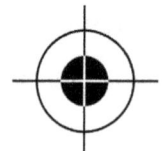

CHAPTER FIFTY-TWO

Scrambling, I hurry back to the room I entered, going out the hole in the window and using the cord from my grappling gun to fly to the ground. The second my feet hit the concrete, I'm sending Lincoln all the information I gathered and calling him.

So many cities. So many people.

But I need to focus on Las Vegas right now.

He quickly answers. "Harper, what am I looking at?"

"They're blowing up Las Vegas. Wyatt was right. The shooting was just a distraction to move our attention elsewhere." It also made us involve the FBI, so all police activity will be at the event. I sprint down the street, heading for the first building on the list. "Where are the Ito brothers?"

"They're probably about a hundred miles from here," Wyatt says in the background.

Lincoln spins to face him, showing him on my projection.

Wyatt smiles. "I already told you. They're long gone, moving on to their next target."

"Salt Lake?" I ask, huffing as I run.

"You're out of your element here," he says. "You can't stop this, Harper. In a matter of minutes, the buildings will be blown to pieces, taking down practically everything around them."

I stop outside the first building, using my watch to scan the perimeter until I catch a heap in the center of the first floor. "You knew this was going to happen and you came here anyway?"

Wyatt shifts uncomfortably. "I thought I'd be on the jet with them, not stuck here with you."

Dwayne all of a sudden appears in the projection, picks Wyatt up—chair and all—and chucks him at the window of the room. With the bulletproof glass, Wyatt just smashes against it and then falls to the floor, unconscious. At least, he isn't moving.

Dwayne dusts off his hands. "Sorry. I couldn't listen to him anymore."

I skid to a stop in the lobby of the building I'm in. "Lincoln, send the bomb coordinates to every building on the list and dispatch their security."

"That will blow our operation wide open," Lincoln says.

"It's either that, or we all go boom. Your choice." I end

the call and use my watch to navigate me to the first bomb, which is behind a locked door.

I rifle through my bag, trying to find something I can use. The door requires hand and facial recognition.

"What are you doing?" a shaky voice sounds behind me.

I whip around to see a girl in her early twenties, short curly hair, and a rose in her cheeks that I'm not sure is natural or a blush.

Her name tag says Meg.

Since I don't have time for niceties, I pull out my tranq gun and point it at her. Meg's eyes go wide with fear, and she sticks her hands into the air. I'm banking on the fact that she thinks I'm holding a real gun.

"I need this door open, now," I say in the most Rigg-like commanding voice I can.

She squeaks before she nods, presses her palm against the datapad, then lets it scan her eyes. A green light flashes, and the door hisses open.

I rush inside, frantically moving my watch around, until I spot the lump in the corner of the room. I hurry over, finding an old cabinet. The bomb is sitting in the third drawer I check.

Meg gasps behind me. "You weren't kidding."

"About what?" I shake my head, not having the time. "Do you have security here you can contact?"

She swallows and nods. "I already did when you said, 'bomb' in the lobby."

"Smart girl."

Four guards suddenly appear behind her, their wide eyes taking in the scene.

I stand as tall as I can. "I don't have time to explain, but you have three bombs in your building that we need to disable if we want to live." I point to the man and woman closest to me. "I'm going to disable this bomb, and you're going to watch and record the whole thing."

I move to the other man and woman, syncing my watch with theirs. "I'm sending you the coordinates of two other bombs in this building." Their watches ping, getting my message. I look at the woman. "Head for the one in the middle and find its exact location." I turn to the man. "Go to the one on the roof and do the same." I point to the two guards behind me and turn my attention back to the woman. "They'll be there in a few minutes to disarm that bomb." I look at the man. "I'll head up to the roof when I'm done with this one. Now, go!"

The two take off, not looking back or questioning me. Must be a Vegas thing. Why can't everyone be like this?

Squashing my annoyance, I turn back to the bomb in the cabinet. "Are you recording this?"

"Yes," the woman guard says. "Are you sure we'll be able to do this?"

I look her straight in the eye. "You follow every step I take, you'll do fine. The two of you combined can do this. I know you can."

She nods, determination setting in her eyes.

"Watch everything I do, repeating each step under your breath, which will help you remember."

I get to work, scanning the bomb with my watch to identify the model. It's U.S. made. By the government. Maybe there's a government official in on the whole thing, like we thought earlier. It would make sense, making sure you have spies everywhere.

But having a U.S. made bomb means I can easily shut it down. I unscrew the back, revealing the wires. Following the directions on my watch, I cut them one by one. After I cut the last one, I gently take it into my hands.

"Where's your bomb box?" I ask the woman security guard.

"Follow me," she says.

After having so many terrorist attacks, most major buildings like this one are required to have a bomb box where a bomb can be detonated safely. Though I cut the wires, we can't take any risks.

We go into a room in the back, and she unlocks the box for me. I gently set the bomb inside and have her lock it back up.

"Couldn't we just bring the other bombs straight here?" she asks.

I quickly shake my head. "You move them, you risk setting them off. The best way is to cut the wires, then bring them here as a back-up measure." I put a hand on the shoulder of the two security guards with me. "Head to the middle bomb and cut the wires in the right order. Take deep breaths, don't rush it, but act quick, and I promise everything will be fine."

They both firmly nod and take off.

I turn to Meg, who has a newfound energy. "Get me to the roof."

She takes off toward the elevator, scanning her hand and eye to grant us access once we get inside. The elevator soars upward, going fast. Ten seconds later, we're on the floor before the roof.

She guides me down the hall and to the staircase, which we take two steps at a time. Meg's moving swiftly for wearing a skirt, and I'm really impressed.

I shove open the door when we get to the roof.

"Over here!" the security guard yells.

We take off, finding him near the center of the roof. The bomb is inside an air duct. The guard has already cut the duct back, giving me room to work.

My watch vibrates and Lincoln's face pops up from my watch. "Every building has been notified. Security has been dispatched. Everything should be disarmed within the next five minutes."

I lick my lips, focusing on the bomb before me. "Good. We have one disabled here, and we're working on two and three."

"Keep me posted," Lincoln says before ending the call.

"How many more buildings have bombs?" Meg asks.

"Nine," I say.

She and the guard share a scared look.

"Who did this?" the guard asks.

"It's too complicated to explain right now," I say. "The important thing is to stop them."

I unscrew the back of the box so I can see the wires. A few seconds after I do, the bomb beeps and a countdown pops up, the green numbers hovering in the air above the bomb. It's counting down from two minutes.

As I make my first cut, I call Lincoln once again. "A timer started on mine. Contact all the others and tell them they have a minute to disable."

"On it," Lincoln says before he ends the call.

"Why a minute?" Meg asks.

"Because by the time he contacts them, that's all they'll have left."

I work my way through the maze of wires, cutting them swiftly and surely.

"Forty-five seconds," the guard says.

"I can see that," I say. "The reminder really isn't going to help."

"Sorry," he mumbles.

Ten seconds later, the bomb is disabled. I stand up, placing my hands on the top of my head and walking to the edge of the roof.

"Should we take the bomb down to the box?" the guard yells behind me.

"We have less than thirty seconds," I say. "You won't make it in time. It's either going to go off, or it won't."

Meg sniffs next to me. "Well, that's comforting."

I place my hand on her arm. "We did everything we could. Thank you for your help."

She offers a soft smile. "Hopefully it works."

I stare out at Las Vegas, seeing all the lively colors and the floating billboards. In ten seconds, it will still be here, or we'll be blown to smithereens. At least if it's the latter, having this view as the last thing I see is not too shabby. Plus, I'll be reunited with my mom. That's a plus, right?

"Five seconds," I whisper.

My fingers tap along my leg, counting down the seconds. When I get to one, I suck in a sharp breath, all my attention on the city before me.

CHAPTER FIFTY-THREE_

IT'S WEIRD, standing here waiting for something horrific to happen. There's this moment where everything goes still, like a freeze-frame. Everything around me is shut out. I can feel the wind, but I can't hear it. I know there are other people on the roof with me, but it feels like I'm alone.

I watch the skyline, waiting for billows of smoke to rise into the air, making the already bright night blinding. I wait for the ground to shake, tremble at the detonation.

But none of that happens.

It's silent in these moments. Just my heavy breaths loud in my ear.

"Nothing happened," Meg whispers, her words finally getting through to me. "That's good, right?"

I nod, though my stomach is tight with worry. "Yep. They disabled them in time."

Meg looks at me. "Why don't you sound happy?"

I tear my gaze from the skyline and turn to her. "Because the guys who did this are long gone."

Or, not. They'll want confirmation of the bombs going off. Once they find out nothing happened, they might circle back. Or speed up their attack in Salt Lake.

I place a hand on Meg's arm. "Thanks again for your help." I look over my shoulder at the security guard. "And yours."

"What now?" Meg asks.

A small smile breaks across my face. "I'm going to hunt down the terrorists and see that justice is served."

"Good luck," the security guard says.

My lungs constrict, and I know I'm about to lose it. "Can I have a minute alone?"

They both nod and leave me alone on the roof top.

The sobs start in shudders, shaking my body. I fall to my knees, placing the back of my hand against my mouth.

I almost died. Everyone I loved, aside from my dad, almost died.

The dam inside me breaks, and I let out a roar that fills the night. My arms are thrown wide as I scream every inch of air out of me.

I thought I'd been ready to join mom on the other side, but I'm not. There's still so much in my life I want to accomplish. I know, deep in my soul, my purpose here isn't over.

Dad. I'm not ready to leave him.

Rigg. Scarlett. Lincoln. Pearl. The burlesque show. Akiro.

Akiro.

I need these people in my life.

I *need* them.

As soon as I'm out of the building, I call Lincoln again.

"By the fact that Vegas is still in one piece," I say, "I take it everyone disarmed their bombs?"

Lincoln nods, his face a mix of elation and worry. "With only seconds to spare. That was a close one." He takes a deep breath. "There's no way to keep this quiet now, though. Too many people know what happened."

"And people saw my face," I say.

"And mine," Lincoln puts in.

"How do you do damage control for this?" I ask.

Lincoln sighs, his shoulders deflating. "You don't."

I'm not sure what that means for my future at DPS, but there's still something that needs to be done. "Linc, can you double-check that Raiden Ito is on the way to Salt Lake? We still need to capture the Corbox Clan."

"I've been working on undoing the damage Bo did, including disabling Raiden's locator." He's looking at the computer next to him. "I don't think they'd come back here just yet. The city is already on lockdown."

I lean my back against the building. "What about the charity event? What ever happened?"

"Nothing, thankfully. President Poulson has been moved to a secure location in light of the threat." He pauses, holding something back. I can see the war in his eyes, even with him looking at the computer and not me. He's avoiding me.

"What?" I ask.

Lincoln rubs the back of his neck. "Rigg and Scarlett have been detained by the FBI, just like Wyatt said would happen."

My heart stops. We've always said we wouldn't reveal anything to the FBI. If they keep their mouths closed, they could be detained for a long time. We don't have that kind of time. The Ito brothers need to be stopped now.

The people coming in from Japan had been dispersed to other major cities in the west. Wyatt said the Ito brothers are already heading to their next target. It's odd they started with the most difficult one to breach, but maybe they thought with the capital destroyed, the country would be so focused on that, they wouldn't think other cities would be in danger.

I never try to figure out the mind of a terrorist, because I figured out a long time ago, you can't. They're delusional, and whatever plan they have concocted makes perfect sense to them, even if it seems asinine to everyone else in the world.

"Stay at your location," Lincoln says, breaking through

my thoughts. "We're loading up here and then we'll come and get you."

"And then what?" I ask.

"We're going home."

"What?" I yell so loud, a person walking near me jumps into the air. I smile at him and turn my attention back to Lincoln. "We can't just leave them here and go home."

Lincoln removes his glasses and rubs his eye. "It's protocol if any of us ever gets caught. Our mission now is to get back to Headquarters and make sure nothing is compromised."

"Our mission is to hunt down the Ito brothers and stop this attack once and for all."

Lincoln sets his glasses back on his face, his eyes tired. "Harper, the attack is over. We stopped it. I know you want to catch the Ito brothers, but—"

"But nothing, Linc. You saw the plans. They're on their way to Salt Lake, and we have to stop them. I'll go by myself if I have to, but I could really use the backup." I sigh. "And the jet."

Dwayne appears in the projection behind Lincoln. "I agree with Harper. We need to stop this now."

Lincoln loses his resolve at Dwayne's words.

"I agree." Akiro's sudden voice from behind me catches me off guard, and I find myself shoving him against the wall, my tranq gun pressed against his neck. He grins. "Miss me?"

CHAPTER FIFTY-FOUR

As SOON AS I lower the gun, Akiro is apologizing profusely. He keeps using the words, *idiot* and *moron*, and I don't try to stop him. He's pretty much hitting it right on the nose.

I just let him ramble (and at some point, he ends up on his knees and the whole display is pretty embarrassing) until the jet arrives, and we climb aboard.

Lincoln has the auto-pilot set, taking us north toward Salt Lake City, where Raiden Ito's location pinged seconds ago. The brilliant Lincoln—who Bo underestimated—restored the locator and found him.

After I change into my DPS uniform, I join the others around the table in the center of the jet, and I try not to let the sight of the people with me be discouraging. They aren't as trained as me.

Lincoln is at the head of the table, tired and looking like he's regretting his decision to go with us.

Dwayne sits opposite me, rubbing his hands together, all smiles. He's still in his bright pink suit, saying if he was going to die tonight, he wanted to at least look nice. His pecs twitch, like they're eager to do some damage. I'm glad he's here, but he's just one person, and we've never worked together before. With Rigg and Scarlett, our system is flawless. We can read each other so well, because we've run countless missions together. We know how the others think. With Dwayne, it's uncharted territory, and this is pretty much the worst time to try to figure it out.

Akiro is on my right, and while he apologized like a million times, the trust between us has cracked. What if he changes his mind once we find the Ito brothers and bows out? I can't have someone bail on me in a time this crucial.

Then there's Wyatt, shackled to a chair, still unconscious (mostly because I knocked him out again once he came to and wouldn't offer any information), his head hanging down, a waste of space. But we couldn't leave him in Vegas alone. I hate having the deadweight with us, but such is life.

Basically, our chances of winning this thing and coming out alive are smaller than me wearing a dress to Homecoming.

Lincoln's trusty fingers go to work, pulling up images and layouts of Salt Lake's airport and downtown. "Looks like they landed about an hour ago."

"Which gave them plenty of time to place bombs around town," Dwayne says. His eyes narrow in on the image of downtown, and he points to it. "Makes most sense for them to go here."

I nod. "I agree."

Akiro scratches the side of his head. "We still have another hour until *we'll* get there. They could be long gone by then."

"And with Vegas still standing," Dwayne says, "they're going to be working fast. Once the bombs are securely in every location, they'll be on the jet, flying to the next location."

I look at Lincoln. "Can you speed this thing up?"

"I can try." With that, he spins around and heads into the cockpit. He could change the speed from his datapad, but I think the guy needs a moment alone. Our odds of survival are low, which I've dealt with before, but not Lincoln. He's always stationed at Headquarters, away from the line of fire. Where we're headed, he'll be practically dancing in the fire.

Dwayne looks at me. "What's our plan of attack?"

I plop down on the chair behind me, kicking my feet up on the table. "I think by the time we get there, the Ito brothers will be headed back to the airport. I'm thinking we intercept them before they can get on the plane."

"What about all the bombs?" Dwayne asks. "We need to disarm them."

"The Ito brothers won't be setting them off while they're still in town," I say. "If we can keep them on the ground, we should be safe."

Akiro arcs an eyebrow. "Should? Should isn't going to cut it for me."

I hop to my feet, rounding on him, straining my neck to look up at him. "I swear, Akiro, I can't have you bailing on me again. I need you now more than ever. If we don't stop this attack, thousands will die." I lightly punch him in the chest. "This isn't about *you*. It's bigger than any of us. Stop thinking about your own butt, and think of all the innocent people in Salt Lake. They're your number one concern right now."

Akiro rubs his chest. "I hate when you're logical."

Sighing, Dwayne rests his palms on the table. "I know DPS isn't used to working with the cops, but I think this is a situation that calls for it. Especially with all these cities involved."

Lincoln walks out from the cockpit, frowning. "I don't think that's a very good idea."

"Why?" I ask.

He uses the bottom of his index finger to push up his glasses. "Because every major city in the western United States has been ordered to arrest us on sight."

CHAPTER FIFTY-FIVE_

AKIRO CLAPS his hands together in frustration. "Well, that's just great."

"Which means we can't land at the Salt Lake airport," Lincoln says, approaching the table.

I rub my forehead. "Okay. Let's go through this." My mind starts whirling, and instead of keeping my thoughts to myself, I spew them out as they come. "Airport is out. Working with law enforcement is out. No way we can get them to trust us in such a short amount of time. We have to stop the Ito brothers. If Lincoln hacks into Salt Lake's police database and puts an arrest warrant on the Ito brothers, they'll know we're heading to the airport where they might detain us before we can stop Corbox. We're on our own." I look at the supply room. "We each need a parachute and all the weapons we can carry." I pat Lincoln on the shoulder. "Get us as close as you can without being detected. You'll stay on the plane and circle the area until we're ready to be picked up."

He lets out a breath of relief. "I like that plan."

I look at Akiro and then Dwayne. "It's just the three of us. Once we hit the ground, we need to move as quickly as we can to the airport. Our main goals are to stay invisible and stop the Corbox Clan once and for all."

Dwayne cracks a smile. "You make it sound so easy."

"Oh, it's not," I say. "But we have no other option."

"I hate that it's just the three of us," Akiro mumbles.

"Four," a hoarse voice says from the corner of the jet.

I spin around to see Wyatt has come to. I laugh. "Yeah, you're staying here with Lincoln."

Wyatt spits a little bit of blood on the ground, causing me to flinch. "You need my help."

"No, we don't," I say.

He glares at me. "I know how the Ito brothers think. I know their plan, including what part of the airport they'll be at."

I fold my arms. "It can't be that difficult to find them."

"It's a big airport," Wyatt says. "Biggest one in the west, and you won't have time to just mosey around until you find them."

I hold up a palm, heading toward the storage room. "Enough, Wyatt. I'm not letting you loose."

"The moment any member of the Corbox Clan spots you," Wyatt says, "they'll start shooting. That will draw the attention of airport security in seconds. If you don't want to be caught, and you want to stop the destruction of downtown Salt Lake, you need to be quiet and stealthy."

I point a finger at my chest. "Something I'm quite good at, thank you very much."

Wyatt hops a little in his chair, coming closer to me, his snarl somehow magnifying. "Raiden and Kazumi know me. I can approach them as an ally. It's your best bet, Harper. Stop being so stubborn."

I run to him, bending down to look him straight in the eyes. "I can't trust you."

"You can," he says, his eyes softening and taking me by surprise. "I want freedom, Harper. I want out of prison. I haven't backed out of my side of the arrangement. I take you to the Ito brothers, and DPS sets me free." He swallows. "And I finally get to see my daughter."

We weren't going to actually set Wyatt free, but Wyatt doesn't know that.

"I hate the thought of you walking this earth a free man," I say.

"It's either that, or we all die." His eyes soften even more. "When I first started working with Tomi Fukunaga, I was put in contact with the Ito brothers back in Japan. I liked the way they thought and wanted in on their mission."

"Let me guess," I say, "they didn't want your gold-tie-clip-wearing self."

He shakes his head. "Said it was a brotherhood. Surely, I'd understand."

"But you didn't."

He shakes his head once again. "A member of a brotherhood should be anyone willing to throw down his life for the cause. There are blood pacts that can be made. But I let them think I was fine with it." He pauses for a few seconds. "They used me. The only reason they wanted me in their operation was because of my access to Everly, the Fukunagas, and Afah, which in turn got them access to Bo."

"Who in the world is Afah?" I ask.

"The man you met at Alcatraz," he says.

I snort. "Ah, the guy who takes the phrase 'man's best friend' a little too seriously." I still can't shake the image of him at Pup Mates from my mind.

Wyatt furrows his eyebrows in confusion. "I don't know what that means, but he's Bo's cousin."

Everything starts piecing together. I'll never forgive Bo for doing this to us.

"I hate those guys as much as you do, Harper, and would love the chance to show them what happens when someone messes with me."

The frustration inside me builds. I know he's right, and I hate it. I keep telling Akiro to look at the grand scheme of things. Wyatt's life compared to thousands of innocent people in Salt Lake? They don't even compare.

With everything in me, I let out a scream of rage, my hands balling into fists, my muscles clenching, my voice reverberating around the jet. My eyes are squeezed so tight tears form at the corners. I keep screaming until it's all out, leaving me heaving for air.

Silence sits around us, the energy of my scream still vibrating the air. The quiet is almost deafening.

Wiping the tears from my cheeks, I stare at Wyatt. "If you step out of line even once, I will end you, understand?"

He nods. "I know you will. But right now, we share a common interest: living."

Cursing the day I ever met Wyatt Mitchell, I unshackle him, letting the chains fall to the ground with a sickening thud.

CHAPTER FIFTY-SIX

"ARE YOU INSANE?" Akiro hisses over my shoulder as we enter the storage room.

I immediately go to a parachute and strap on the vest. "I think that's already been established."

Akiro throws a parachute pack on his back. "What if he orders the Corbox Clan to kill us?"

"What if he's telling the truth about hating them and wanting to turn on them?" I ask, grabbing a tranq gun from the cabinet and shoving it into Akiro's chest. The one Scarlett made especially for me already sits in the holster at my side, my two darts calling Raiden and Kazumi Ito's names.

"What if he kills them?" Akiro asks. "DPS doesn't kill, unless it's a last resort."

"I know the DPS rules!" I take in a deep breath. "What if Wyatt is lying? What if we can't stop the bomb? What if thousands of people die tonight?" I take a step toward him. "What if we can stop it from happening? What if we can arrest the most ruthless gang in Japan and stop them for good?"

Akiro nods. "Those last 'what ifs' really outweigh the others."

"This is my job. To stop these attacks from happening, no matter the cost. I can't just sit back and let the Corbox Clan take over the western United States, because I'm worried about failing."

"Or dying," Akiro puts in, as if it's helpful.

"I need you, Akiro," I say, placing my hands on his warm cheeks. "You know I wouldn't let just anyone fight beside me."

He arches his bushy eyebrows. "It's not like you have a lot of options."

"True," I say, "but if I thought any of you were capable of ruining the mission because of your stupidity, I'd lock you up and leave you on the jet." I draw closer to him. "We can do this, Akiro. I have faith in us. Question is, do you?"

He answers by kissing me firmly on the lips, his arms sliding around my back and pulling me into him, my body melting into his. His fingers tickle the back of my neck, and I shiver despite the heat in the small storage room.

His lips pull back from mine, and he stares deeply into my eyes. "I do." His lips quirk into a small smile. "Now, let's go kick some Corbox butt."

"As adorable as this is," Wyatt says from behind Akiro. "We don't have time."

I push away from Akiro so I can see Wyatt better. He's got a parachute strapped to his back, a rifle in one hand, and a Colt handgun in the other.

"We don't kill, Wyatt," I say. "Not if we don't have to."

"I know," he says. "But I do. And if you think you can take down the entire Corbox Clan with your measly tranquilizer guns, you're more naïve than I thought."

I've never had to kill someone, and I really don't want to start right now. It's a line I don't want to cross. I'm in the game of stopping death, not causing it. But I do understand that sometimes it's the only option. It comes down to your life or theirs. I just try to avoid putting myself in that situation if possible.

"Get ready to jump in five minutes," Lincoln says from a speaker overhead.

Dwayne takes real guns like Wyatt has, but Akiro sticks with the tranq guns and tasers like I do.

Obviously, the Corbox Clan will have real guns on them—ya know, ones that shoot bullets and kill—but if I can get close enough to use my fists and a tranq, the bullets won't be needed. I prefer hand-to-hand combat anyway. Makes me feel like I'm accomplishing something, and when I say, "yeah, I took that guy down," it means I was the one who actually took the guy down, not some bullets.

There's just one more thing I need to do before we jump. Going over to a storage bin, I use facial recognition to open the door and pull out a pair of handcuffs. Before Wyatt can realize what I'm doing, I slap them on his wrists.

He growls. "You've got to be kidding me."

I snort. "You really thought I'd let you walk out of here completely free?"

Lincoln showed me how to use the invisible handcuffs after we landed in Vegas. Mostly because I wouldn't stop asking him questions about them. Using software on my watch, I change the cuffs to invisible, so no one can see them. The electrocution range is set to five feet.

Wyatt looks over my shoulder at the hovering projection. "Five feet? If we end up in a fight with the Corbox Clan—which *we will*—I'm going to need a bigger radius than that."

He's right. No way he could stay that close to me. I broaden the range to twenty feet. "That's all your getting. Deal with it."

We huddle near the door.

"We jump at the same time," I say, eying all of them, and waiting for them to nod in agreement before I go on. "Coordinates for landing have already been programmed into your chute. We'll land a mile out from the airport."

"A mile?" Akiro asks.

"Yep," I say. "We'll run the rest of the way. Keep the same pace as me." Again, I wait for them all to nod. "Once we arrive at the airport, Wyatt will guide us to where their plane will be. We'll scope it out and go from there."

Dwayne rubs his massive hands together. "Let's get this party started." Even with all the confidence radiating off the guy, I can hear some of the worry lacing his tone. We could be walking into our deaths.

I steal a glance at Wyatt, really hoping I can trust this guy. He bares his sharp canine tooth, not helping. Then I remember that he's doing all of this to see his daughter, and it settles my nerves. Just a little.

The door hisses open, the sudden air from outside blowing in. I stand in the middle of the pack, Dwayne and Akiro on my right, Wyatt on my left.

Standing on my tiptoes, I whisper into Dwayne's ear. "If Wyatt steps even a hair out of line—"

Dwayne looks down at me. "I've got it."

As much as I don't want to, I make everyone clasp hands—which leaves me holding Wyatt's hand. Thank goodness for the gloves providing a barrier for our skin.

A countdown starts above us, going down from ten seconds. At zero, the five of us jump out of the jet and into air, plummeting toward the earth.

CHAPTER FIFTY-SEVEN

I WANT to enjoy this moment of freedom like I did with my jump to get Wyatt out of prison. But having Wyatt at my side, the unknown of what exactly we're about to face, and the thought of my dad having to bury me alongside my mom so soon makes my stomach clench.

I know I go into every mission with the possibility of dying, but I *can't* die right now. It would destroy Dad. And everyone else in San Diego and all the other cities they're planning on attacking. So, I have to do everything in my power to live.

I mean, I know that should always be my goal, but it's usually placed on the back burner. My job is my number one priority. This is the first time that I can remember where living and stopping a terrorist attack are coming in tied.

My plan: do both. Live and stop the Corbox Clan from taking over the U.S.

Our chutes open, the dark material blending in with the night. With the coordinates of our landing spot already entered, the system automatically guides us toward it, adjusting for wind and velocity when needed.

When our feet hit solid ground, we unstrap our chutes and they immediately disintegrate.

Wyatt moves toward the north, but I grab the back of his shirt and yank him back. I huddle everyone around me.

"I know our situation sucks," I say. "There are only three and a half of us and countless of them."

Akiro arches an eyebrow. "Three and a half? Is somebody pregnant?" His gaze slides to me, his eyes going wild. "You cheated on me, and *this* is how you tell me?"

I roll my eyes and then punch Wyatt's arm. "I'm only counting him as half a person because I don't trust him. There's a fifty-fifty chance he'll turn on us."

Akiro sighs in relief. "Thank goodness."

I rub my hands together. "We *have* to stop this attack from happening. The Ito brothers, or any member of the Corbox Clan, can*not* get back on the plane. Those bombs can*not* go off. I know I always say we need to stop attacks or die trying, but dying is *not* an option tonight. Rigg, Scarlett, Everly and the others *need* us to help them. We can't forget they've been detained and need rescuing as well."

Dwayne and Akiro are nodding fiercely, soaking up every word I say. Wyatt just keeps grunting like he wants to say something, but he's smart enough not to.

"We are going to the airport, and we're going to stop

the Corbox Clan"—I take a deep breath, hating the next words out of my mouth—"by whatever means necessary. We don't have a lot of time. This needs to be as quick and clean as possible."

"What happened to not killing anyone?" Wyatt asks with a smirk.

I resist the urge to punch him in the face. I can do that afterward. "I know I can't control any of you. I also can't ignore the fact that some will die. Guns will be going off, and that's that. Lincoln isn't nearby, so it's not like we can take them all as hostages on the jet. But I would like Kazumi and Raiden alive at the end if possible. They're a fountain of knowledge that needs to be drained."

Using my watch, I do a quick scan of the area, making sure there are no heat signatures nearby. I glance at everyone with me. "Let's head out."

I take off at a trot, slowly working up my speed into a steady run. Everyone keeps up with me. For the most part. Wyatt—being completely out of shape and having been stabbed—has a difficult time keeping up with us. Dwayne stays behind him, kicking him forward when needed. Each grunt from Wyatt's mouth makes me smile.

Ten minutes later, we're at the edge of the Salt Lake airport. If it hadn't been for Wyatt and the others, I could have been here in five.

"We need to go to the east side," Wyatt says next to me in his scratchy growl.

As he moves in that direction, I take him out of our

communication channel so he can't hear what I say to the others. "Keep a close eye on Wyatt."

Akiro and Dwayne mumble their agreements, trying to keep quiet.

With reluctance, I let Wyatt lead the way. We stay in a straight line, our steps quiet and light. As much as the man drives me crazy, he knows how to move stealthily. I'm banking on the fact that he really does want to be let free, not team up with the Corbox Clan.

Everything I've read about them tells me they are very exclusive and don't let just anyone into their group, which coincides with what Wyatt was saying about them rejecting him. And Wyatt *hates* rejection.

Once we arrive, Wyatt puts up a fist to stop us, and I can't help but roll my eyes. The guy is not leading this op, no matter what he thinks.

With two fingers, he motions to the wire fence in front of us. I look over to see a high voltage sign, telling me that if we attempt to climb, we'll be dead in about two seconds.

Reaching into my bag, I pull out a pulse-field device and set a perimeter about five feet wide and as tall as the fence.

"We need to climb as quickly as we can," I say. "If I don't turn it back off in one minute, they'll be alerted of the jam and send workers out to investigate."

The three of them nod, letting me know they heard me.

With a press of a button, the device jams the current,

leaving the area safe to scale. I climb first, showing them how it's done. Akiro is quickly behind me, scaling the fence easily.

Wyatt has a difficult time, but Dwayne basically climbs up right below him, hefting him up the whole way. I can't help but smile when Wyatt lands on my side of the fence with absolutely no grace, stumbling around like an idiot.

Once Dwayne lands on the ground, we move toward a jet about fifty yards out. As we approach, the jet is completely silent, but I can see small lights lining the bottom, letting me know it's powered up and ready to go.

There aren't any vehicles in the area, so the Corbox Clan hasn't gotten back from planting the bombs.

"What's the plan?" Akiro asks next to me. "We can't just stand out here in the open. We'll be spotted."

There's a ramp on the other side of the jet, so I hustle over there—keeping my feet light—and look to see it's leading to an open door.

I turn to the others, who are all right behind me. "I'm going up first. Dwayne, stay with Wyatt down here until I give the signal to enter the jet. Akiro, watch the perimeter for incoming vehicles."

I don't wait for verification this time around. I just head up the plank, knowing they'll listen to my command. There's no time for them to argue or question it.

Removing my tranq gun from its holster, I hold it at my side, barrel facing down, my finger along the side right above the trigger. I go up the ramp at an angle, watching my every step while also keeping an eye on the door.

As I near the top of the ramp, I hear low voices talking inside. Japanese. I immediately flip on the translate function on my watch.

"They're on their way," one voice says. My system pings on the voice. Raiden Ito. Overlord of the Corbox Clan. I'm only a few yards away from the most notorious crime boss on this earth.

My whole career has been building to this day. This is the moment I've been living for, why I started in the field. Taking down these morons is why I do my job.

I just hope I'm ready for it. I wish Scarlett and Rigg were at my side. Not because I can't do this without them and need them to hold my hand, but because we work best when we're together, and I'd love to experience this moment with them.

I can't let them down. They've trained me to handle these situations. They've taught me everything they know. I can do this. I *will* do this.

Lifting my tranq gun, I hold it close to my chest the last couple of steps up the ramp, then extend my arm, pushing my back into the side of the door and peering inside the jet.

There, sitting on cushy leather chairs, are the Ito brothers.

Raiden and Kazumi, here in the flesh.

CHAPTER FIFTY-EIGHT

Taking a light step back, I let my mind whiz through my options. Not only are the Ito brothers in there, but four of their security guards, who look tougher than the original burlesque show. I mean, when I first met the burlesque show, that really wouldn't have meant much. I thought they were just there for looks. Turns out, though, the guys are pretty skilled.

Then there are the Ito brothers themselves. The guys are built rock solid. Their necks alone are thicker than my torso.

If I just go in guns—er, tranq—blazing, I'd be lucky to get off two shots before I go down.

I glance down the ramp at Wyatt, who's staring at me, probably knowing what I'm thinking. Letting him go in first might be the best option.

Actually, it's the smartest option.

If Wyatt goes in first, and alone, and the Ito brothers

aren't happy to see him, they'll kill him right away, taking him off my list of problems, and distracting the Corbox members enough for the rest of us to make a move.

If they *are* happy to see him, then the rest of us can get really close, seeing as the jet isn't that big. Easier to tranq a few people when they're right next to you.

If we could knock them all off, we could steal *this* jet. Lincoln could probably talk us through how to fly it. Maybe. Then we'd have our own getaway, plus have the key Corbox members in our custody.

We could be heroes.

Yeah, Wyatt is so going in first.

I motion for Wyatt and Dwayne to join us on the ramp. They come up slowly, keeping to the right. I can't risk anyone inside hearing us, so I sweep my hand, telling Wyatt to enter.

As he passes me on the ramp, I whisper as quietly as I can, "Raiden and Kazumi are inside. Get them to let us inside with you."

Wyatt nods, his face all business, no snark to be found. He kinda looks hungry, like he can't wait to get a crack at the Ito brothers. They really did piss him off.

I so wouldn't want to be the Ito brothers right now. They could end up like poor Ned.

Wyatt pauses at the threshold, takes a deep breath— his shoulders moving up and down—and takes a step inside the plane, both his hands raised in the air.

There are a few shouts from within, but then they shut off once Wyatt is fully inside the jet, facing the brothers.

From where I stand, I can only see Wyatt. He only needs to take a few steps forward to be out of my sight.

Dwayne, and Akiro line up behind me, weapons drawn and ready to use.

"Wyatt Mitchell," Raiden Ito says, his tone a mix of amusement and shock. My software translates everything from Japanese. "I thought you were still in Vegas."

Wyatt grins. "I couldn't make our meet-up point, so I found my own way here." He says it in Japanese, which doesn't surprise me. If the guy really wants to work with them, he better speak their language.

"How?" Kazumi asks in Japanese. "No commercial airline could get you here that quick."

"If you have the right help, then it's possible," Wyatt says, taking a couple of steps forward. One more and he'll be out of my line of sight, which I don't like at all.

"Help?" Raiden asks.

Wyatt tips his head to the side, motioning to outside the jet. "I have some friends I'd like you to meet. Like me, they want to help your cause."

Raiden chuckles. "We don't need your help."

"You sure about that?" Wyatt asks. "Obviously, Vegas didn't go as planned."

Someone stomps toward Wyatt, so all of us duck out of the line of sight. Which means I can't see Wyatt.

"What do you know about Vegas?" Kazumi asks.

351

Wyatt takes a couple of steps back, so I can now see just a fraction of his back. "I heard they're in lockdown, because of a failed terrorist attack."

"You wouldn't have anything to do with the attack failing, would you?" Raiden calmly asks.

While I've read up on the Ito brothers, you learn so much more from being near them. Just from their short interaction with Wyatt, I've deciphered a crucial piece of information. Raiden is the calm one, not even flinching in intense situations. Kazumi can fly off the handle in the blink of an eye. That's probably why Raiden is the leader. Honestly, it makes him more intimidating than his brother. It's the calm ones you have to watch out for. They can do the most ruthless things without batting an eye.

Too much emotion can get you in trouble. Rigg taught me that. No matter how intense it gets in that jet, I need to keep myself in check.

"Of course not," Wyatt says. His hand comes into my line of sight, pointing outside the plane. "Would you like to meet the people who helped me?"

"How do we know we can trust them?" Kazumi asks.

"Kill them if you don't," Wyatt says with a slight laugh. "Not my problem."

My fingers itch to pull the trigger on my tranq gun and knock Wyatt out. I'm relying on a traitor and murderer to help me out.

I hate this.

"Come in," Raiden says smoothly.

I motion for Akiro to stay outside the plane. I can't take the risk of them recognizing him. They've worked with his uncle, so they've probably researched his family. Hopefully, they didn't dive too deep into the Fukunaga family and find I'm the nephew's girlfriend.

With a deep breath, I step inside the jet and come face to face with the leaders of the Corbox Clan.

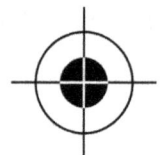

CHAPTER FIFTY-NINE

As a spy, you dream of these days. Coming face to face with some of the most ruthless criminals in history. I mean, how many people can say they've stood on a jet with the leaders of the Corbox Clan?

Having both the Ito brothers stare at me is a little unnerving and not even close to what I was expecting. There is a sense of flattery since they're only looking at me and completely ignoring Dwayne. It's not often that happens. The guy is huge and all smiles. People's eyes are usually drawn to him when he walks in the room. Plus, he's wearing a bright pink suit.

But the Ito brothers only have eyes for me. Maybe Bo told them all about me.

Kazumi stands in the middle of the jet, a wild look in his eyes that make Wyatt's fierce canine ways seem like a little puppy with a bow tied around his neck. Well, in

Wyatt's case, the puppy would have a tie and a gold tie clip, which would be downright adorable.

Kazumi's deep brown eyes size me up, his thick fingers flexing like he's calculating how long it would take to get his massive hands around me and snap me in half. He stands with such an arrogance that I have to hold in my gag. He has a topknot, everything else shaved completely smooth.

The weirdest thing, though, is that he's wearing a pair of really tight pants and a maroon satin vest. Like, just the vest. No undershirt or anything. His arm muscles are clenched tight, the massive veins ready to pop.

When we make eye contact, the guy smiles, showing off his three platinum teeth. Then the guy winks at me. *Winks.*

Dwayne inhales sharply next to me and speaks in such a low voice I'm pretty sure I'm the only one who can hear him. "Oh, he's going to regret that."

Oh, he is.

My gaze slides to Raiden, who's sitting in a leather chair off to the side, his legs crossed, his clasped hands resting in his lap. A subtle smirk settles on his thin lips, the pencil-thin mustache above his lips twitching. The ends of his mustache curl down the sides of his lips, hanging down to the bottom of his chin.

He's the complete opposite of his brother. He's all cool and collected, the air around him calm and light. While his brown eyes aren't wild, they're definitely calculating. Strategic. Which confirms that he's so much more dangerous that Kazumi.

His eyes slowly wander over my body from my feet up to my head, his smirk never leaving. He's already assessed me: a joke, non-threatening, weak.

I can't fault him, though. I did the same when I first met the burlesque show—even though Rigg taught me to treat every suspect as a high-threat until you know the truth—and it turned out I was wrong.

Raiden's opted for a turtleneck sweater that I'm pretty sure is cashmere. Something I wouldn't have known before I met Pearl. Last year, I would have mocked someone for knowing that. But Pearl taught me that clothes say a lot about the person. This man is all about the soft and frivolous things. He takes his appearance as seriously he does his business.

Just like his brother makes his appearance as obnoxious as his personality.

Two guards stand near the front, flanking the sides of Wyatt, me, and Dwayne. The other two guards are behind the Ito brothers.

"You brought a little girl with you?" Raiden asks Wyatt in Japanese, his eyes not leaving mine.

Dwayne inhales again, his voice low. "Oh, he's going to regret that."

Yep.

"Don't underestimate her," Wyatt says back in Japanese. "She got me out of Calloway and saved my life tonight."

Kazumi breaks out into a laugh, clapping his hands together. "This *girl* got you out of prison? You expect us to believe that?"

"They really need to stop talking," Dwayne whispers.

My hands are in fists, ready to pummel the brothers. But I keep my face cool and collected, just like Raiden. Acting like Kazumi will only get me in trouble. I need to change the topic for that to happen, though.

My Japanese isn't quite perfect yet, and these guys won't settle for less than perfect. Their files said they know English, even though they usually act like they don't.

So, I speak in English. "You have a traitor in your clan."

Kazumi's eyes practically bulge out of his sockets, but not about my statement. He's mad that I had the audacity to speak directly to them.

Raiden holds up a hand, and it's then I notice that Kazumi has taken a couple of steps closer to me. Thank goodness he stops at his brother's signal.

"What makes you think that?" Raiden asks, of course, in perfect English.

Wyatt looks shocked to hear him speak so clearly. Maybe he didn't know they spoke English. There's probably a lot of things about them that he doesn't know.

The fact that he's bold enough to reveal the truth about his English tells me one thing: they're not planning on letting us leave this jet alive.

CHAPTER SIXTY

I LEAN CASUALLY against the wall, crossing one ankle over the other and folding my arms. "Your operation was stopped before it could play out. They knew you were coming."

Raiden leans his elbow on the armrest, his chin resting in his palm as his index finger taps the side of his face like he's thinking. "They?"

I scoff. "The U.S. government? You know, the people who run Vegas? You did do your research before you came here, right? If not, rookie mistake, man."

A low, guttural growl emerges from Kazumi, and it takes everything in me to keep my focus on Raiden, whose laughing eyes tell me he's clearly amused by my comment.

I unfold my arms long enough to whack Wyatt in the stomach. "Is this why you two are friends? You share a love of growling. A cute little dog pack."

Wyatt and Kazumi both move like they want to maul

me, but Dwayne steps in front of me, pushing me to the side. He holds up his arms. "Let's take a few, deep breaths and calm ourselves." He lowers his arms to his sides. "I know she's snarky, but that's how she was packaged. Non-returnable."

Dwayne's move made it so I'm now directly in front of Raiden. I miss being sandwiched between the guys, an equal distance between the two brothers.

Raiden is still staring at me. "I do enjoy a little snark now and again."

"Best served with a side of sarcasm, if you ask me," I say.

Dwayne glares down at me, telling me to zip it, but I never listen to grown men. Aside from Rigg and my dad. Even then, it depends on the moment.

Raiden finally tears his gaze away from me and looks at Wyatt, sticking with English. "Why are you here?"

"Like I said, I thought you could use some help," Wyatt says. "I know you thought you could do this without the help of Americans, but it looks like you could use it now."

"We have everything under control," Raiden says, but there's an edge to his voice.

"Right," I say. I point at Kazumi. "And he actually looks good in that vest."

Dwayne sighs once again, his shoulders deflating like he's completely given up all hope for me.

Raiden, though, breaks out into a fit of laughter.

"I'm going to kill you, little girl," Kazumi says in Japanese.

I give him a thumbs up. "Good luck with that."

"Are you trying to get yourself killed?" Akiro suddenly asks through my earpiece.

No. But if I *do* die in the next couple of minutes, I want to go out with style, just like Dwayne in his bright pink suit. I want the Ito brothers to remember me for the rest of their pathetic lives.

Wyatt, who hasn't said much since we stepped on the plane, takes a few steps forward, coming into view. "You don't have much time. The CTB has already caught wind of the Salt Lake attack. Let's get to Boise before they can stop us."

"Us?" Raiden has finally stopped laughing, but there's a tiny tear resting at the corner of his eye. I wonder how long it's been since he laughed? Like, a good, hearty laugh. "There is no *us*."

"The CTB knows we are here?" Kazumi asks in broken English. Nowhere near polished like his brother.

Wyatt nods his head toward me. "Like she said, you have a leak." He looks at his watch. Watch? Where did he get a watch? I take a quick glance at the guard next to him and notice his wrist is bare. Wyatt stole his watch. Wow. The guy is ballsy, I'll give him that.

"You don't have much time until the cops swarm this place," Wyatt says. "Your best bet would be to take off right now."

"Our men aren't back," Raiden says coolly.

I wave my hand. "That's what we're here for. We can help plant the bombs and get off to Boise, then the other cities." I shrug. "Honestly, your route is kinda weird. I would have started in San Diego and then worked clockwise, but whatever."

"Uh," Akiro's voice comes through my earpiece, "we have company."

"You need to be more specific," I say.

"What?" Raiden asks, quirking an eyebrow.

"The rest of the Corbox Clan is here," Akiro says. Then he swears in Japanese. "Including my uncle and his *friend*."

"Ah," I say, nodding. "Thank you for the clarification."

Raiden suddenly stands. "Who are you talking to?"

I glare at him. "Anyone tell you it's rude to interrupt a conversation?"

When his nostrils flare and his hand moves for the gun at his hip, I know the fight has just begun.

CHAPTER SIXTY-ONE

I DIVE into a roll toward Raiden, shooting my tranq gun into the guard at my side, wanting to minimize the threat around me. Raiden's gun went off, but I dove just before it could hit me in the head.

I figure Dwayne and Wyatt are working on the other guards and Kazumi, so my main focus is Raiden.

Which totally sucks. But is also cool.

I really hope I don't die.

Coming out of my roll, I jump onto my feet, pointing the gun at Raiden's stomach, but before I can pull the trigger, he comes flying out of nowhere, his leg connecting with my wrist and sending the gun flying to the back of the jet.

Which leaves me with a taser I can't get to right now, because Raiden-freaking-Ito just landed a kick to my face, making me stumble backward, seeing stars.

I've been training hard, day after day, but the man is a

freaking ninja. Not just Akiro style, but, like, 'I've been trained in the art of ninjutsu since I was in the womb because both my parents are ninjas and it's in my blood' style.

A whirl of cashmere is coming at me again, but I'm already falling to the ground just from the one kick. Which would normally make me mad that I fell after *one* kick, but it saved me from another one that surely would have knocked me unconscious and that would be the death of me.

So not going out that way.

I swing my legs, connecting with Raiden's, making him stumble, but not fall. He leans his palm against the wall of the jet and then goes to kick me in the stomach. My hands barely clasp onto his foot before he can land the blow, and I twist his ankle, sending him flailing toward the cushy leather chair he'd been sitting in.

His face smacks against the back of the chair right as I scramble to my feet and jump onto his back, reaching for the taser at my side. His hand grabs mine before I can get there, and with just a yank of my arm, the guy sends me flying over his head, landing in a thump on the chair behind his.

Man, these leather seats are really soft. Nice for landing in a fight.

Raiden is already moving toward me, so I don't have time to bask in the luxury of it all. I get onto my feet, standing on the chair so I can at least be taller than the guy.

He's holding a gun, but he just tosses it to the side, all smirks. "Don't want to ruin my jet."

I nod. "I bet blood is difficult to get out. Guess I'll find out once you're dead, and it's mine." Leaping into the air, I twist to the side, jamming my foot into his throat. His hands grab my foot, and though he's gasping for air, he doesn't let me go.

My back falls onto the seat of the chair and I'm staring up at his raging eyes as his hands squeeze my foot tighter and tighter. Thank goodness for my DPS boots, because, otherwise, the bones in my feet would be snapping like exploding firecrackers.

I try to pull my foot away from him, but the man is strong. I'll be stuck in this position if I don't make a move.

Raiden stares down at me like he has me right where he wants me. He's probably thinking how he can kill me with his bare hands, and he can. A thick vein is popping out from his neck, pulsating like crazy, like it's mocking me.

He's taking his precious time, really living in the moment. Enjoying it. He slowly lifts me off the chair, dangling me in the air like fresh bait.

I need to find a way out, but I'll have to be quick. The second I move, Raiden will be watching and make his own move, so I won't have a second to spare.

Being upside down, the blood is rushing to my head.

Raiden bounces me up and down, like he's shaking every-thing into my head. His hold on my foot is still strong, the pain radiating fiercely. With all the extra weight on my lungs, it's difficult to breathe, not to mention my eyes are starting to go a little blurry.

I need to move *now*. As fast as I can, I reach for two things: the taser at my side, and a spare tranquilizer dart in my pants' pocket.

Raiden notices my movement and starts to lower me back onto the chair, giving me my opening. Jamming the taser into his leg, he starts convulsing, slowly releasing his hold on my foot, but not letting go completely. Man, this is one tough guy. The wattage in this baby is no joke.

But he starts to lean down, grunting from the pain. Just a little bit lower, that's all I need. His neck vein is worming around like it knows what I'm about to do. Sorry, little worm, but it's me or you, and tonight, it's not going to be me.

With a battle cry, I lift my body up and slam my hand into his neck, the needle of the tranquilizer piercing his skin. I hold it there as we stare at each other, Raiden still convulsing, spit forming at the corner of his mouth, his eyes saying he wants to ravage me.

I could match his glare, but, instead, I smile. "Never underestimate." I switch to Japanese. *"Little girls."*

His eyes flutter, the tranquilizer finally kicking in. I don't know what this guy does for his exercise regimen, but I really need to find out. Most people would be out by now.

We slowly sink to the ground, me not stopping the taser or pulling the needle out of his neck. Just keeping them there gives me a firm hold on the guy, and I don't want him slipping through my fingers.

It's basically a slow-motion descent, letting me soak in the moment of 'I'm taking down the Overlord of the Corbox Clan without drawing blood.'

The second he falls unconscious, the precious moment is over, because I look up just in time to see Kazumi driving a knife toward Dwayne's heart.

CHAPTER SIXTY-TWO_

My BRAIN IS a whirl of thoughts and colors. Blood is still engulfing my head, but now that I'm upright, everything is slowly descending to where it belongs. My eyesight comes back into full focus.

I'm already sprinting toward them, pulling another tranquilizer dart out of my pocket. When I'm a few feet away, I leap into the air, kick my legs into a leather seat, push off, and hurl myself at Kazumi's back, the tranquilizer ready for action.

The needle sinks into his neck as I land against his back, my other arm wrapping around the front of his neck.

Kazumi twists back and forth, my legs swinging behind me, but I latch onto him tight. Pushing against gravity, I move my legs to the front so I can wrap them around his thick torso and get a better grip.

He pounds on my arm, fighting against the tranquilizer like his brother. He's trying to scream, but it's coming out in a gurgled wheeze like a dying chipmunk. Our descent is slow as well, Kazumi falling to his knees with a *thunk*, jarring me.

My arm is burning from his punches, but I can't let go. Not until he passes out. His hits get softer, turning into light pats. Much more manageable.

When his limp body finally hits the ground, I stand up, panting.

"I gotta crank up my work-out routine when we get back home," I say, looking over at Dwayne.

He's kneeling on the floor, blood pooling on his chest.

I fall on my knees next to him, placing my hand over his that's pressed against his chest. "Dwayne!"

He smiles, showing his pearly whites. "Just got me below the collarbone. Should be fine." He winces. "If I can get to a doctor."

Crawling over to my bag near the door, I rummage through it until I find some gauze and tape. I hurry back to Dwayne and pull his hand away from his chest. His skin is pierced just below his collarbone like he said, relieving me just a little. The hole is deep, though, and he'll need stitches.

I press the gauze against the wound and tape it in place. "I've already done one set of stitches tonight. Why not two?"

"Probably should check on Akiro first," he says.

"Right." I stand, looking around the jet.

The guard I got, plus the Ito brothers, are all unconscious on the ground. The other guards, unfortunately, are dead. They're lying face first in a pool of blood.

"Wyatt got to them," Dwayne says, his teeth clenched in pain.

"Where is he?"

"Don't know," Dwayne says. "My bet is that he ran."

Pulling up the data on my watch, I check for his handcuffs. They ping near the door to the cockpit. I quickly switch them to visible, revealing the cuffs lying there on the ground, undone, with no Wyatt in sight. How he took them off, and without alerting me, I have no idea, but I've always underestimated the man.

When I go to check his tracker, it has been disabled.

Swearing under my breath, I hurry out of the jet and down the steps, taking them two at a time.

When my feet land on the asphalt, I take in everything at once.

Akiro is sitting on the ground near me, bleeding from a wound on his head, but otherwise looks unharmed.

Akiro's Uncle Hitoshi is unconscious near Akiro. I don't see any blood, so I'm hoping that means Akiro was able to use a tranquilizer on him. Nozomu is sprawled out next to Hitoshi, all the blood telling me he didn't get the same fate as Hitoshi.

The rest of the Corbox Clan—at least twenty of them —are either unconscious, dead, or in handcuffs.

370

Bo is nowhere in sight. Where did he go?

I reach my hand up, trying to block out the blinding lights blaring on me. Cops are everywhere, circling the perimeter, all their guns trained on me.

The thing that really pisses me off?

Wyatt is gone.

CHAPTER SIXTY-THREE_

THE COPS ARREST DWAYNE, Akiro, and me. They cuff the unconscious Corbox members, including the Ito brothers.

It's weird being the one handcuffed. I always knew this day would come, but I wasn't expecting it to be like this. It's a grand spectacle, cops and lights everywhere, ambulances and coroners. These people don't waste time.

They took my watch from me, along with all my weapons. I hate that DPS gear is now in the hands of law enforcement.

A woman—Detective Pierce, I think—makes me sit down on the ground after they examine me to make sure I don't have any wounds. Dwayne and Akiro are getting stitched up in nearby ambulances.

Drones hover over the bodies on the ground, taking digital scans and the coordinates of their location, already setting up the crime scene and cause of death in the cops' database.

Detective Pierce saunters over to me, tossing my watch on the ground. Dad's horrified face hovers above it, the call live.

"You have two minutes," Detective Pierce says.

"Thanks," I say before I turn my attention to Dad.

"Harper?" Dad licks his dry lips. "What on earth is going on?"

I clear my throat, trying to stall. I can't say too much, because the detective hasn't moved from her spot. Plus, they'll be recording the whole thing.

"I, uh." I swallow, wishing I had some water to wet my throat. "Let's say my trip to Vegas got a little out of hand."

Dad closes his eyes and sighs. "For who else?"

"Basically, everyone who came with me."

His eyes open, his hand landing on his thinning hair. "This is bad, Harper."

"Yeah, I know."

"Are you with the others?"

"Just some," I say. "We took a little detour. We're in Salt Lake."

Dad's hands run down his face, pulling at his skin. He looks so tired. "What should I do? Do you want me to call Forest? He's nearby."

I shake my head. "Not until I know what's going on. I'll keep you posted, I promise."

Tears well in his eyes. "I can't lose you, too, Harper. I just can't."

I blink back my own tears. "You won't. We'll get this sorted out."

"Time's about up," Detective Pierce says.

I keep my eyes on Dad. "I love you. I'll—"

A deep cough comes from behind me, one I'd know from anywhere. I turn my head, taking in the tall figure lurking in the dark. It brings me back to all the nights he caught me in the alleyway, trying to sneak back into my apartment. He's just missing a cig in his hand.

He steps forward, coming into the light. "Tell your father to come to Vegas."

I turn back to the projection. "You heard the man. Pack your bags and come to Vegas." I don't know if this is a good thing or a bad thing, but considering it's Ike, I'm going out on a limb that it will be a good thing in the end.

Dad squints his eyes, trying to look past me. Since my watch is on the asphalt and I'm handcuffed, I can't change the angle so he can see Ike. He probably just sees Ike's pant legs.

"Ike's here," I say quietly. "I'll see you in Vegas."

There's a meow in the background, and suddenly Casper jumps onto Dad's shoulder, awkwardly sitting there, even though he's way too big to be a shoulder cat.

"What about Casper?" Dad asks. "Think Mrs. Fuku-naga will watch him?"

Ike leans down and picks my watch off the ground,

holding it up so Dad can see him. "Bring him with you. In fact, pack all the essentials for you and Harper. I have a feeling you'll be needing them in Vegas."

Pearl's chipper voice pops into my head, and I hear myself saying, "Extended vacay!"

Dad and Ike both chuckle lightly. Detective Pierce looks at me like I'm crazy weird.

After Dad and I exchange goodbyes, the detective goes to take my watch back, but Ike holds onto it. "I'll take it from here." She's about to say something, but he flashes his CTB badge, and she thinks better of it.

Ike reaches down, grabs my arm, and helps me to my feet. "I knew I'd find you in handcuffs one day."

There's a beep behind me, and the cuffs unlock, falling into Ike's hands. I move my hands in front of me, rubbing my wrists. "Thanks."

"Don't thank me yet," Ike grumbles. "We have a lot of red tape to cut through."

"Sounds like something I'm good at."

Ike shakes his head but smiles. "I've already touched base with Rigg and Scarlett. We'll be meeting them in Vegas for a meeting."

Relief floods me.

"Pearl will be there as well," he says, "along with Everly and her crew."

Why is Pearl coming? Did they fly her in?

It's then that I suddenly remember Lincoln. I hope he was able to get away. He has the jet. He could get back to

DPS Headquarters and wipe everything clean. Unless the CTB intercepted him as well. I don't want to ask and give him any ideas in case they haven't found him.

Ike sets a hand on my shoulder. "You took down the Ito brothers?"

I shrug under his hand. "Just a day in the life, you know?"

"No, I don't. The CTB has been trying to get their hands on them for *years*." He drops his hand. "We have so much to talk about."

My stomach growls, so I place my hand on it. "Does this talk involve food? Because I'm *starving*."

Ike stares at me a second before he laughs, good and deep. He points a finger at me. "I've missed you, Harper."

"Same," I say.

He steers me toward Akiro and the others. "Once we get the clear to take them, I'll make sure we get some food aboard our jet back to Vegas."

"Can it involve bacon?" I ask. "Everything is better with bacon. Like serious talks."

"Bacon it is."

CHAPTER SIXTY-FOUR

I ACTUALLY DON'T GET to talk that much on the flight. I'm too busy stuffing my face with pancakes and bacon while Akiro yaps on and on about what happened outside the plane, which has to be more than exaggerated.

When the Corbox Clan members showed up, a few moved to shoot Akiro, but Hitoshi talked them down. They had a little chat, similar to what we had in the jet with the Ito brothers, before Akiro had to make a move. He wasn't talking his way out of anything, just like Dwayne and me.

Akiro went for Hitoshi first, using a tranquilizer dart on him. Then things went crazy from there. Guns blazing. Fists being thrown. Legs being kicked. Akiro is pretty much on an adrenaline high, getting way animated with the retelling. He's basically reenacting the entire event for us on the jet. I wonder if it was really as mind-blowing as he's making it seem.

Ike leans toward me, keeping his voice low as to not ruin Akiro's high. "Cops showed up just as Akiro used the tranquilizer dart, which shifted the Corbox's attention to them. Cops took care of everything."

I choke back a laugh, and just let Akiro have this one.

After we land, we head to the CTB headquarters. I've barely walked into the meeting room when two arms are thrown around me, the person squeezing me tight.

"I'm so happy to see you," Pearl says, sniffing. She's crying. Why are people always crying?

I pat her back. "I'd say the same, but I can't see you. You're invading my personal space."

With a laugh, she releases me and pulls back so I can see her beaming face. There are tears at the corner of her eyes, but she looks unbelievably happy. Considering the predicament we're in, I'm not sure why she's so happy.

I don't get to ask, though, because she's attacking Akiro now, and he's soaking it up like he just did the most heroic thing in the world and barely came out alive.

Okay, so he did. But he's really milking it, and Pearl can't drink it fast enough.

After hugs from Scarlett, Everly, and Paul, and a quick wave to Echols and Rigg, we all take a seat around the long table.

Minutes later, Dad walks into the room, holding a panicked Casper in his arms. I hurry out of my chair and over to them, wrapping my arms around them.

Dad hugs me back with one arm, while Casper growls

and puts his paw on my cheek, trying to push away from the affection.

"He doesn't like to fly," Dad says as he releases me. He rubs the back of his head. "In fact, neither do I."

I scratch under Casper's chin, calming the guy just a little. "I'm just glad you both made it."

"Dad?" Akiro asks.

I glance behind my dad to see Mr. Fukunaga come into the room. He and Akiro quickly embrace before Ike motions for all of us to sit down.

He stands at the head of the table, looking out over all of us.

I take a moment to do the same.

This whole situation is weird. I've got Akiro and Mr. Fukunaga on one side of me. Dad—with Casper curled up in his lap—and P-squared are on the other side of me.

Across the table are Rigg, Scarlett, Everly, Echols, Dwayne—he's all patched up and doing well—and Mayleen.

Then there's Ike, my old building manager and school janitor. That has to be one of the worst undercover jobs, ever. I'd hate it.

I finger the angel wing earrings I have on, thinking of Mom. I'm hoping she's here in spirit as well, because I'm going to need all the support I can get. I have no idea what to think of this whole situation.

Ike clears his throat, catching everyone's attention.

"First of all, the CTB would like to thank all of you who helped stop the bombings in Las Vegas and Salt Lake."

I shift uncomfortably in my seat, just waiting for the 'but' to come. Like, you'll be arrested and will never see the light of day again.

"The search for Wyatt has already begun," Ike says, his gaze sliding to me.

I growl quietly, deep in my throat, but loud enough for Casper to perk up and scan the room, looking for the threat. When he realizes there isn't one, he settles back into Dad's lap, clearly annoyed that I disrupted his nap.

"The Ito brothers and the rest of the Corbox Clan that remain alive," Ike continues, "are being transferred to an undisclosed underground facility." He quirks an eyebrow. "Apparently, the security at Calloway isn't as great as we thought."

Scarlett looks across the table at me and winks, her nose scrunching.

Ike takes a seat, positioning his tie so it rests perfectly against him. "Teams have been dispatched to the other major cities in the west, rounding up other Corbox Clan members that have come here from Japan." His tight gaze goes to Mr. Fukunaga. "Your brother, Hitoshi, is providing a list of everyone smuggled in on your shipments."

Mr. Fukunaga looks at the table, a mixture of emotions on his face. His brother lied to him, turned on him, used his operation to smuggle terrorists into America, but he himself has been doing illegal things just by letting regular

Japanese citizens step onto our soil. I can't imagine the amount of trouble he's in.

"Unfortunately," Ike says, "Bo is also in the wind. We're thinking he took off with Wyatt. This means we don't know his motives or how he got involved with the Corbox Clan to begin with."

Great. Just freaking great. Both Wyatt and Bo got away. I bet Bo was the one who disabled Wyatt's tracker.

Ike leans back in his chair, clasping his hands together and resting them against his stomach. "I'm going to cut to the chase. Every single person sitting at this table has broken the law in some way currently or in the past."

It's Dad's turn to shift uncomfortably, and it makes me wonder what he used to do for President Boggs.

"I'm giving you two options," Ike says, completely calm and even. "One, you can go to jail, the length of time depending on the gravity of your crime."

Pearl chokes on a sob. I look over at her to see Paul handing Pearl a handkerchief, which she accepts with a weak smile. Why did they sit P-squared next to each other? Pearl's unrequited crush is painfully obvious to everyone but Paul. Pearl blows her nose into the handkerchief, magnifying the awkwardness floating in the air like a bad dating site ad.

"And our other option?" Akiro asks, sitting tall and strong, though the crack in his voice gives away his nerves.

Ike taps the table. "You come to work for the CTB."

CHAPTER SIXTY-FIVE

IKE'S DECLARATION basically sucks the room of air. I've never heard so many gasps at once. Then there's an outbreak of voices, everyone talking over one another, shouting out questions and concerns.

I just sit back and watch it all, letting my brain rifle through it. Work for the CTB. Honestly, I'd be honored to work for them. I've always loved DPS and what they do, but I wasn't sure if it was a forever job.

I want something my mom would be proud of. Dad and I never told her what I did, because we didn't think she'd understand. Working for the CTB, though? That would make her proud. My heart warms at the thought, and I wonder if that's her way of telling me I'm right.

Also, I wouldn't go to jail, so that part's nice.

But it means I might not work with Rigg and Scarlett as much as I do now. I look across the table and Scarlett's looking at me, probably thinking the same thing. Like me, she's staying silent, probably processing everything like I am.

Working for the CTB means our sources would be limited. We couldn't do the same thing DPS does, since a lot of what DPS does is illegal. The government can't just bug someone's home and life, then break-in and steal their weapons.

I do something I don't even do at school. I raise my hand, waiting to be called on.

"Silence!" Ike blares, and the room goes still.

Except for Casper, who jumps out of Dad's lap and runs to one corner of the room, then another, then another, searching for somewhere to hide, but there's nowhere for the poor kitty to go.

Ike points at me. "Harper."

I lower my arm. "What exactly would we be doing?"

Ike takes a deep breath, getting ready to dive into a speech. I get comfortable in my chair. Casper moseys back over and curls up between Dad's and my feet.

"The CTB has been at a standstill for a while," Ike begins. "We've been working on a secret project, which led me to go undercover, spying on the Chandler family."

All heads whip toward me and my dad.

I wave my hand. "Hey."

"It revealed some things," Ike says. "One, that Miles has information that can help our project. And two, that Harper wasn't any ordinary kid."

I place my hand against my chest. "Oh, stop. I'm sure loads of kids at my school can do what I can."

Dwayne chuckles. "I saw you with Raiden. Kind of. I was a little busy myself, but you..." He points his thick finger at me. "No kid at your school could take on the Overlord of the Corbox Clan."

Ike nods. "I quickly caught on that there was more to you and DPS."

Rigg glares at me, like this whole thing is *my* fault. How was I supposed to know that Ike actually worked for the CTB? I mean, isn't that something *Rigg* should have figured out with his all-knowing software?

Ike leans forward, resting his clasped hands on the table. "I think if we combine some aspects of DPS with the CTB, we can make it unstoppable."

Rigg's glare drops and he turns to Ike. "What aspects are we talking about here?"

Ike nods at Scarlett. "Her creations. Lincoln's software." He leans his head to the side. "Yes, some adjustments would have to be made." He quirks an eyebrow at me. "Like getting a warrant to search someone's house."

"Warrants are totally overrated," I say.

"I want to create a couple of new units in the CTB," Ike says. "A program development group that will be run by Lincoln. Technology creation run by Scarlett." He looks at Rigg. "And special ops run by you." His gaze slides to me. "With Harper second in command."

Second in command? Me? Holy freaking crap.

Scarlett can't help but beam at me, her nose so scrunched it's practically disappeared.

Everly leans forward, finally speaking up. She uses her business voice, not her sugary tone she turns on for the residents of San Diego. "How do I fit into this equation?"

"Excellent question," Ike says, leaning back. "We have limited funds."

Everly quirks an eyebrow. "You want me to *fund* the CTB?"

He shakes his head. "I want you to fund the new units." He motions to the members of her burlesque show. "I want your team to help out on missions when needed. I want you to move Anchorage Corp's headquarters to Vegas. Change your vision to solely technology." He waves a hand. "You're good with people. I think you could have a nice sway on some of the members of our government, helping them see the CTB's vision." He looks at Mr. Fukunaga. "You would work side-by-side with Everly to see that all the departments run smoothly. You'll be the communications liaison, helping us work with members in our government, along with foreign governments."

Everly glances briefly at Echols before turning her attention back to Ike. "When do you need an answer?"

Ike stands, and so does everyone else in the room. "You all have forty-eight hours to decide what you want to do." Then he looks at Dad. "You'll be working under Mr. Fukunaga, the two of you using your knowledge from your time with President Boggs." His attention goes back to

everyone in the room. "Forty-eight hours. No exceptions."
With a nod from Ike, almost everyone in the room moves
to leave, some looking like they can't get out the door fast
enough.

Pearl and Akiro linger, though, since he didn't assign
them anything.

Ike motions for them to sit back down. "I'd like to
speak with the two of you in private."

I pat Akiro's shoulder. "Good luck."

I hustle out of the room, needing some water and
fresh air.

CHAPTER SIXTY-SIX

SINCE PEARL HADN'T BEEN at DPS long, Ike gave her the option of going back to San Diego and resuming her normal life, no jail time. Pearl never really did anything illegal while at DPS, unless you count those horrendous pink paisley holsters she tried to bring into play.

Akiro's a little trickier, though. He knew of his dad's illegal shipments, and he did help DPS on this mission. But Ike wanted to give him the benefit of the doubt. Just a couple of months of community service, and all would be settled.

Pearl and I are sitting in my hotel room, me lying on the couch, Pearl lying on her stomach on the bed.

Akiro's sitting on the other end of the couch, resting my feet in his lap.

"Pearl," I gently say, bringing her out of her reverie. "What are you going to do?"

She shakes her head, her unfocused eyes on the

comforter. "I don't know. I mean, I want to have my senior year at school. I want to continue being student body president and going to school dances." She looks up at me, tears welling in her eyes. "But I've always wanted my life to mean something, you know? Ever since my brother died, life has been rough at home. It just hasn't been the same. I've been trying to cover it up, but—" She cuts off, pressing a shaking hand to her mouth.

Getting up, I go over to her and lie next to her on the bed, taking her hand. She leans her head against my shoulder.

"Mom and Dad are fighting a ton," she whispers. "It's like a war zone in our house. Even if I stayed, I don't think I would be truly happy." She squeezes my hand. "I've had fun working for DPS. It's made me feel like I'm worth something. Like I'm doing good for mankind, which I know sounds totally stupid."

"It doesn't," I say, cutting in. "That's who you are."

Akiro kneels on the ground in front of the bed, smiling softly at Pearl. "You're worth a lot, Pearl." He breaks out into a grin. "Like a whole clam full of pearls!"

She laughs as I roll my eyes.

"You have us," Akiro says. "And I know everyone at school looks up to you. No matter where you go, you'll be doing good."

She nods. "This just feels more real. Legitimate."

"Scarlett would be lucky to have you on her team," I say. "I think your fashion designs will come in so handy."

She looks at me with so much sincerity in her eyes that it pulls at my heart strings. I didn't even know they could be pulled like this. "You think so?"

"I know so," I say, hoping my eyes are showing I'm as sincere as her. "I don't want to be selfish, but I like the thought of you being here with me."

"You're staying?" Akiro asks, looking at me. "You're not going to talk to your dad or Rigg or anything?"

I shake my head. "Dad and I need a fresh start." I tug at a loose thread on the comforter. "Dad and I already talked, just through a look. We both want to be here."

"I wish I had that kind of relationship with my parents," Pearl says.

"When you've been through what we have," I say, "being practically broke and scrounging for every meal, having to watch my mom slowly die, and both of us having a kind of spy background, we can read each other pretty well." I give a strained laugh. "Makes it nice on the days I don't want to talk." I look at Akiro, raising my eyebrows.

He throws up his palms. "I'm trying, okay? I'll figure you out. Eventually. Probably." He shrugs. "Hopefully."

"What about you?" Pearl asks Akiro.

"I gotta talk to my dad and mom," he says, "but I'm betting Dad's going to take the job. He'd be good at it, and no way he'd want to go to jail and tarnish the family name like that." He grunts. "Hitoshi already did enough of that. We have a lot of repairing to do." He plops down on the ground, folding his legs. "If Dad stays here, Mom will come, which means I will come. By my talk with Ike, I don't think there will be a position for me available at the CTB. At least, not yet."

I reach out, and he takes my hand. "But you'll be here with me, and that's what matters." I look at Pearl. "You should talk to your parents."

She sits up. "What if they say no?"

Letting go of Akiro's hand, I sit up next to her. "You'll be eighteen in a couple of months anyway. I'm sure Ike will hold the job for you. You can live with me and my dad."

Her eyes light up. "You'd be okay with that?"

I smile, loving that she's more worried about me being okay with it than my dad. "Yeah, I would."

Squealing, she throws her arms around me. "Thank you, Harper."

I pat her back awkwardly until I finally settle into a hug. I hate how nice they are. Hugs shouldn't be this nice. "Anytime, Pearl."

She sits back, pulling up her parents' number on her watch. "I hope I don't start another battle at home."

"It won't be your fault," I say. "You can't control how your parents react. Just make sure to trust your gut."

With a nod, she leaves the room.

Akiro sits down next to me on the bed. "I told you I was sorry, right? For everything I said on that street ..."

I lean my side against him, throwing my arm around his back. "Like a million times. We're both passionate people. Fights are bound to happen. We just gotta work through them."

Placing his hand on my chin, he turns my head toward him, his eyes soft and warm. "I always work through them for you, Harper. Always."

Leaning in, I kiss him gently at first. Then I remember I almost died a few hours ago. Life is too precious to be gentle.

I throw myself into him, knocking him back on the bed, and we tangle together, kissing each other like we may never see each other again.

Until Pearl bounds into the room ten minutes later, screaming that she's moving to Vegas.

LIVING in Las Vegas is pretty much amazing. It feels like I was born to live here. All the technology, the way of life, it basically completes me, and I'm head-over-heels in love.

Dad, Casper, and I found an apartment in a skyrise about two miles from the CTB building. I was a little hesitant moving back into an apartment since the one I lived in for most my life was a pile of junk with hardly any room, but this is different. I mean, it's over two-thousand square feet of advanced technology and living space that doesn't make it feel like we're walking all over each other.

And the major perk: no duct tape anywhere to be found.

We were able to acquire a three-bedroom place so Pearl could live with us. It was a little awkward at first, adjusting to having her bubbly personality bouncing all over the place, but it kind of reminds Dad and me of Mom before she got sick. She was so full of life and energy, always smiling and happy.

Don't get me wrong. Pearl can't fill the void Mom left. But she's certainly helping keep Dad and me out of a state of depression.

The three of us work full-time for the CTB. Pearl and I are taking online courses to finish our high school degrees. Then, on to college classes.

It's taken some adjustment, working for a company that actually obeys the laws. I've already been reprimanded three times since I started. Which is a better record than when I started at DPS, so I'm taking this as a win.

Mrs. Fukunaga wants Akiro to finish high school in San Diego. She wants him to have the full teenage experience. Akiro wasn't too happy at first, but I think he likes being back there, especially since he took over Pearl's role of student body president.

Mr. Fukunaga is here in Vegas, so Akiro and his mom usually spend the weekends here anyway, so I still get to see him. Plus, we talk every day via projection.

I haven't told him this, but it's been kind of nice for me to have the break. It's giving me time to fully deal with the loss of my mom and focus on the woman I want to be. I've gained so much perspective in just two months that its mind-blowing.

I love Akiro. I truly do. He's made me into a better person and taught me so much about myself and life. I didn't realize what an impact he'd have on me when he first walked into my life. Well, I walked into his. And by walk, I mean I broke into his house and got caught drooling over a baseball. But I've been lucky to have him by my side.

In the end, though, we have two very different outlooks on life. We want different things for our futures. Akiro wants the full college experience, plus a family, fully equipped with cute little kids wearing matching snarky tees. My life is dedicated to stopping the bad guys, and that's never going to change, even though I would make killer shirts for the kids. Besides, there's no way I'm bringing a kid into this crazy world. Not when I have the abilities to fix it.

As much as I love Akiro, I don't see him as a boyfriend in my future.

Only Pearl knows this. She's been a great sounding board as I've sorted through my thoughts. I just need to figure out what it all means.

For now, I'm just living life day by day, going wherever it takes me.

It's Monday morning—seriously, the best day of the week. It's the start of new cases and problems to be solved. I absolutely love it.

Ike pulls Rigg, Scarlett, Dad, Mr. Fukunaga, Lincoln,

and me into a meeting. Everly and her burlesque show are currently wrapping things up in San Diego as Anchorage Corp's new headquarters is being built in Vegas.

Ike sits at the head of the table, his pinstripe suit perfectly pressed. "Now that everyone is settled into their new positions, I want to get started on our first major task as a unit."

I'm giddy inside, bouncing in anticipation.

"Everything said in this room will be left in this room, understood?" Ike waits for everyone to verbally agree before he continues. "As you all know, the U.S. has been in a state of disarray for quite some time now. The amount of terrorist attacks is getting out of hand and a lot harder for us to control." He claps his hands together and rests them on the table, leaning forward. "I need everyone to be honest right now. What are your feelings toward President Boggs?"

Mr. Fukunaga is the first to speak. "Gladys did an amazing job as president. The EMP was a surprise for everyone, and honestly, I don't think it could have been stopped no matter who was in office. She's good for this country."

Dad nods. "President Poulson is an idiot and has no idea what he's doing. He's a tiny fish swimming in a big ocean, barely staying afloat. I think Gladys should be given a chance to finish out her term as president."

Ike looks at Rigg and Scarlett. "Thoughts?"

Scarlett is leaning back in her chair, her left leg up and

resting on her right. "I agree. I think she'd do a better job. She has the right mindset and was taking this country in the right direction before the EMP."

"Poulson has completely ruined what she created," Rigg says in a gruff tone. "Is Boggs the perfect person for the job? I don't know. I think she'd do great, though."

"We need someone reliable right now," Lincoln says, using the top of his index finger to push up the bottom of his glasses. "Someone we can trust."

I lean forward. "Not just reliable, but relatable. No one can relate to Poulson. He's lived a privileged life, everything being practically handed to him on a silver platter. He's selfish and arrogant, creating a bigger divide between the rich and the poor." I tap the table. "President Boggs is the total opposite. She came from nothing, worked her butt off to get in the president's seat, making sure that everyone around her was taken care of."

Dad looks at me. "Our family was living a lot better life when she was in power. And if she hadn't been chased out, I honestly don't think our family would have been in such a dire situation when your mom got sick."

"Healthcare alone is worth bringing her back," Mr. Fukunaga says.

"Could other people do what she did?" I say. "Yes. But I think we need *her*. We need that familiar face. The one that makes you feel comfortable and like you're at home. The one you would trust with your life. She has our best interests at heart and could help put our country at ease."

Dad takes my hand. "No one should live like we had to the past few years." He looks at Ike. "Having worked with Gladys for many years, I know she can fix this."

Mr. Fukunaga nods. "I agree."

Ike smiles, happy at all our declarations. "I'm assuming that means if I assemble a task force to get her out of hiding and put her back in power, you'd all be on board?"

"Is that even legal?" Scarlett asks.

"Leave that part to me," Ike says. "Everyone in agreement?"

"Yes," we all say at the same time.

"Good." Ike sends a quick message on his watch, so fast I don't see what it says.

A minute later, two people walk into the room.

The first I recognize from Salt Lake. Detective Pierce. Her curly auburn hair is pinned up, highlighting her green eyes.

Ike stands, so we all do the same. He smiles at her. "This is Detective Pierce. She'll be working with Tomi and Miles on getting the intel on where Gladys Boggs is currently located and how we can safely bring her back into the light."

She walks over and shakes my dad's hand, then Mr. Fukunaga's. "I'm excited to work with the two of you."

My gaze goes to the second person, and my breath hitches. Like, an actual hitch that I hope no one heard, but when I steal a glance at Scarlett, she's smirking at me, and I'll never hear the end of this.

I'm not one to swoon. I don't get gooey over guys, even my own boyfriend. Boyfriend. I have a boyfriend. And his dad is like two feet away from me. I gotta keep myself together.

But then I look back at the guy, and I can't help but stare.

His curly black hair is in a small fro around his head. He's got gorgeous hazel eyes that are staring straight at me. And his thick lips? They're curled into a small smile, revealing a dimple on his cheek.

He's tall and strong, perfectly muscled without being obnoxious like Rigg's and Bo's, and he carries himself with a confidence that's incredibly hot.

He's maybe nineteen or twenty, so only a couple of years older than me. I mean, I'll be eighteen in three months.

Wait, why does that matter? He's just a guy standing in the room with me. And many others. Including my boyfriend's dad.

I steal a glance at Scarlett again, and she puts her finger under her hanging jaw, pushing it closed like I should do the same.

I'm not gawking at the guy.

Then I realize my jaw is dropped, and I coolly put it back in place, not moving too fast for it to be noticeable.

"Everyone, this is my son, Brax," Ike says, motioning to super-hot guy.

My head swivels toward Ike. "You have a *son?*"

Ike raises his eyebrows. "Two, actually. And a daughter. Brax is my youngest."

Brax steps closer to the table, smiling. "I was the perfect surprise."

Ike chuckles. "You were certainly a surprise. Perfect? Not too sure on that." Ike's gaze goes toward Rigg. "Brax is highly skilled in special ops and will be helping your team when it comes time to extract Boggs from hiding."

Which means he'll be working closely with me. I mean, with me. Not closely. There will definitely be a gap between us. A large one.

What's wrong with me? Has Pearl melted my brain?

I hate this.

"Alright," Ike says. "Let's get started."

We all take a seat, everyone getting comfortable in their chairs and pulling up the op notes on our datapads.

As much as I try not to, I can't help but steal glances at Brax. And I can't help but notice him doing the same to me. Probably because I'm staring at him like a fool.

I'm going to kill Pearl.

ACKNOWLEDGMENTS_

As always, a monster shout-out to Cammie Larsen and Mary Gray at Monster Ivy Publishing. These Harper books are always my most complex, and I appreciate all the insight and help weaving the story. And, Cammie, LOVE the cover. Again. I'm sensing a pattern here.

A special thanks to Isaac Dotson for your edits and molding Harper: Unhinged into an even better story.

Douglas, you're the perfect husband, travel buddy, and emotional support system. I wouldn't survive writing and editing these Harper books without you.

Harper and Aviendha, you're the best cats ever. You keep me on my toes, always.

And, of course, YOU, dear reader, for your continuing and ever-growing support.

ABOUT THE AUTHOR_

Jo Cassidy is a YA thriller author who loves all things creepy. Bates Motel is one of her all-time favorite shows, but Prodigal Son is on its way to climbing to the top of her list. Anything with deeply disturbing characters draws her in and captivates her in a way she can't explain.

Jo grew up in Yorba Linda, California but now resides in Utah with her husband and their two crazy cats, Harper and Aviendha, AKA Lil Punk and Lil Chunk. When she's not writing, she and her husband love to travel, going to new places around the globe. You can subscribe to her newsletter at www.authorjocassidy.com.

Good Girls Stay Quiet - Fifteen-year-old Cora has a secret only her "daddy" and journal know about... until a blackmailer finds out the truth and demands test answers and money.

Willow Marsh - When seventeen-year-old Tessa uses séances to contact her brother and mom, renegade spirits slip through the gateway, taking over her mind and town.

I ran my fingers along the white eyelet canopy surrounding my bed. Daddy said it would protect me at night while I slept but still allow me to breathe. Sometimes I liked to sit on the bed with the canopy closed, soaking in the comfort and safety it provided.

I'd already finished my homework for the day. It was

always the first thing I did when I came home from school so I'd have the evening free to spend with Daddy.

My leg bounced, my fingers drumming along with the motion. I glanced at the twin bell alarm clock on my nightstand. Only twenty more minutes until Daddy came home and unlocked my bedroom door. I could hold my bladder that long. I'd done it before. I needed to distract myself so I wouldn't think about it.

I leaned over the side of my bed, the canopy draping over my hair, and retrieved the journal tucked under my mattress.

Noah, my stuffed elephant, cleared his throat, which did nothing for the rasp in his tone. "Oh, Cora dear. You know not to write in that during the day. *He* may come home and see it."

I glared at the elephant sitting on my bed, his bright, blue eyes staring back at me. "I know that, *Noah dear*. I was just seeing how much room I had left." I thumbed through the empty pages in the back. "I'll have to steal another journal soon."

Noah guffawed. "So you can write more thrilling stories about me?"

Whoever manufactured the stuffed animal didn't bother with getting the facts straight. I'd never seen an elephant with blue eyes that sparkled. It certainly didn't match with Noah's sometimes rough and sarcastic demeanor.

Daddy had bought him for me when I was eight. He'd

said the elephant's eyes matched mine. Little did he know, he'd brought me home an elephant with a soul that came alive when we were alone.

"Or is this about brushing up on your shoplifting skills?" Noah asked.

I put my hand on my hip. "Please don't judge me. There are extenuating circumstances."

"Keep telling yourself that." He laughed louder, though his stuffed body remained completely still on the bed.

I was about to flick his trunk when I heard footfalls in the hallway. Daddy was home early. Shoving the journal back under my bed, I surveyed the room to make sure nothing had been left out that I didn't want Daddy to see. I fumbled to refasten the top button on my shirt so only half of my neck was exposed. Then I rolled down my sleeves and buttoned the cuffs. Daddy liked his little girl to look a certain way.

"Are you going to start hiding me?" Noah asked.

Daddy didn't know about my relationship with Noah, and I wanted it to remain that way. Luckily, I was the only one who could hear Noah. It was the main reason our relationship was special and why I confided in him so much.

Right as the lock unlatched on the outside of my door, I settled into place on my bed holding a regency book I'd brought home from the school library. At the last second, I moved my braid so it rested on my right shoulder. The door opened, and Daddy stepped inside the room. He still wore his blue work coveralls, and I immediately took in the scent of grease and sweat. I noticed his pomade had held his perfectly brushed hair in place all day.

Even though his presence caused unease to swirl inside, I plastered on the smile he loved so I wouldn't have to deal with his explosive anger. It was why I referred to him as Daddy in my head. I never wanted to accidentally call him something else to his face.

"Hi Daddy!" I set the book on my nightstand and went to him. I put my arms out to hug him, but he took a step back.

"I need a shower." He rubbed at his tired eyes. "My last appointment was a bit of a mess."

"Why don't I cook dinner while you wash up and then you can tell me all about your day over our meal?"

Daddy leaned forward and kissed my forehead, his dry lips causing my stomach to roll. "What would I do without you, Cora?"

"Not be such a creepy old man?" Noah offered in a haughty tone.

It took everything in me to not turn around and scold Noah. He shouldn't talk about Daddy like that. Thank goodness Daddy couldn't hear him, or we'd both be locked in the basement for the night.

"I could really use a decent BLT," Daddy said.

"Consider it done." My tone was as sweet as honey, but my insides were heavy like molasses.

He turned to leave, but then faced me and raised his

eyebrows. "Make sure the bacon is crispy, but not over-cooked." He placed his hand on my arm and squeezed as a small storm brewed in his eyes. "Last time it was practically burnt."

I clasped my hands tightly in front of me so I wouldn't flinch from the pain. "Of course, Daddy."

The storm in his eyes retreated, and Daddy left the room. I wanted to yell at Noah, but I really needed to use the bathroom. It had been hours. As soon as I finished, though, I headed back into my room.

"Don't say things like that about him," I hissed. When it came to Daddy, Noah and I didn't see eye to eye. He didn't like the way Daddy treated me.

"The truth?" Noah whistled. "Fine. I'll feed myself lies like you do."

Going to the bed, I put my face in front of his. "Being nice to him makes him happy. He's done so much for us, Noah." I poked his trunk. "Remember that."

"That's right. All the things he does out of *love*. Well, if you want him happy, then you should start dinner and stop lecturing me."

I gave him one last glaring look before I went into the kitchen to prepare dinner. I put on an apron so the grease wouldn't splatter my shirt. That would make Daddy real mad. I kept a close eye on the bacon, making sure every inch turned brown but had no hint of black. Once it was perfectly cooked, I took the plate of bacon and gently placed it on the table. I used a towel to wipe away a drop of grease on the edge of the plate.

After smoothing out a wrinkle in the tablecloth, I used my hand to measure the length of the material hanging over the edge, double checking it was even all the way around, just how Daddy liked it. We had a round table so the chairs could be spaced perfectly apart; far enough so Daddy could look at me, but not too far so he could reach out and touch me if he needed to. It had been almost a year since I'd stepped out of line at the dinner table and he'd sent me to timeout. I planned on keeping it that way.

The white ceramic plates and bowls were on their placemats, with a fork on the left, fork above for the salad – even though we weren't having salad, it always had to be there – and a spoon and knife to the right. The glasses were up and to the right, with the cloth napkins flawlessly folded in a standing triangle on the center of our plates. It was perfect.

"Smells delicious, angel," Daddy said, joining me in the kitchen. He'd switched to his usual button-down shirt tucked tightly into his casual slacks. His shirt was buttoned all the way to the top like mine. My chest tightened at the sight of his leather belt.

He wrapped his arm around my shoulder and kissed the side of my head, my hair creating a barrier between his lips and my skin. His sweat and grease stench had been replaced by soap and Selsun Blue shampoo and his brown hair hung down, still wet from the shower. I preferred that look to his perfectly sculpted hair. It made him appear carefree.

"So, tell me about this last client of yours," I said, hanging up my apron in the pantry and softly closing the door.

Daddy grabbed a bottled beer from the fridge. "Not much to tell. A guy inherited everything in his dad's garage, which included some tools that hadn't been used in a very long time."

Keeping my hands steady, I pulled out his chair for him. He sat down, his thin lips turning into a smile as he did. I returned the smile, though my stomach fluttered. I hoped I cooked the bacon just right.

"Did you get them working again?" I sat down and tucked my napkin into the top of my shirt, just like Daddy had done. Then I made sure my braid hung over my right shoulder.

He winked. "Always do."

I grabbed two pieces of bread and spread mayo on them. "*Never leave a client unsatisfied.*"

He laughed. "So you *do* listen to me."

I tilted my head to the side and winked at him. "Always do."

The laughter reached all the way to his eyes and some of the tension released inside me. His eyes were much kinder when they weren't housing a storm.

I loaded up his sandwich with bacon, lettuce, and fresh tomatoes I had picked from the backyard the day before. I tried to keep my hands stable as I placed the BLT in the center of his plate.

Clasping my hands in my lap, I waited patiently for Daddy to take a bite of his sandwich.

"It's perfect, angel." He wiped his mouth with the napkin and nodded at the bread. "Go ahead and make yourself a sandwich now."

My heart calmed. "Thanks, Daddy."

"You deserve it," he said. "Having you gives me a reason to wake up every morning."

Tears welled up behind my eyelids. I was lucky to have a father who loved me so much.

After dinner and cleaning up under Daddy's watchful eye, I grabbed the playing cards from the closet in the hall. It was tradition to play every night. I let him win all the time because he hated to lose. The last time I won, he didn't let me out of the basement for two whole days.

Once Daddy locked me in my room for the night, I switched to my long sleeve crew neck shirt and cotton pants. It was what Daddy liked me to wear to bed. They were comfortable, so I didn't mind. I waited for him to go to bed before I pulled out my journal. I sat down on the floor next to the large dollhouse and used the flower-shaped nightlight as my guide.

I wrote in my journal every night. I recounted everything that happened to me during the day, not leaving a single detail out. At the end of the entry, I'd sketch a drawing of my favorite event from the day, whether it was something that happened or someone I saw that I thought looked interesting. Sometimes I wrote poems or song lyrics imagining myself in a happier life.

"Don't forget to mention my charming personality," Noah said from the bed.

"Hush!" I whispered.

"Why?" he asked. "It's not like someone else can hear me." He raised his volume. "I could shout all night long, and nothing would happen. Maybe I'll sing you a few songs. Except I'd have to make up the words since you can't listen to music."

I reached for my backpack, fished out an eraser, and threw it at Noah. "You're distracting me. Now please be quiet."

He grunted. "Was that necessary? Hitting me? Please don't turn into your precious *Daddy*."

His words punched me right in the gut. I was trying to be playful with him, not intentionally harm him. I never wanted to resort to violence to get my way. Noah had just proved that words could be more powerful than actions.

Suddenly the latch on the outside of my door lifted. Daddy. I wasn't close enough to the bed, so I stuffed the journal inside my backpack and pulled out my math book as the door opened.

Daddy flicked on the light and stared at my empty bed. He was still in his regular clothes. He never liked me to see him in anything less.

"I'm here, Daddy," I said.

He turned his attention to me on the floor, his voice coming out low and rough. "Were you just talking to someone?"

I held up my math book, holding tight so my hands wouldn't tremble. "I have a test tomorrow, and I wanted to review the material one more time. It helps me to repeat it out loud."

His eyes scanned the room, looking for anything out of place. He folded his arms. "Why are you doing it in the dark?"

I thumbed the pages of my math book. "I didn't want to wake you, Daddy. You work so hard for our family, and I wanted you to be able to have a good night's sleep for work tomorrow."

The strain in his face relaxed. "That's very thoughtful of you. But it's late. You also need your sleep."

I stood, hoping my legs didn't look as shaky as they felt. "Of course, Daddy."

He waited until I climbed back into bed. He tucked in the sides of my sheets, snuggling me in. "You're smart, angel. You'll do fine on your test." Grabbing my braid, he pulled it forward to its proper place. He kissed my forehead, but dark clouds flew into the back of his eyes as he squeezed my shoulder. "I never want to catch you outside of bed at night again, do you hear me?"

A painful lump landed in my throat, and it took me a second before I could speak. "Yes, Daddy."

"Sleep tight, my angel girl." His low, breathy voice caused me to shiver.

Once Daddy was out of the room, I took Noah and held him in my arms. His soft fur was soothing to the touch. My heart thudded in my chest from how close I'd been to being caught. Daddy would be furious if he knew I had journals that held our family secret.

He could never know I had them.